THE UNWINDING: GIN'S STORY

The Unwinding Series Book 1

JULIANA REW

Cover Art by Keely Rew

The Unwinding: Gin's Story
The Unwinding Series Book 1

by Juliana Rew

Copyright 2019 Sophont Press
ISBN #978-1-7322189-9-4

Discover other titles by Juliana Rew:
(1) Erenarch Academy: Under the Dragon Banner
(2) Daris Moon
(3) Miranda of Daris
(4) Mountain Ma'am
(5) The Adventures of Mountain Ma'am

Cover: Keely Rew

www.julianarew.com

Dedication

This book is dedicated to Orlando James (Bud) Rew, who was the Watchman in our family.

Contents

Prologue 7

PART I. THE LABYRINTH
Chapter 1. Virginia 9
Chapter 2. Quantum Opposable Singularity 13
Chapter 3. Families 15
Chapter 4. Shipwrecked 21
Chapter 5. Impossible Things 33
Chapter 6. Wreckers 37
Chapter 7. Lost in Heaven 47
Chapter 8. The Unwinding 59
Chapter 9. Natural One 77
Chapter 10. Back to the Future 81
Chapter 11. How to Be a Badass 93
Chapter 12. Hello, Goodbye 107
Chapter 13. Recurring Cauchemar 123
Chapter 14. Sally, Go 'Round the Roses 131
Chapter 15. Into the Mystic 139
Chapter 16. Drop Me in the Water 157

Part II. THE BREACH
Chapter 17. Recursion 169
Chapter 18. Blackmail 179
Chapter 19. Parental Issues 189
Chapter 20. Baby Blue Horizon 201
Chapter 21. Living Cintamani 203
Chapter 22. An Opening 213

Chapter 23. Synergies and Dreams 223
Chapter 24. Unholy War....................................235
Chapter 25. Capitulation...................................245
Chapter 26. I've Come Undone 251
Chapter 27. Empty Nest 261
About Juliana Rew 269
Art Credits 269

*****~~~~~*****

Prologue

First off, riding a whiskered dragon following a breadcrumb trail across time and space is not for everyone. I wouldn't have said it's even for me, but nobody asked for my opinion.

My name is Virginia, Gin for short. Lately, I've spent a lot of time either alone or with strangers, untethered to the demands of family. In the 21st century, I would have given my eyeteeth to have so much freedom, such anonymity. I dedicated my life trying to balance being a proper daughter to my Korean parents and a supportive faculty wife for my American husband. But since I've been chosen, I ache, I want, I burn for... my people. I'm sitting on a sandy beach, while gray-blue waves gently roll in from a distant winter horizon. It looks enough like the Outer Banks to pass muster. Now and then, I repeat my name, to keep it mine.

Are there mystical ley lines that align places and times? I don't know. I do know that I can travel from place to place, sometimes even across galaxies, and from time to time, from now to then. I can stay wherever—or whenever—I want. It's just that I dare not remain anywhere for very long. I've got to keep looking. I'm not a time traveling vacationer, visiting people and places of my design, like Dr. Who. I'm closer to a clueless detective on a short deadline, grasping at any possible lead. I pray my family are alive and looking for me too.

Sometimes I feel optimistic. The scientific theories in my world said there might be an infinite number of universes, each having its own physical laws. I tell myself that I am a creature of my own universe, and that if I were in a very different universe I would not still be alive. That narrows it down to a mere infinite number of possibilities. I can't chase every breaking wave, yet I will know it when I see it.

Other times I despair. That way madness lies. I've been completely mad several times. But the universe always reveals something that catches my eye, giving me the courage once again to venture away from the safety of this little haven.

Why should the universe care about me, or for any human, for that matter? Earth is an infinitesimally small speck in the vastness of things. What's so special about this place? This galaxy, even? But in spite of the sheer enormousness of the cosmic realm, I think we must be rare and precious. At least, that's how I feel about my family. Alan and I tried for years to have Grace, and when she was born, I knew she was God's gift to the universe, not just to me and Alan. So even though life on Earth seems plentiful, such pockets of life may be rare. They're worth preserving, aren't they? I can't shake the feeling that with recent events the universe suddenly has a personal interest in what's been happening to me.

I call it the Unwinding. Like a needle caught in the feed dogs of a sewing machine, threads are snarling, then breaking. If it's not fixed, the needle will break too. But how can the needle get clear of the teeth so the fabric can move freely again?

Since the Unwinding began, I've gradually come to realize a strange truth: the universe is alive in the midst of all-hell-breaking-loose, it wants love just as badly as I do, and for some reason it thinks we can help each other. God, I hope it's right.

*****~~~~~*****

PART I. THE LABYRINTH

Chapter 1.

Virginia

I was sitting on a beach very like this, on Christmas morning, enjoying a picnic with my family. My daughter was back home visiting with her new husband, and we were all celebrating the future. I began unpacking a special basket I'd prepared to both please the palate and impress Eric, the rich boy that Grace had finally married after a rocky engagement. A nice bottle of 2015 Mouton Cadet, some tangy Irish cheddar, salty Greek olives, and pork-stuffed Cuban sandwiches, and, not to leave out the great cuisine of Korea, my homemade *banchan,* which I'd slaved over all week. I'd even slept well the night before, instead of tossing and turning with assorted hormone-fueled nightmares, like I usually do.

I was admiring my handiwork, when I spotted a newspaper blowing down the beach. Full of more energy than I'd felt in a long time, I chased it as it skipped along in the shore breeze, not wanting it to escape, finally grabbing it in triumph and looking for a trash or recycling bin. I glanced down, trying to read what it said. It was a broadside poster, printed in old-fashioned type, with those tall esses that look like effs. The wind kept blowing at it, and I wished I had a rock to hold it in place. A rock appeared in my hand. At first, that didn't strike me as unusual.

The sheet was dated March 28, 1827, a publication called "Freedom's Journal." The banner read:

"We wish to plead our own cause. Too long have others spoken for us."

"Hey, everybody, look at this. It looks like an antique newspaper. How do you suppose it got here?" I called.

"Hmm," my husband Alan said. "Maybe it's from the Nag's Head historical museum, a mile or so toward town, but I have no idea how it got here." Eric and Grace didn't show much interest. They were already digging in to the goodies.

The sky had an unusual greenish cast, so I thought we should get on with the picnic before the weather turned wintry. Climate change was welcome, at least on Christmas, even if it meant the beach was eroding away at a fast clip.

"Hey, leave some for the rest of us. I want to propose a toast—" I started to say.

Suddenly I was alone, while the sky grew dark and lightning and thunder crashed around me. A huge wall cloud loomed impossibly close, shedding sheets of black rain and staring down at me. A storm surge rose up and knocked me off my feet, pulling me under gray, bubbling surf. I tumbled over and over.

I clawed for the surface, until with a gasp I surfaced and struggled against the insistent undertow. Finally reaching solid sand, I rested on my hands and knees, alternately panting for air and coughing up salt water. Rain cascaded off the tips of my bare breasts; the powerful wave had completely turned my halter top around and ripped off my wedding ring. Embarrassed—but still alive—I retrieved what missing clothing I could find and surveyed the beach. The picnic basket was gone, and so was my family. I ran up and down the beach, holding my baseball cap on while the wind and rain lashed my face.

I cried their names: Alan, my beloved husband, Grace, my daughter, Eric, my son-in-law.

"Alan! Grace! Eric! Where are you? Can you hear me? Let me know if you can hear me!" If there was any answer, the bellowing tempest would certainly have drowned it out. Then, as quickly as it had happened, the storm subsided, and I stood alone on the beach. The only evidence there had been a storm was my dripping hair and clothes. A moment later, I was completely dry. I turned around and around, feeling my arms, my hair, my dry shorts, over and over. I have a tendency toward OCD, I've been told. Taking its cue from my inner ear, my stomach began to revolt.

What was happening to me? I screamed, while my mind took a short intermission.

*****~~~~~*****

Chapter 2.

Quantum Opposable Singularity

"She seems safe for the moment," QoS said. "I don't want to tell you what you already know, but that probably won't last long. I calculate your brother's next incursion in a day or two at most, her time. As usual, Golaeth has said it's done everything it can and we're on our own. I told it we were about to try repairing the anomaly, but then we'd lost track of it. Virginia may be our last chance."
"**"

"Well, how do you propose I do that? Yes, I realize that you're the divine one, and it wouldn't do to talk to her directly. I manifested the Cintamani pearl and an Earth newspaper as you instructed, but I think it went right over her head. Giving her the Cintamani makes her incredibly powerful. And unpredictable."
"**"

"Yes, she loves detective stories, but I think this was a bit obtuse, don't you? Why ask her to do all this ratiocination? Why not just broadcast it in lights on a big marquee—you know, "WORLD ENDING!"
"**"

"Oh, that's a good idea. A big flying one, that'll get everyone's attention. At least until we can find her daughter. I'll get right to manufacturing one. Meanwhile, I'll keep up with the missives, for what good they'll do. Maybe keeping up with the clues will keep her engaged. We've got to hurry. Humans die quickly—and easily."
"**"

I didn't mean to imply she's a complete dunce, but she has primitive ideas about how the universe works. Every time you let her bend the rules, it's just going to confuse her more. I'll do what I can to get her up to speed and help release us from this maze we've made for ourselves. And for the love of—You—please keep a low profile while I'm away. Build some castles in the sand or something. This stasis point can't last forever."

*****~~~*****

Chapter 3.

Families

Bluish light flickered across the faces of the four family members locked in the hypnotic trance of the "Trollhunter" movie, their eyes intent on the hairy creature with venom dripping from its rotting teeth. It lashed out with lethal-looking claws and prepared to spring. Virginia pushed the pause button.

"Does anyone want to take a break? They had a ton of snacks on Christmas special at the Go-Mart."

"I could eat some," said her husband Alan, "and could you bring me a beer?"

"Anybody else want a drink? Eric?"

"No thanks, Mrs. Jones. I'm trying to lay off the booze lately."

"Hmm, I see. And would you please call me Virginia, or Mom, or something less formal? You and Grace have been married nearly two months, for God's sake. Grace, I've got your favorite, the Tia Maria liqueur. Want a shot?"

"No, thanks, Mom. Just some chai tea for me and Eric." Her new husband put his arm around her.

"On second thought, let me help you, Mom," Grace said, jumping up from the couch. "Then it'll only take one trip." They went to the kitchen, and Gin's taller daughter began busying herself pulling mugs from the cabinet. A large tin of polar-bear-themed popcorn sat on the gleaming granite counter.

"Thanks for watching the movie Eric brought," Grace said. "It was either that, or video games, and I know how you hate those."

"Not hate, exactly, but truth be told," Gin said, "I prefer mysteries and detective stories, you know, like Edgar Allen Poe. Somebody gets killed, and you have to find the bastard who dunnit."

"Well, you do have a competitive streak," Grace said. Look at all the Tae Kwon Do stuff you've got."

Gin glanced up at the glass ornament hanging in the kitchen transom light. Perhaps she *had* overdone the martial arts thing a bit. She'd had the tricolored *taeguk* symbol commissioned recently by a friend who'd taken up stained glass as a hobby. The yin and the yang were supposed to aid understanding of change in the world as the interactions of the heavens, the Earth, and Man. But, sometimes, Gin just wished she had even a little control over the universe. Like a crazed game of Whack-a-Mole, change seemed to pop up faster than she could bat it down. Here Grace was all grown up and married, and now she was moving away...

"It's helped me keep my girlish figure," Gin said. "My hands are a mess, though, between the TKD and twenty-five years of doing your laundry."

"Very funny. You know, we're really looking forward to the picnic on the beach tomorrow at Nag's Head. Eric and I have both had our noses to the grindstone with me teaching and him trying to finish his degree, and that's not counting writing all those thank-you notes for the wedding gifts."

"I can hardly wait, either," Gin said. She reached under the kitchen table and pulled out a large wicker basket. "I've got a great spread planned, with expensive French wine and everything, though I'm glad to hear you and Eric are cutting back on the drinking."

"You know, Mom, I'd appreciate it if you would stop commenting on how Eric's not drinking," Grace said.

"He's working on it. We don't need you to bring it up constantly. When he had his accident, I wished so hard for him to live, I— I don't think I could have survived if he hadn't."

"I'm sorry, don't get all emotional," Virginia said. "Your father and I just want you two to be happy."

"I know, but sometimes you can seem too hands-on. Dad seems to get along fine with Eric," Grace said.

"You're right," Gin replied. "Let's change the subject. The forecast is for the low seventies, so it'll be the warmest Christmas in years. It'll probably be mobbed tomorrow, so we should get there early. What's a good time?"

"Two o'clock?"

Gin chuckled. "I actually reserved a picnic site for noon, figuring no one would ever think of sleeping through Christmas morning. Oh, and look what I found on the beach when I was scoping out sites."

"Oooh, very pretty. What is it? Pearl?"

"Yes, I think so, or mother-of-pearl. I bent down to pick a piece of nacre off the sand. At first I thought it might be a broken piece of shell from a nautilus, but when I looked more closely, it turned out to be this little beauty. I'm thinking of having it set in a pendant or something, but that will have to wait until after the holidays."

The electric kettle lever snapped, indicating the water was at the boil. Gin spooned the chai into the screened basket in the dark red cast iron teapot and poured steaming water in.

Eric entered the kitchen. "How's it going in here?"

"We're making tea," Grace responded. "Mom, is that Grandma Sun's kettle she brought from Korea? I've always loved the dragon on it, especially his whiskers."

"Me too," Gin said. "It reminds me of her stories about the magical Korean water dragon, which was controlled by a mystical jewel, called the Cintamani."

"Hmm," Eric said. "Well, it reminds *me* a little of Dragon Ball Z."

"You're going to have to learn some Korean mythology, if you want to be in this family, Eric," Grace teased. "Hey Mom, maybe your dragon could give Eric's Kraken a run for its money."

"I've heard of it, but never understood what the 'Ball' or the 'Z' stood for," Virginia said. "Yet another one of you kids's arcane cultural references."

Grace frowned. "You want us punks to get off your lawn, eh?"

"No, just the opposite," Gin said. "In fact, I have to admit that a dragon does feel more like the real me. If at first you don't succeed, try, try another avatar."

"I know you're trying, Mom," Grace said. "Give us a hug, dragon lady."

Savoring the spicy smell of cinnamon and cloves, Gin piled the cups and kettle onto a tray and followed Grace and Eric back to the living room.

"All right, let's kill us some trolls."

☺

Watching its charges in the immense disk-shaped Hatchery of universes, Golaeth pondered the current crisis.

It had guarded the embryo until the dark energy within caused it to germinate. A pitifully small bud, not nearly as fine as its parent universe, but, still, it deserved protection, like all the others. Each cosmos was unique, though descended of the same parent components. Finally, there was motion. The bud began to swell, slowly at first, then suddenly mushrooming. The bud was growing much too fast. At this rate, Golaeth knew it would run into the other broodmates, especially the Black Universe, possibly breaching its sheath and provoking an immunity reaction.

Golaeth spun a delicate tendril of 510-nanometer radiation and reached out to touch the boundaries of the new universe, checking its specifications and spinning it into the proper flattened shape indicated by its metadata. It was not enough. The infant universe collapsed into a spinning platter of viscous matter and began to vomit heavy elements never seen before in the other universes. If these new elements were to infect the other universes, Golaeth feared they might all die of the contagion. Hot gases coalesced into galaxies and spiraled outward at impossibly fast speeds, hurtling toward the face of the Golaeth.

For billions of years, Golaeth continued to shoot tendril after tendril after the runaway matter, in an effort to cauterize the expansion and restore the out-of-control detonation to a more orderly pace. It pumped out dark energy to fill and cushion the voids between the spilling galaxies. But it was falling behind. Golaeth pondered whether it was time to terminate the unhealthy universe. Incursions into the Black Universe could not be permitted.

Just before its oldest galaxy exceeded the unruly universe's permitted range, Golaeth heard the cry of a helpless infant.

*****〜〜〜*****

Chapter 4.

Shipwrecked

When I come to my senses, I'm still alone. The sun's struggling to make an appearance through gray overcast, but it looks like it is losing the battle. The waves have left the beach sparkling as they deposited fine new silica crystals and retreated. I feel in the pocket of my shorts. Empty. Nothing but that little pearl.

I feel empty, but oddly, I've lost my appetite. I'd been looking forward to that picnic with Alan and Grace for a long time. Where are they, anyway? I wait a while longer, unwilling to admit they have vanished before my eyes. My heart begins to thud against my ribs. Finally, I set off back toward town, prepared to report them lost in the mysterious disaster.

The beach is deserted. It is usually crawling with locals and tourists. Everyone but me and my family seems to have had the good sense to get off the beach when the storm came up. I don't see the parking lot; it is usually overflowing, cars circling and fuming the beachgoers trying to escape civilization. The lack of wreckage after such a big storm is remarkable. I would expect the boardwalk to be a pile of lumber, but there is nothing, as though the boardwalk also has been swept out to sea. And the lighthouse isn't visible in the distance. I must really be turned around. I walk for what seems like hours along the line of sand dunes. I don't have any water, and the Mouton Cadet has vanished along with my family. I tell myself I'm not thirsty anyway. Clouds begin to thicken and move inland, and soon it is raining. I'm soaking wet again, but happy to be cool. I begin to fantasize that the storm has returned, bringing the irrational premonition that it will carry my family to me.

So I turn around and run back to the picnic spot. No one there. I fall to my knees, all of my short burst of energy drained. It's quiet, no wind, like this little spot has no weather. Wiping my face, I stumble to my feet and begin to trudge back toward the town I failed to reach before. Obviously help is not coming, so I will have to go and get it myself.

The town seems to elude me for a long while. Where has the marina gone? Surely there should at least be some pier pylons poking out of the water.

"There should at least be some footprints around here somewhere," I mumble. Sure enough, a set of footprints leads inland, toward a thicket of bushes obscuring anything beyond. I follow the footprints, in case this little social trail offers a shortcut into town.

A narrow opening in the hedge reveals itself when I get closer, and I hesitantly step through into a small garden, with crossed sticks propping up a variety of vegetables. Off to the side, a goat stands tethered, chewing on a small pile of hay. So, there should be a house nearby.

"Where's the house?" I demand, as if the universe has an answer for me. A weathered gray clapboard shack shimmers into existence, surrounded by pieces of driftwood, in a feeble attempt at front yard decoration. Not quite believing them, I rub my eyes. They feel bloodshot, like I was up all night drinking. How could this house appear right in front of me without my seeing it from afar? I run to the porch and pound on the door, yanking my baseball cap off and running my fingers through my matted, cropped hair to make myself more presentable.

The door opens a crack.

"Johnny, that you?" a woman's voice asks.

"No, my name's Virginia," I say. "There's been an accident in the storm. May I use your phone?"

The door opens wider.

"Did you see my husband on your way up?" She wears a long dress covered by a dirty apron. She looks hardly older than sixteen.

"No, sorry."

"Well, that's good, what with you going around half-naked like that," she says, seeming equally surprised at my clothes. I have on my favorite Quik-Dry nylon shorts, beach thongs, and a sleeveless blouse. She stares down at my bare legs.

"Are you all right, you poor thing?" It's as if she assumes I've been attacked and some of my clothes torn off or stolen.

"I'm fine, but I need help," I say. "Have you got a phone? I'd be happy to pay for the call." Of course, I don't have a cent on me.

Surmising this immediately, she offers, "I ain't got one of them 'foam' things, but I'll lend you my other dress. I'll take you to the Reverend. Maybe he can spare something from the poorbox. Did you say you saw Johnny?"

"No, I didn't see anyone for the longest time. I'm so glad I finally saw you."

"Well, Ginny, is it? I'm Hope. Let's see if we can get you back on your feet." She reaches under the mattress on the floor to pull out a blue dress. It's wrinkled, but nicer than what she's wearing, probably her good Sunday dress.

I used to think I'd be too proud to accept charity, but at that moment I am so grateful I could hug her. For a split second I think that maybe she's a figment of my overheated imagination, and maybe I invented her house, and I invented her. She's the kind of person I'd want to meet if I were in trouble. Or else, she is real, and I've called her up, because I need a kind, generous woman like her right now to give me hope. Either way, it seems too bizarre, and I've got more important things to think about. I slip into Hope's dress and put my sole possession in the pocket. I roll my outfit into a small bundle.

"Hope!" a man's voice calls. "We got a good haul last night. And I got some rabbits for supper." His heavy footsteps sound on the porch.

Hope grabs my arm and pulls me behind a curtain to their sleeping corner. She puts her finger across her lips to signal me to be quiet. Why is she hiding me? I realize this young woman is actually afraid of her husband. Alan has always treated me as an equal. I nod assent, and she returns to the front room.

The screen door slams, and I can hear him drop something on the table.

"Those are some fine coneys, Johnny," Hope says. "I'll cook 'em with some carrots and spuds from the garden."

Rabbits. Suddenly my appetite is back with a vengeance.

I can't resist a peek. A lean young man with a lined face wearing a tricorner hat is leaning his musket next to the door. A musket, not a rifle. And it's not something that blew away from a museum.

"But first," Johnny replies, "I've been up all night, but I ain't too tired to get some of your sweet potato pie. Come here, woman."

"Wait a sec, Johnny. I got something to tell you."

I hold my breath. Just how is she going to explain me? And how can I explain to *myself* that I appear to be in the 1800s, like in the newspaper on the beach? I feel sick. Maybe it is just *me* who's missing—everybody else is where I left them, in 2019, and nearly 200 years separate us. That seems crazy. But it feels real. How will I ever get back to Alan and the kids? Oh, God.

"Yeah, what is it? You know, you look good enough to eat, *chérie*," Johnny says.

"I found a gal on our porch..."

"*Damn* it, woman. Where's she at?"

"Here," I say, stepping out from the corner.

Johnny's hand slides off Hope's waist, and he turns to look at me, anger on his face. His expression turns to one of relief.

"A colored gal," he pronounces. "Not an escaped slave, are you?"

"Um, Asian-American, actually," I say. Then I realize that makes no sense to him. "From China." That is close enough to Korea, where my mother was born, I figure.

"Ain't never seen one of those," he avers, staring at me. "How'd she get here?"

"There was a storm—" I begin.

"And you lost your way," Hope finishes for me. "I been helping her with some food and clothes. Reckon we can take her over to the church? The Reverend could help her find a place to stay."

"She ain't seen anything, has she?" Johnny asks. His eyes flick over to the musket propped against the wall.

"Just some biscuits and chickory coffee," Hope says. I can tell she is trying to cover up something Johnny has inadvertently said, but I put on my blankest expression and play dumb.

"All right, you get her on over to Reverend Remy, though I don't know what he'll do with her, either. I'll be waitin' for you to get back, so don't dawdle."

Hope leads me out the door and waves goodbye to Johnny. I hold my wadded-up shorts, ballcap, and sandals in a bundle. Hope and Johnny seem to be going barefoot, and I'm pretty sure baseball caps haven't been invented yet. She leads me down to the beach again, where we continue in the direction I'd travelled before looking for town. I grab a stick and thread it through my clothes, leaving my right hand free to catch myself when I flounder through the soft sand of the dunes.

The beach looks entirely different than it did just an hour ago. A lot of debris has washed up, like flotsam or jetsam from a ship.

"What is all this stuff?" I ask Hope.

"Oh, jist junk from the sea," she says.

"Is it from the storm?" I ask. "Look, there are some boxes. Some have broken open. And—are those coins?" Hope just shrugs. We walk another mile or so before arriving at a small cluster of tiny frame houses. A slightly larger house has been whitewashed, evidently the church. I'm Catholic, but I haven't been observant lately, and my mind is racing furiously against my heart about just exactly what to ask God at this point.

A man scratches a hoe in the dirt beside the building, tending a garden a lot like Hope and Johnny's. I recognize tomatoes and beans. Gardening isn't just a hobby, everyone here grows their own food.

"Reverend Remy," Hope says, "this pore gal was washed up on shore and has got no place to go." That doesn't seem strictly true, but I want to find out where I am. Am I still in North Carolina, even? Even if I tell them where I want to go, they probably won't know how to get me there. Even if I came here for a reason, I don't know what that is. But I damn well am going to find out.

The man pulls out a grimy rag from his pocket and mops at his face, regarding me for the first time.

"You ain't a runaway, are you?" he asks. "We can't shelter anybody who's part of a rebellion."

I shake my head vigorously and say nothing. I know that's wrong, but it's hard to be a rebel when you're alone.

"She's Chinese," Hope says. "She cain't hardly speak English at all," she adds, poker-faced. "Probably washed up in last night's storm." Hope finally acknowledges there was a storm.

"Oh, well, then maybe we can find her a place with one of the freed slaves," Reverend Remy says. "I've got to finish my hoeing before I can take her, though."

"Thanks, Reverend. That's what I was hoping," Hope says with a grin. "I've got to git back to Johnny. He's starvin' after bein' out all night, so I'll just leave her here, all right?"

"What's her name?" the Reverend asks.

"Virginia, I think."

"Jin-Yi," I interrupt, bowing to the clergyman in what I hope is a good imitation of Chinese courtesy. Hope squeezes my hand and then runs off.

"Here, grab a hoe, Virginie," the Reverend says, pointing to the row of rusty tools along the wall. I do so, and set about scuffing up the sand-caked ground. Luckily, I've had my tetanus shots. As we hoe, a few of the local residents wander by, obviously curious about what I am doing there. The Reverend says nothing to satisfy their curiosity about this sweating visitor.

An hour later, the Reverend puts his hand on my shoulder and hands me a ladle. He points to the buckets on the church porch.

"Let's get cleaned up a little, and I'll take you up to Freetown," he says. I am glad to hear this, as blisters are forming on my fingers. I've always enjoyed gardening, but only in my mostly nonexistent spare time.

We begin marching farther north up the beach, until we come upon another small settlement, even poorer than the one we've left. A woman wearing a big gingham bonnet calls to the Reverend from the side of her house. It seems like all the arable land around here has been put to use growing vegetables.

"Fine day, isn't it, Reverend? Who you got with you?"

"This here is Virginie," he says. "She's Chinese." That seems to be all anyone knows or cares to know about me. I'm crestfallen, about to be left off with some

27

strangers somewhere in the far distant past, in a place I have no real idea where is. At least I can understand them.

The woman takes off her bonnet and fans herself with it. A mass of gray-streaked dark hair winds in soft rolls at the nape of her neck. Intelligent brown eyes take the measure of me.

"I'm Pauline Bernard," the black woman says, holding out her hand. I take it and repeat, "Paw-Leen."

She grins and without looking away says, "What brings Virginie here?"

"Hope found her, and we thought maybe you could use a hand," the Reverend said. "She doesn't have anything except the clothes we gave her. And those rags," he added, looking at my hobo bundle.

"Well, maybe she can stay with me. Since Reg died I could use the help, like you say—" Pauline says. I smile hopefully. "—at least until my son gets back from Raleigh. He's up buying a freedom."

"Where's he getting the money?" the Reverend asks bluntly. I'd be curious to hear the answer too.

"George is share cropping, and any extra money, we put towards buying freedoms," she says, standing up straighter.

"Well, tell him he ain't gonna get a share of last night's pickings, since he wasn't there to help with the work. And tell him to come over to church once in a while," the Reverend says. "I'd be happy to hold a service for the coloreds on Sunday afternoons." I think he is also hinting that this George could contribute some cash toward finding a cheap worker for him.

"I'll do that, Reverend," Pauline says, watching the Reverend's retreat. She turns to me.

"Hungry?"

"Am I!" I exclaim.

"Hah, I knew you spoke English," Pauline laughs. "Let's get you some biscuits, and you can tell me how you got here. Do you drink coffee?"

28

"I love coffee!"

Pauline laughs again. She takes a pottery mug from a hook on the wall and hands it to me.

"You can have Georgy's mug for now. Coffee pot's in the fireplace."

In the fireplace? A soot-covered fireplace sits on the floor against the wall, lined loosely with clay bricks. There's no chimney. The nearest vent must be an open window. No wonder they used to burn the house down back in the day. An open pot hangs from a tent-shaped frame set right in the middle of the coals, which have gone out long ago. Well, beggars can't be choosers. I pour myself a cup of lukewarm, murky sludge. It's delicious. A thought crosses my mind. Why haven't I just *asked?*

"Pauline, before I tell you my story, could you tell me where and when I am?"

"You're in Freetown, North Carolina, Ginny. You don't even know what day of the week it is, you poor girl?"

"No, I mean what *year* is this?"

"1827, of course," she says.

I was afraid of that.

"And could you tell me if you read newspapers? I saw a newspaper blowing down the beach before the storm."

"Well, of course," she says. "Georgy edits *Freedom's Journal* that argues to free all slaves. He gets them printed in Raleigh and delivers them all over. I read books, too," she says proudly, "so if you're real careful, I might let you borrow one."

Just like that, I am living on an old-fashioned farmstead. Up to now, I've been pretty passive, letting everything happen to me. No one has tried to kill me or exploit me, but on the other hand, none of these people have anything I want, either.

That night, on a pallet prepared for me by the kind Pauline, I lie awake, suffering silently, fearful that I might

29

never have what I desire most. I think about Hope and Johnny, probably breeding like bunnies, making a family of their own. I may be nearing the end of my child-bearing days, but I still hunger for the taste of my husband's kiss and the feel of his hands on my body.

The next morning, Pauline rises early and shakes me by the shoulder. Still groggy, I feel like I just dropped off. It's still practically dark out.

"Get on up, we've got a lot of chores to do," Pauline says. She sits in the corner and lets her hair down to her waist and combs it with a wide-toothed wooden comb. She dips her fingers in a pot of grease and smoothes it down her hair before rolling it back into coils and pinning them up. She dons her sunbonnet and an apron. I'm already dressed—I've slept in my poorbox dress, which is my sole article of clothing and much dirtier than the one Hope loaned me. My short hair is probably a scandal of some sort, but at least it's easy-care. I've never been able to keep a decent hair-do.

We set to work setting up the food supplies for the day. Pauline shows me how to milk the goat, which does not want to be milked by an amateur like me. Pauline laughs as I jump up and down after having my foot stomped upon.

"She'll like you better once she knows you'll be feeding her," Pauline says. She shows me a patch of tall grass and hands me a bushel basket. "Trim enough to fill this up. You can give it to her tonight."

"We're going to need more biscuits," Pauline says. "You do know how to cook, don't you?"

"Of course," I say. "But I may need some help figuring out your oven."

"You're completely useless is what you're saying," Pauline says. She sets me to work the rest of the morning harvesting tomatoes and plucking hornworms off the plants. The little monsters look much bigger up close, as they cling stubbornly to the vine, eating it down to a bare skeleton. It's a gruesome job dislodging them one at a time then hacking squeamishly at their soft bodies with a hoe until the green blood fertilizes the ground. It's a cruel world out there, and I've become soft and weak. By afternoon, I'm so tired I've almost forgotten to worry. My back is killing me, and my hands and feet are throbbing from myriad tiny cuts from the sandy soil.

"God, I'd give anything for a hot bath, or at least to be clean again," I murmur. "I'll try to do something when I get home, but it looks hopeless."

When I get back to the house, Pauline does a double take.

"What the devil happened to you? Did you jump in the creek? How did you get so clean?"

I glance down. My homespun dress looks like it's been to the Laundromat, and my hands—there's not a speck of dirt under my fingernails.

*****~~~~*****

Chapter 5.

Impossible Things

That night, Pauline cooks a wonderful stew of tomatoes, peppers, and squash, the fruits of my labors.

"You did a good job today, Ginny," she says, ladling out a big steaming bowl and offering me a plate of biscuits. After supper, she gives me a slim volume to read. It's a poem called *Tamerlane*, by a young author named Edgar Allen Poe, which she says is about finding independence and pride, as well as loss and exile. I'd forgotten that Poe started out as a poet before he began writing his wonderful detective stories.

"Thanks, Pauline," I say. "Having something to read will help a lot. I'm feeling so sad and hopeless, afraid that I'm always going to be lost."

Pauline reaches out and holds my hand. "Before I thought of dedicating my life to freeing my people, I felt the same way, but look at me now. You're just looking to find your way, child. You'll know it when you see it. Now get some rest. We have a big day tomorrow."

As I drift off to sleep, I wonder if I am going to die here, forgotten in a godforsaken backwater. I think about the vanished colony of Roanoke and the legend of the Croatoan name carved into a tree. That happened around here somewhere, didn't it? Damn it, now I can't sleep again.

The next day, Pauline's son George arrives. I'm helping out in the garden, pulling weeds, which seems to pretty much be the routine around here. Crows fly overhead, checking out the pickings, their black wings temporarily blotting out the sun. I stand up to rub my back, reminded of the time I made a pilgrimage to a Philadelphia museum to see Grip, the raven that inspired Poe's poem, "The Raven." He wouldn't write it for eight more years. Noting my inattention, a squirrel runs off with one of Pauline's prize ears of corn. She's been babying that stalk for a week, waiting for the tassels to age just right. She lets out a shriek of distress when she sees the bushy tail retreating rapidly. Without thinking, I blurt, "You stop right there, you little rascal." The squirrel *bounces*, like it has run into a wall. Confused, it drops the ear and dashes off to the side, vanishing into the adjoining field.

"Darn varmint," Pauline says, running over to pick up the corn cob. "Luckily, he dropped it," she says.

"Well, I'll be—," a deep voice says. A tall black man appears from the forest of cornstalks and drops his bag. "Who's this, Momma?"

"Georgy!" Pauline exclaims, throwing her arms around him. "This here's Virginie, and she's been shipwrecked."

I rock back a little on the balls of my feet. He's seen the squirrel fly into the air. I remember how a rock suddenly appeared in my hand when I wished for it back on the beach the previous week. Something is very strange here, and not just the disappearance of my family.

I seem to be able to do a lot of impossible things now—everything but go home.

☺

These are the clues: I have found myself inexplicably transported to a beach on the North Carolina coast in the year 1827. My family has disappeared. I can move things with my mind. But I can't get home. I've tried. Believe me, I've tried.

I've been taken in by a family of black sharecroppers, and the work is hard. At least now I can fall asleep most nights, exhausted. Troubled dreams invade my sleep, however, until I wake and spring to my feet in the dark, the tarry smell of burnt-up pine logs clinging to the hairs in my nostrils and threatening to suffocate me.

Just an anxiety attack, I remind myself. I read a theory somewhere that some nighttime panic attacks are a reaction to a lack of oxygen. The body just tries to wake you up and get you breathing some fresh air.

I pull my shawl tight and step outside the house, gulping in buckets of air and waiting for my pulse to slow. A feeling of impending doom and fright hangs over me.

"You all right, gal?" Apparently George can't sleep, either.

"Oh, fine, thank you," I reply. "Just had a little nightmare."

"Ah, *cauchemar*," he says, using the French word for night terrors. "Very bad. They are very common here." A pitch match flares to life as he lights a hand-rolled tobacco cigarette. The Bernards have a small stand of tobacco, but they mostly save the valuable crop to sell up in Virginia.

I nod, although this hasn't been your common, everyday nightmare, like the one where you show up for school not wearing any clothes. We stand there looking out at the night, too uncomfortable to say anything. I can tell he is curious about me, but he doesn't ask.

"Best get inside," he says, finally. "Be sunup in a few hours."

I thank him and return to my bed on the floor. A *cauchemar*. Is that what I'm living in now? Will I ever wake up?

☉

Pauline and George and I spread ourselves in rows along the cotton patch, peeling the ripe cotton puffs from their pods and stuffing them into our shoulder sacks. My harvesting skills are minimal, at best, but I want to help in any way I can. Pauline's been complaining about the corn borers, weevils, and tobacco crickets, and I've decided to try an experiment.

"Get on out of here, weevils," I say. "Go pick on someone else's field." A bright flash, like lightning in the distance, briefly lights the corner of my eye.

"Did you see that?" Pauline asks. George nods, casting a look my way. I bite my lip. Why did I open my mouth?

"Maybe we should finish up, in case there's a storm coming," George says.

The wind is picking up, teasing my hair into knots. It's grown an inch during my two-month stay and no longer stays neatly tucked behind my ears. We gather our bags and hurry into the house.

*****~~~~~*****

Chapter 6.

Wreckers

And they are gone: aye, ages long ago
These lovers fled away into the storm.
—The Eve of St. Agnes, John Keats

"Captain! There's a light! We must be near the shore, thank the Lord!"

Captain Blauw frowned at the horizon, obscured by sheets of driving rain. He too thought he detected a faint glimmer.

"Bring us closer, bosun, but watch out for rocks. We want to get there in one piece. If we don't, there'll be hell to pay."

The bosun understood all too well. The red-headed Captain Blauw was famous for his Irish temper and would brook no failure. Of course, it was the Captain's fault that the *Albion* was lost and in trouble. He refused to take advice and had insisted they veer off course in the first place. Then the storm hit, and they were in unmapped waters.

"Get on with it, or I'll have you keelhauled," the Captain blustered.

"Aye, aye, Sir." The bosun tried to turn on his heel with some dignity but was tossed off his feet as the ship lurched to starboard. He sniffed, mumbling, "It would hardly be possible to keelhaul anyone in this weather."

Blauw almost felt a sense of despair. Here he was, back in his own time, and a miserable time it was. He'd always been an outsider. He'd sailed the seven seas—and the seven galaxies, for that matter—and this was a disgusting demotion in his eyes. He especially despised America. He'd been totally loyal to Calaneris, ever since being pulled out of his own era to serve a powerful galactic empire. About to die in a battle where life had no meaning, all around him he saw faces bloodied, guts exposed, and legs shattered—and he was next. Miraculously, he'd risen from being a lowly infantryman to a powerful Renaissance man capable of the most exquisite mayhem. He gained even greater favor when he suggested that the petty despot Calaneris call himself "Emperor" and add Roman numerals implying a long pedigree. Blauw'd become a master spy and provocateur, but to what end? Now he realized that Calaneris had just wanted to send him back to do dirty jobs on Earth.

Calaneris had dismissed his objections, assuring Blauw that this was an important mission. But he was being tight-lipped about it, which was unusual. Blauw only knew that when he took command of the ship, he already had a fearsome reputation, and that was good enough for a start. His assignment was simply to land hereabouts, locate a particular woman, and capture her quickly. Killing sounded simpler, but either way the job was totally beneath him.

"There it is again!" a voice shouted. "The light's moved!"

A grinding noise rose from under the keel.

"We're breaching!" the bosun yelled. "We don't have a lot of boats. What are we going to do, Captain?"

"Captain?"

"We're probably going to drown, I expect," Blauw said. He cursed Calaneris and all of his forebears.

☽

Two days of steadily worsening rain is beginning to cause us all to go stir crazy. George announces he is going out.

"I'm going over to the town, Momma. Don't wait dinner for me."

I envy him getting away, but not the two-mile walk in the mud.

Much to my surprise, he asks, "Want to come along? Maybe the Reverend has some news." Perhaps they find my castaway story believable after all.

I jump at the chance and ask Pauline if there is anything she wants from town.

"No, you go on, gal," she says with a smile. "I hope they've heard something about your kin." Turning to George, she says, "Not a very nice day for a walk, though."

George tucks a knife and a small shovel in his belt and shrugs into his coat. I don't have a coat, so Pauline hands me a tarp coated in pine pitch. The thing stinks to high heaven of turpentine, but I take it gratefully. Together, George and I step out into the rain, blowing almost sideways at just below gale force.

It is almost impossible to talk during the long slog, as the wind howls and lightning continues to jump from cloud to cloud. Just before we reach the settlement, George stops suddenly. I skid to a muddy halt beside him.

"Why are we stopping?" I ask. He pulls out his shovel and sets about digging.

"Making a trench to channel some of the water away from the path," he yells, his voice barely registering above the wind.

"Oh," I say, relieved that the shovel isn't for me. But then he says it.

"I know what you are."

"What—I'm sorry?"

"I seen you doing witchy things."

"I'm not a witch," I say. I don't know what I am, but that certainly isn't it.

"This coast attracts 'em," he states flatly. "I seen your hat, with the pentacle on it. You're one of them."

39

I wonder when he had been going through my things. I come from a family of computer geeks, and we are not a superstitious lot.

"That's just a hat. You know, for the sun?" I ask, Valley Girl style, pointing to my head. He is having none of it.

"Just growing sot-weed isn't enough to keep us. Knowing you were a witch was the only reason I decided to keep you around. If you help us, I won't tell them what you are."

As I stand there sopping like a drowned rat, I have a sinking feeling in the pit of my stomach. Logic isn't going to work here. I don't have any logical explanation, anyway. I'm about to be blackmailed.

"What do you want me to do?"

"We's wreckers."

"Wreckers?" If that is some Creole word, I don't know it.

"We wreck ships."

"Why, that's terrib—" I start to blurt, but think better of it. "What do you mean? You and Pauline?"

"Of course not, you fool. We men—he emphasizes the word 'men'—put lights on mules to lead ships to be shipwrecked near shore, so's we can loot them of their valuables. This weather's perfect."

I think about the lighthouse that I'd never found. It is in the future. This is a treacherous coast, and someday they'll put one up, and George and his friends will be put out of business. Until then, I am about to be pressed into service as a criminal.

A rustling in the bushes catches our attention. Through the dripping foliage, Johnny emerges.

"Let's go, George. Peter's got the gear ready— What's *she* doin' here?"

"This here's Ginny," George says.

"I know that. Why did you bring a woman?"

"She's a *cauchemar*," George says.

Johnny takes a step back and crosses himself. "I knew she wasn't a castaway," he says.

I almost laugh. A corrupt pirate crossing himself? His hand creeps to a knife in his belt, and he fingers it speculatively. I stifle myself, knowing my self-defense skills might not stand up to his practiced blade.

"I'll help you, but after that I'm gone," I say.

"Suits me." Johnny grabs me roughly by the arm, and we set off toward the beach.

A group of men are clustered under a tarp on the beach, barely visible in the driving rain. They have lanterns, but they are unlit. No fire. Miserable. We wait for darkness.

Johnny calls out, "There's one! Let's get it over here." He lights several lanterns and hands one to each of the men, who begin to pace back and forth along the strand.

A barely visible dark hulk of a ship approaches. Haloes of violet light hover off the mast as lightning streaks through the clouds. It's St. Elmo's Fire, usually considered a good luck sign. Sailors take it as a sign that God's on their side.

"Are they going to be all right?" I ask. "The ship, I mean."

"No, this here's the worst rocks on the whole coast," George replies with a grin. "They think we're signaling them to safety off the reef."

"What about the people?" I exclaim.

"How do you think they found you?" Johnny says, echoing Hope's impromptu story. There could have been a wreck the night before I arrived, but with George having been gone, I'm not sure. "We'll take care of any that survive," Johnny adds.

I don't tell them that I am not the victim of a shipwreck but of something much worse. "What's the best route to have survivors?" I ask, desperate.

George points. A small frothy current snakes in and out of the rocks.

"Then I hope the ship follows that current," I say.

A huge crunching sound hits our ears as the ship strikes the first of a series of rocks. Maybe these pirates have misled me. A sliver of moonlight pokes through the heavy clouds.

"Oh, no, not on the rocks!" I yell. The ship suddenly vanishes.

George grabs me and holds a knife dangerously close to my face. He yells, "What did you do, *cauchemar*? Bring it back right now, or die right here."

"All right!" I say, pulling away. "There it is."

Visible again, the prow of the ship heaves upward and lands on a sandspit, grounded. Lightning continues to strike all around, alternately brilliant white, then turning green. I can see a lifeboat hit the water, and man after man jump alongside into the water.

"You'll all swim safely to the boat," I say under my breath.

"You half will be the welcoming committee," Johnny shouts to his companions. Half the men run to wave the lifeboat passengers in, while the other half pull out a rowboat and head for the ship. I've read about this in the history books. The law allows people to scavenge shipwrecks, but these men will have caused the shipwreck. They'll strip the ship of all its goods and push the ship back out to sink. The survivors will just be grateful to make it to land and be none the wiser.

⊘

The next morning shortly after sunrise, George and I return to the house in Freetown. Pauline is starting a fire to make breakfast.

"Look what I brought you back from town, Momma. It's a fancy gold watch from Paris, a Louis Moinet chronograph. I know how you like French things.

See, you pull out the stem to set the time, then you push it back in, wind it, and it starts ticking."

"You're a good boy, Georgie," Pauline says. "I was worried about you out in that storm."

"Well, there was a shipwreck, and we got caught up helping the survivors," George replies. "I'm going back to help with the cleanup."

Turning to me, Pauline says, "Did you hear any news from the Reverend?" I suspect Pauline really knows about the wrecking. It's a small place, after all. And that watch isn't something you just pick up lying about.

"I sure did," I reply, glancing warily at George. "I'm going to have to be going soon to look for my people."

That day, the shipwreck is all the news. I help Pauline clean up some of the damage to the farm from the storm. The tomatoes look beaten down but still alive.

"Well, at least the storm must've wiped out all the weevils," she says. "I ain't never seen the fields look so good." The raindrops indeed sparkle on the cornstalks.

I go back inside to pack up my bundle. I slip on my shorts and 21st century clothes and pull on my 19th century dress over it all. I leave the *Freedom's Journal* I'd found on the beach beside the bed, along with Pauline's copy of *Tamerlane*. I'd been surprised to find that the Bernards could read. Silently, I wish I'd met Edgar Allen Poe, instead of coming here.

When I finish packing, I go outside. George stands in my way.

"You know you can't keep doing this, don't you, George?"

"It pays for freedoms," he says.

"Yes, I suppose it does, but it's time I was free of you. That knife trick you pulled was the last straw." He hovers over me, but finally turns his back, not acknowledging that I could break him like I broke that ship last night. At least I think I can.

That is going to be the last I ever want to see of George, though I'll miss Pauline. If I ever get home, I'll have to look up what happened with the slave rebellions. We Americans tend to forget so much of history that we don't find pleasant to recall. Right now, though, I don't know if history is the same as it was. Maybe I've changed some things just by being here.

When I leave, George is gathering his tools and baskets to go help glean the last of the goods that are washing up on shore. I walk ahead toward the town of Nags Head, where people are scrambling to pile items up. A group of ship survivors huddle in blankets near the church.

I think about lending a hand with the refugees, but shake my head. Besides, it looks like the wind is picking back up, and I have to be moving on. I look over at the broken ship, which is disintegrating rapidly. Maybe it is my imagination, but I'd swear I see a giant head rise over it. A sea creature with glistening scales shakes the iridescent spray off its whiskers and disappears beneath the waves. I stare. The wreckers turn to see what I am looking at, but there is nothing there. And nothing for me here. I made few friends, except for Pauline.

I smile a little, reminded of the creamy iridescence of the pearl I found on the beach. The wreckers won't get everything.

I continue past Nags Head back to my spot on the beach and sit down. The rolling gray waves look the same as ever. It could even be the same day I left, except it is a little sunnier.

As the sun sets, a green spot glows above the sun, reflecting on the ocean surface. This is a treat, seeing a rare green flash. Suddenly a green ray shoots up from the spot and begins to move. I stand up. The sea boils all around the beam as it cuts its way toward the shore. Toward *me*.

Involuntarily, I finger my pearl, which I've grown to suspect is my magic good luck token. I begin to pray.

"God, save me, please. I promise if you'll get me out of here, I'll do anything you want. Anywhere but North Carolina 1827."

A fresh wind comes up. I pull out my baseball cap and stick it on.

The green ray vanishes. So does the sun.

🌀

I've finished constructing Hangul the dragon, as requested, QoS *reports.*

"*****"

"Yes, I agree that this will be a good vehicle. She's going to be traveling longer distances and times from now on, and she'll need him to help her get there, while still feeling a connection to her own mythos. The dragon answers to the Cintamani pearl that we've given Virginia. She's already had a glimpse of it and can manifest it anytime she wants."

"******"

"It will seem part magic and part technological miracle. Each of the scales is an individual peripheral device linked to the mainframe that is Virginia's Cintamani. Some handle dimensional shifts, while others handle construction of wormholes. I've patterned it after an Earth-style Korean dragon, so it can fly through the air or swim in the sea, but it will just as efficiently convey the rider through vacuum or through any sort of turbulent flow. Its 'whiskers' will be capable of forming a protective radiation barrier."

"******"

"Thanks, I'm rather proud of it, myself," QoS says.

🌀

The green ray has disappeared, but the beach is still here, a calm and gray late winter afternoon. Somehow I know I'm not in Freetown anymore. I'm afraid to sit down again, expecting another weird storm or event at any minute. And was I hallucinating a sea monster?

"What? What?" I say, to no one and nothing. "Who are you? What do you want? Where am I, and why am I here?"

I scan the skyline, but it is just me, alone again, waiting. Presently, a broadsheet blows cartwheels toward me down the beach.

"Is this for me?"

I reach out to take a look. The headline draws my eye. It says, "Babbage Difference Engine Announced." I hold my breath. My husband Alan is a computer scientist. Maybe this will lead me to Alan! I clear my throat.

"Rock," I say. My trusty paperweight appears in my hand. I lay the broadsheet flat on the sand and look for the date. Then I read the whole thing very, very carefully.

*****~~~~~*****

Chapter 7.

Lost in Heaven

Your pain is the breaking of the shell that encloses your understanding.
—Khalil Gibran

I hear faint music, a mixture of open-string droning violins and voices sauntering up and down the harmonic scale, then switching to the minor. Is it the pure minor or the minor of a mode, I wonder? I would like to record it, but my fancy smartphone disappeared along with my family. I was in my sixth year of musical studies when I lost the idea of home. I suppose learning all of that theory was a waste, but now it is coming to me as I sit on this beach in the middle of nowhere and nowhen.

"Knowing your modes is the key to improvisation," my teacher said. All those modes, with their Greek names—Dorian, Ionian, Lydian, Phrygian... Phrygian's the one I don't understand, though she tried patiently to explain it over and over. The name comes from the wild lands of Anatolia bounded by the Black and Mediterranean Seas. Is that what I am listening to? Would I know it if I heard it? Would it take me home if I could play my thoughts in that scale? What scale does the universe play in, anyway?

This place looks and sounds suspiciously like how I imagine heaven, but it's not a place I want to be, at least not yet.

"Don't get lost in heaven," I warn myself. "Heaven's going to have to wait." I stand and brush the sand off my hopsacking dress. Opening my bundle of 21st

47

century clothes, I slip on my sandals and begin to walk "north." I'm not going back to Freetown if I can help it. How I got there in the first place remains a mystery to me. All I want is to get back to my husband and family, but I've lost the way back. No GPS here, for sure. The broadsheet in my hand is an 1870 London newspaper, the *Daily Universal Register,* and it reports on the recent invention of the Babbage Difference Engine. Like the 1827 newspaper, it looks freshly printed. Surely a clue? But if 1827 was a clue, I fail to see what it was trying to tell me. Maybe that I've become a witch? Or that I have a superpower, like telekinesis?

If I can move ships, I'm pretty sure I can move myself, maybe all the way to London. Then I could find out if anyone named Alan has been seen there. My husband was always proud of having the same first name as the famous Turing. I'm sure a mathematical society is where Alan would belong if he could pick anywhere in the Anno Domini 1870 universe. Unless he is just as lost as I am. But am I still in 1827? What if I have to wait forty-three years to see him? I'll just have to take that chance.

"I wish I was in front of the Royal Mathematical Society," I say. Suddenly I am standing on a busy city boulevard filled with horses and carriages.

"Hey, watch yourself, twirlie," a voice shouts. I step back and narrowly miss being trampled by a huge bay carthorse. Throngs of men and women crowd the edges of the street, dressed in somber browns and blacks.

Am I in London? The driver spoke English. I turn around. The building behind me is an ornate arched edifice surrounded by a wrought iron fence. I enter the gate and climb the short stone stairway to read the small sign, hidden behind one of the columns: "London Mathematical Society, est. 1865."

I've successfully made the jump from 1827 to 1870, and I'm not 85 years old. "That's not possible," I say, but it looks that way. I can travel in both time and space, nice to know. A map would be nice, though, so I could see exactly where I've come. There's no address, so I head back to the street. Turning to a passerby, I ask, "Excuse me, can you tell me where I am?"

"Piccadilly, of course," he replies, curling his lip a little and hurrying on.

I realize that I still look like a beachcomber—or a castaway, which I am—and mumble, "Sorry I'm not better dressed." Shivering in the moist London air, I realize I'm still human. "I wish I had something warmer on."

Well, all right. I could get used to this. My hopsacking dress is now tweed wool, with a large, full skirt and a ruffled train attached at the back. Grace would love this; she was into Victorian Goth. I correct myself. Grace *is* into Victorian Goth. She's not dead, only missing. I can feel some bloomers underneath, too, and a corset restraining my middle parts. Good, I won't freeze—it is quite chilly here. I touch my head. My baseball cap has turned into a felt bonnet. I wish mightily for a mirror so I could see myself but find the large plate of shining brass the door reflects my image quite nicely, thank you. I carry a little velvet purse with a drawstring. It isn't even big enough to hold a cell phone, and therefore seems quite useless. I look inside, and notice that the little pearl I found on the beach is nestled in one corner. Might come in useful if I need to bribe anyone.

A man sitting on the sidewalk holds out his hand. I look inside, and notice that the little pearl I found on the beach is nestled in one corner. No money, though.

"Would a pound do?" I ask. The man's eyes widen at the sight of the silver coin, and he jumps up and runs off.

Well, if I can get whatever I wish for, I will try again. I always try again.

"I want to be home, back before all this happened. Make everything all right again. You know what I mean,"

I add, in case this is like a case of making your wishes to a genie very specific.

"Do you need help getting home, madam?" a middle-aged man asks me, tipping his hat. I jump, startled. I haven't gone anywhere. What is the deal here?

"No, I've got an appointment here at the Royal Society, it appears," I reply. I chafe a little at being called "madam." Sure, I'm almost 50 years old, but I don't enjoy being reminded of it all the time.

"I am just opening up," the man says, pulling out out a key on a chain and unlocking the door. "Reggie Pierson, at your service. Is there something I can help you with?" Colors dance through stained glass panels onto the parquet floor of the entry.

"I'm looking for one of your members," I say. Pierson leads me into a library. I savor the smell of polished leather couches and reach out to touch one to make sure it is real. He lights some gaslight sconces on the wall and sets hurricane lamps out on the reading tables.

"Have you encountered anyone by the name of Alan Jones, a quite talented mathematician?" I ask.

"That's a very common name," Pierson says. "Let me look in the membership roster. We've only been in existence for five years, so it shouldn't take long." He pulls out two heavy volumes and drops them on the reading table. But before opening them, he says, "Please excuse me for inquiring, but are you from the Orient?"

"Not for a long time," I reply. Truthfully, I only know what my grandmother's told me about Korea. Was it called Korea in 1870? Did they eat Kim Chee then?

Reggie's claim seems to be correct. Each register contains biographies of 50 members, along with names and addresses.

None are Alan Jones.

"Was he ever associated with the University of London?" Reggie asks.

Lost in Heaven

I don't know. I lived with the man every day for nearly 30 years, but who he talked to when he went to work was sort of a black box. Alan and I mostly talked about recent physics discoveries that were making the news. Disappointed, I gather up my monster skirt and prepare to leave.

"Do you by any chance have a tintype in your reticule?" he asks, eyeing my little velvet pouch, which wouldn't hold anything bigger than a thumb drive at most. "It's possible I might recognize him."

"A picture," I say. A sharp corner protrudes from my bag, and I tug the drawstring open. Inside is a small sepia-toned image of Alan. I feel an adrenalin rush, and my hand shakes as I hold it out to Reggie.

"No," he says. "Wait, he does look a bit like the magician at the Spring Gardens in Kennington. My fiancée and I were there years ago. The place is horribly run down now, but the man was a marvel. No one knew how he did all of his tricks."

"When was this, exactly?"

"Oh, it must have been back in '59," Reggie says.

I wonder if this is another cruel trick of fate. "Ha, you've missed him by 10 years, lady," it whispers to me.

"Do you think he's still in London?" I ask, trying to disguise a quiver in my voice. This just tears it—I've journeyed on a hunch to the Royal Mathematical Society, but Alan is not there. More to the point, he is not *when*.

"Well, you could ask around Kennington," Reggie suggests. "Hmm... Let's see. We pride ourselves on having the most up-to-date maps." He selects another bound volume, which turns out to contain a map of the Greater London area. He points to Kennington. "Would you like me to call you a cab?"

I demur, knowing I could probably get there in an instant.

"You know, it's odd, because I remember seeing another nicely dressed Oriental lady at Spring Gardens," he says. "She made quite an impression on me. You're only the second one I've seen in my entire life. Interesting coincidence, though."

"Thank you so much for your help," I reply, and hastily open the door to the noisy street. The tang of horse manure wafts in. Breathing through my mouth, I step out and feel the door close behind me. Where can I find a quiet, private spot for my transport? Offhand, I can think of but one.

"The Beach, please." I am there, moist sand threating to ruin my dainty suede boots. The music and the soothing sound of the ocean are mesmerizing, but I have to concentrate.

"Kennington, 1859," I say, "requesting a free transfer." I know sarcasm won't help, and I don't know where the hell I'm going precisely, but I figure the universe does. I've read about the place in an old English novel, where they called it "Vanity Fair."

Promptly, I am deposited on a rural roadway beside a large park. Smog-shrouded London is barely visible off in the distance, though it appears that development has begun encroaching on the countryside. In its heyday, this was the remote hideaway of pleasure seekers of all kinds, and Vauxhall Gardens were the amusement park of the rich. Under new management, the sign now reads "Spring Gardens." A woman carved in white stone lies on her face beside a hedgerow that obscures whatever is beyond. Shards of flower pots are strewn about, covered in slimy moss and about to be buried by the training wallflower vines that spring up all around. I hope I'm not just on the long road to nowhere. But the air is clear here, and a light breeze caresses my face.

A tuneless whistle make its way to my ears. Definitely not Phrygian, I decide. More like Mixolydian. A ragged citizen is picking his way along the rutted road, eyes fixed to the ground in front of him. A tuft of red hair sticks out from his cap. He has nearly come right up to me, until I say, "Hey there, you."

Startled, he stops. "Beg your pardon, m'lady."

"No problem," I say. Might as well get right to it. "May I ask, are they still doing shows here?"

"Yes, there's a magic show every night, and it's only sixpence to get in."

"Do you work here?" I ask.

He chuckles. "Naw..."

"So you live around here, then?"

He glances around, not answering.

"Just waiting for the show, then?"

"Aye, that's it," he replies with a wink. I consider myself lucky not to have any pockets to pick and tighten my grasp on my little bag.

"When does it start?"

"After sunset. It doesn't look like much right now, but with the lights and all, the gardens are still pretty. Oh, and they've got a new replica of the Hampton Court Maze. That's really something."

The sun is fairly low in the sky, and I figure I can wait until evening. But it wouldn't do to loiter about here, so I thank him and set off in the direction I'd seen him coming from. After a bit I turn around again to wait. That's when I come upon the maze attraction. The shrubbery is only about a foot and a half high, and you can see all the way to the center. It seems like it would be hard get lost in this maze, so I saunter in. Maybe I've spoken too soon. I've taken several wrong turns, and my feet are beginning to burn. Ah, a little teak bench. I take this opportunity to sit down and take off my right boot. I stare ruefully at the blister burgeoning on my big toe.

"Band-Aid," I say, and peel the sterile wrapper off. Pulling the tabs apart, I center the gauze on my blister and carefully wrap the sticky plastic strip around. The familiar adhesive smell comforts me, as it did when I was a kid. I crumple the wrappings and stash them in my purse.

Wouldn't do to leave my trash in the past. I get back up and trudge on. Reaching the center of the maze, I notice a sign showing a map of the Hampton Court Maze. Below that is a quote:

Our Universe is a labyrinth. We can't see the barriers, but they are there, and they shunt us down many paths, only one of which is right.

—Emperor Calaneris XXIII

I've never heard of this Calaneris, but he has that right. My mind wanders, while I think about all the court intrigues and love affairs that probably took place behind the tall hedges of the real Hampton Court Maze. I lose track of time for the next hour or so; no one intrudes on my fortress of solitude. I begin to see clumps of people approaching, laughing and talking loudly. A few carry flasks and pass them around to their companions. The men have red daisies tucked into their lapels, and the women wear sprays of lilies of the valley in their hair, showing off the pride of their gardens. I hurry back toward the maze entrance, again marveling at how a dinky little hedge could hide the route so effectively.

"Did you like the maze, ma'am?" It's the pickpocket. Where did he come from all of a sudden?

"Um, yes, thanks very much," I say, and hurry to join the latest gaggle of celebrants. Keeping a decent distance, I follow them until I am near the place I first "appeared." I look around and wonder if a younger version of Reggie might show up, fiancée in tow. Would I recognize him if he did? I decide to change the color of my outfit, just in case. Now I am wearing a green damask ensemble, with an even bigger skirt and tighter corset. I scowl, but have to give the universe credit for looking out for me and adjusting to the fashion of the day.

"Where's my little bag?" I say. The outfit adjustment was fine, but I still want my little bag and souvenir pearl. My ensemble is complete.

Lost in Heaven

As dusk arrives, I go with the flow and soon reach a large open-air pavilion covered with awnings and brightly lit by gaslights. A brass band is chuffing out a hearty overture, but it's hardly sufficient to cover the hammering in my chest—ba-room, ba-room, ba-room. Surely everyone can hear it; it's as loud as a bass drum. Is it from the prospect of possibly seeing Alan—if he is indeed the magician of Spring Gardens? I tell myself not to assume too much; you can't always identify someone from a single picture.

To my chagrin, a man is stationed at the broken-down gate, demanding a half-shilling of everyone as the multitudes stream in. I am about to wish for a sixpence coin, if there is such a thing, when the ticket taker waves me in. Either I am overdressed, or he considers me one of the performers. A large playbill has been glued to a tent pole at the side of the entry, "The Great Mathison."

I help myself to a program for an extra tuppence. But when I rummage in my little bag, there's no tuppence, and the pearl seems to be missing. That's disappointing. I should have checked when I asked for a different outfit. Maybe the thief took it? I already miss my lucky jewel— things seemed like they'd been going better since I found it. I put the program back on the pile and concentrate my attention on the playbill.

"The Great Mathison in Spring Gardens," the poster says. "Single-handedly won the War for the British by breaking the Russians' polyalphabetic substitution ciphers." There is a map of the Crimean War theater, but with the exception of the Black Sea I don't recognize most of the landmarks. I'm a typical American—we only know enough geography to get to the grocery store. I wonder if Mathison could be Alan.

Amid much jostling, all of the audience is finally seated. I find a spot in the far left, second row, thanks to being a singleton. Several ushers turn down the lights along the wall and light more at the foot of the stage. A burst of applause causes me to look up. There he is. Alan! Afraid I can't believe my eyes, I stare at him, as if I could will him to look beyond the footlights and see me waiting for him. I study his face, drinking it in. It seems older than I remember. Has he worried about me as much as I have about him? Perhaps, but it appears he has settled into his act, at least for now. It's impossible to be patient, but I wouldn't want to disappoint his fans. Besides, I'm itching with curiosity about what the Great Mathison's act is like.

"My friends!" he shouts. "We are in for a treat tonight. I will need a volunteer from the audience." I jump to my feet immediately, but my foot catches in my voluminous skirt, and another man runs to the stage ahead of me. The ushers pop over and boost him up next to Alan. I sink back down in my seat.

"Let's start with something simple," Mathison says. "What is your favorite food?" The man laughs and says, "Pasties."

"Ah, a lover of savory fare," Alan says, plucking a meat pie seemingly from the air. I can't tell whether Alan's using magic tricks, or real magic like my pearl. My pearl... I feel a sudden shortness of breath that's not due to the corset. The audience laughs and applauds, while the man takes a big bite and nods.

"Are you perhaps a veteran, sir?" Alan asks. The man shakes his head.

"No matter, thank you for your service anyway," Alan says, dismissing him.

"I will now perform for you a rendering of the Siege of Sevastopol," Alan declares. The footlights dim, and a large white sheet drops from the rafters. The ushers secure the bottoms by pounding tent pegs with wooden mallets. A flickering image lights up the sheet, showing a panorama of a battlefield. A projection screen? Yes! At first it appears to be black-and-white, but as my eyes adjust, I discern it is in color—it is just that the smoke from cannons makes everything appear gray. Suddenly, a soldier in the panorama comes to life and begins to run across the screen. The audience gasps, amazed at the Great Mathison's technical expertise in illusions of light and motion.

I too find it fascinating, but the more I look, the more I realize it is not a recreation of the battle, but a *creation*. A number of Russian combatants fall to the ground, as some very realistic blood sprays toward the onlooker. Some of the ladies shriek, and a general murmuring ensues.

"I beg your pardon!" Alan loudly interrupts. "The horrors of war are no way to entertain ladies and gentlemen. Let us see a more pleasant scene. The motion picture switches to one of a rural countryside, with groups of people walking down a road. It is right here in Kennington, I'm willing to bet.

"Let us see who is coming to see the Great Mathison!" The view swings around from face to face, lingering at times upon a particularly pretty face and then moving on.

"Look, there's Mattie!" someone exclaims. "I saw Robert, too. How did he do that? There's been no time to develop tintypes or create images for projection!"

Alan only smiles, allowing his audience to admire him. The red-haired man's face appears, scowls, and disappears.

Another face moves into focus, filling most of the screen. My God, it is *me*!

I stand up.

The smile evaporates from Alan's face, replaced by a look of consternation. "Virginia? Turn up the lights," he demands. "Virginia? Are you here?"

The audience seems confused. This probably isn't part of his normal act. Is the Great Mathison trying to reach someone beyond the veil?

"I'm here, Alan!" I shout, waving my arms.

He looks around frantically, unable to see beyond the stage. "Not the footlights, you fools—turn up the *house* lights!" Alan springs off the platform, landing badly on one ankle. He scrambles to his feet and scans the crowd, seeing me at last. We fight our way the short distance until we can touch. I want so much to touch him.

"You got my message," Alan says.

What message? That doesn't matter to me. I curse at my hoop skirt, which seems to try to keep me from my husband. Just as we are about to embrace, the ground shudders, and Alan's face turns a greenish shade. The awning erupts in flames, as a blinding beam of viridian light cuts through from above, turning the pavilion into a scene of chaos. Abruptly, Alan fades away right in front of me. Muffled screams sound in the distance.

"No! Alan!" But it is no use. I am back again on the damned beach, tears streaming down my face. The pearl I thought I'd lost sparkles cheerily on the sand in front of me. Stupid pearl. Doesn't it know Alan is a part of me? I fill my lungs up to scream at it.

"Take me back!" I demand, but nothing changes. "Kennington 1859!" I repeat, to no luck. There is nothing but the program in my hand. The Great Mathison in Spring Gardens.

What went wrong? The pearl didn't listen to me. Am I back in the 21st century? If so, that man is long dead. I sink to my knees and rip at the green damask skirt that has been my downfall. How can I bear it? I feel like my insides have been ripped out too.

*****~~~~~*****

Chapter 8.

The Unwinding

As before, it is daytime on this beach, a sort of gray, misty, yet warm and pleasant daytime. But it never changes. I feel like I've been marooned on a desert island. I may be safe, but I'm not sound. I know this is some sort of bubble that holds back the universe, or at least protects me whenever the green rays strike. But there's a vast darkness out there, filled with stars and galaxies. Places I could be looking for my family. I've heard it's possible to see stars in the daytime. If I were standing at the bottom of a deep well, it should be possible to look straight upward and see stars. It's tempting to wish for a very deep hole and bury myself in it—to see evidence that there still *are* stars. I'd even settle for just Venus. It is supposed to be visible in the daytime, if you know exactly where to look. I don't. Yet it is always daytime on this beach, and that in itself is strange. There were nighttimes in Freetown and London, telling me that there are normal days and nights somewhere. How many somewheres can I go, I wonder? Apparently London 1859 is barred from me.

I wish I had paid more attention when Alan took me to a physics lecture at the university. They talked about a concept called "Schrödinger's Cat," in which a cat placed in a box with a deadly substance that might kill it can simultaneously be both alive and dead. But if you open the box, the cat will be either alive or dead. I don't see that you have any choice but to open the box. You might kill the cat, but it's going to starve otherwise. Now all you have is a kitty cat, and you haven't observed anything about the quantum physics that was going on in the box. That uncertainty is what they call "quantum entanglement."

So, am I alive or dead, or both? I've been able to move about Earth in time and space by simply wishing aloud, but I don't know how it works, or why sometimes it doesn't work. Am I even in the same space as Alan? It seemed like it in London. But it doesn't seem like it when I'm here, on this beach. Why did Alan fade away right in front of me? Once we were entangled in the true sense of the word. But it seems like something came along and unwound us from our mooring. I've come to call the event that sent me on this quest "the Unwinding."

I'm afraid. I can go somewhere else, but can I get back? Not back here, but back to the here that was the here and now of then. Now you see why I'm afraid. I'm not starving, or anything, in fact, I feel perfectly well when I'm here—but I might be in that box like the cat. Is this a real place?

It's hard to understand if there's a purpose to all this. I thought I could get Alan back with my newfound powers, and that would be an end to it, that I would go from being lost to being found. Now I know my search is just beginning. I thought I could do it alone, and now I know I can't. Being lost in time feels even more dangerous than being lost in space. Like, what was the point of going to 1827 and then 1870?

Maybe 1827 was a retreat, an easy place to stash me while all hell was breaking loose elsewhere. A place that hadn't unwound yet. But then it did. The universe won't let me return to dangerous places or times, yet it's guiding me forward somehow, provisioning me for a long journey into the future. The newspapers and the Hampton Court map seem to be attempts to give me a heads-up of what's coming. The problem is, they're frustratingly inscrutable. I hate those stories where Harry has to solve a stupid riddle before he can save the world. Give me a Poe story anytime. I call up the Hampton Court map and spread it out on the sand. Something about the Emperor Calaneris quote tickles the back of my mind, like *déja vu.* If the emperor is right, everywhere I go takes me a step closer to reaching Alan and my children. I'm being shunted through a maze, but I can't stop or rest. I've returned with nothing but deadly knowledge: There's a killer in the labyrinth, and it's green.

I sit and think for a long time. Night never falls. I see no stars. I cry a lot. Finally, I deduce that there must be *two* forces at work, one that's on my side, and one that wants to destroy me.

I pick up the little pearl from beach. Do I really have magical powers, or is this some sort of advanced technology that's been tailored to me? A pearl couldn't just reappear at will, could it? Someone has to be directing it, or else it's been designed to answer my commands.

I'm not thirsty, but I try an experiment.

"I'd like a glass of cabernet right about now." A glassful appears in my hand.

"No, I want it in a red plastic cup," I say. The wineglass immediately changes to the kind of cup used at fraternity houses—or at picnics. Angrily, I fling the pearl into the surf.

"Find your way back, if you think you can," I say. I look down. There it is, right at my feet. The pearl obeys me. I hate to admit it, but the powers it gives me give me hope. Right now, my pearl feels close enough to magic for practical purposes, but if I think of it logically, like Alan would, I'd conclude it's some sort of steering device, and this beach is like a ship. A really big ship.

Common sense tells me I'll never get anywhere unless I get moving again.

"Alright, you, universe, or heaven, or whoever you are, I'll keep following your tune, and you'll keep tantalizing me with finding my family." *From now on, I'll call you Poe, after Edgar Allan.* Though I can't touch my family, I will take them with me no matter where I go.

They will always exist in my heart, regardless of how we get lost in time, space, or dimensions. My telltale heart.

A new melody begins to form in my mind, playing lightly against the modal backdrop, yet not clashing with it. Humming, I fold up the map and put it in my pocket. I think I'm finally learning to improvise.

"Take me to the top physicist in the world," I say. But that might not be good enough. The green lightning might mean something is happening to the universe, and only I can sense it when I've got this pearl. "Make that the most eminent physicist in the *universe*," I correct. If I know anything about my husband, that is who he would seek too.

☉

Perched on a narrow ledge, I press my chest a little closer against the sheer rock cliff face. Rain is pouring in buckets, and I can hardly see. My fingers grasp at what is an uncertain handhold at best. I look down at my feet, which is a mistake. I groan involuntarily and begin to tremble. I've always been subject to fear of heights, and this is an agoraphobic's nightmare. Is the universe out to get me? I have to be comforted by the thought that the universe probably doesn't really give a damn about my feelings, just my safety. I wait for my shaking to subside and contemplate my next steps. I don't want to take any more steps, but on the other hand, I don't want to go back to the Beach either.

Through the rain, I can make out a big winged reptile flapping its way toward me. A dragon. And not just any dragon. I recognize the scales I saw on the sea creature back in North Carolina. Is this my ride?

His giant head has whiskers like a carp, and his body is long and snakelike. I'm thrilled that this is one of the Korean dragons my mother showed me in the picture books we read when I was a kid. Rather than being evil fire-breathing monsters, Korean dragons were related to water and agriculture. The *Hantul*.

"Nice draggy," I say, as he hovers just below my right foot. He is wearing a leather saddle trimmed in gold that I hope I can slide onto.

"Hold it steady," I plead, and edge my foot out into the air over the saddle toward the stirrup. Suddenly the dragon's wings stop flapping. Oh my God, he is going to plummet from the sky, without me. But he doesn't plummet. He remains in place, seemingly contrary to the laws of gravity. I reach out to grab the pommel of the saddle and throw my leg over. I nearly overshoot, but I soon get my bearings and am sitting on a dragon. I glance again at the scenery below, mostly lost in rain and mist. My head spins, and my stomach lurches. I resolve not to look down again.

Now that I am sitting on my trusty steed, we take off, shooting sparks behind us. Now I wonder if this is a real lizard. Maybe it is a machine of some sort. If he's a machine, I am a little disappointed, because this means he won't be carrying the mythical stone of unimaginable power that would give its possessor the powers of omnipotence and creation at will. I chuckle. I have my lucky pearl for that already.

"Take me to the nearest city," I say. "And cut out the rain, will you? I got enough of that in North Carolina and London."

෨

A wide boulevard lined with Art Deco-style buildings curves ahead, like something out of a 1930s Flash Gordon serial. In the distance is a range of steep, snow- capped mountains, a row of Mount McKinleys jutting splendidly out of the plains to create a postcard-perfect backdrop. But obviously it isn't 1930s Hollywood. The sky is a sherbet shade of orange, and there are two suns, one half the size of our sun, and one that is much smaller. A sign on the pale yellow lawn is written in some lettering that I can't understand. Oh, wait, I can understand it now. It's a pointer to a public park, I think. It seems to say "Place of Contemplation."

It would help if I spoke the local language, I think to myself. We land in the open space, where I dismount. "Hangul—" I've decided to name him Hangul—"why don't you go park yourself somewhere?" I watch as he becomes a tiny speck in the sky.

"Mistress Jones. We have been expecting you." I turn around, and see a tall humanoid (yes, that's the best I can do) person bending over to greet me. He wears a helmet with a divided nosepiece upon his oversized head and sports a cape over a suit of tights and boots. My God, is my imagination really that clichéd?

"Right," I say, with as much sarcasm as I can muster. "Is this what you really look like?"

"Not really," he or she replies. There's no mouth at the bottom of its head. It's spooky hearing sounds coming from a moving mannequin. "We wanted a setting that is acceptable to us both, since we both seek the same thing. We wish to make you as comfortable as possible."

"We seek the same thing?"

"Yes, we believe that is true."

"I'm looking for my family, who disappeared a few months ago on Earth."

"We, too, are looking to return to our home."

"You said, 'we.' Is there someone else here from your home?" I feel that would be a good sign if two people from the same place and time could co-exist.

"My fellow physicist Ralff is here with me. I am Benrus."

An alien named Benrus, like the watch brand. But that reminds me. I'm here to talk to the best physics minds the universe has to offer. This is not exactly what I had pictured the word "best" to mean. I guess I expected it to be a human. How provincial of me.

"Well, thanks very much for meeting with me, Ben." I pause. "You know I just wished myself here, right? I'm here to find out how that is possible. And, by the way, do you know where we are?"

Ben nods. "You've traveled several light years from your home planet, beyond what you call the Oort Cloud."

"What did you mean about having expected me?"

"Well, perhaps not you in particular," Ralff says. "But discrete theory showed the probability of a remote traveler tracing this path during this century was high. We surmise you've visited other discrete points as well, correct?"

I breathlessly launch into a description of my adventures leading up to this point, peppering it with theories about what might be happening, Schrödinger's Cat, mazes, magical pearls, and all. I'm beginning to believe my pearl is the Cintamani of legend.

"Your suppositions are accurate, as far as they go," Ralff says.

"Which ones? The part about our universe unwinding? Or the part about Earth being under attack?"

"Both, but the latter activity may indicate the existence of another universe, one that's incompatible with our own."

Wow. I've phrased my request so that I would be talking to the best physicist in *my* universe, not even supposing there could be more than one universe, like Alan's friends have theorized. Alan was always saying, "We live in the universe that is best suited for us to live in." Is that right, and has that changed?

"Though remarkably uninformed, your questioning mind is quite insightful," Ben says. "We have pondered much the same questions since the Event occurred 800 years ago."

"The Event?"

"That is our name for it. I was a young soldier. Our world had ever been at war. My father was a great warrior-athlete, and it was my turn to carry on the tradition of my family. You can probably see that, from my superior musculature compared to Ralff. But I was beginning to doubt the value of war. Our traditions taught that war built character and physical stamina. War fed the fires of industry, keeping us ever striving for more powerful weapons and employing the population in worthy occupations. We based our pride in ourselves on war. But once I'd traveled to Kantor Prime, where the war was actually waged, I saw that death was everywhere and that the people we were fighting were not all that different from us." He nods at Ralff.

I agree that the physical difference between the two is negligible, though Ben is a little taller.

"You say you traveled to another planet to fight? What did the natives think?"

"The natives had been gone or killed eons ago. I came home on leave and told my father what I had seen. Instead of understanding, he was angry with me, saying I should not talk of such things."

"How so?"

"He said the enemy was pledged to wipe us out and that the winner would inherit our whole world. I asked him why we couldn't share it. After all, both nations originated on Jandalat. My father wouldn't be moved. He insisted I go back to Kantor Prime and finish my duty to kill as many of the enemy as possible."

"How did you get to this other planet? I assume it was in your same solar system?"

"Not at all. We are all skilled at quantum displacement."

"What? Then how far was this planet, anyway?"

"About 20 light years from Jandalat."

"What? If you all can travel that distance that easily, why didn't one of you just pull up stakes and move to another planet?"

"Pride, I'm afraid. Jandalat is the jewel of this quadrant, rich in resources and exceptional beauty. It is the capital of learning and culture. Or, at least it was. Our home planet suffered incursions very similar to the ones you recount. One of our new recruits materialized and told us about widespread destruction on Jandalat caused by ionizing radiation from space. I declined to further engage with the enemy I faced and immediately displaced home. When I arrived home, Jandalat was nearly destroyed and disintegrating fast.

"Wasn't there anything you could do to stop it?" I asked. The idea of Earth being destroyed like that caused a shiver up my spine.

Benrus replied, "I hoped that as a physicist I could determine the problem and do something about it, but knowing the cause doesn't always mean you can directly see the solution. I tried constructing a planetary shield, but it soon failed. Perhaps some of my people managed to displace to other planets, but most didn't survive. I had resolved to stay to the last and had made my peace with death."

"But then I arrived with further bad news from the battle front," Ralff said. "Although we were enemies, we recognized that it was hopeless to stay on Jandalat and decided to retreat to a safer location to contemplate our limited prospects. That's one thing we do really well. Contemplate."

"Ralff and I held hands and displaced here," Benrus said. "We have constructed a limited form of stasis. We tried our best to reproduce our home, but the world which we made for ourselves was rather void and featureless, compared to our colorful and energetic world."

"It rained all the time until you came," Ralff adds.

"It sounds a lot like my beach," I agree.

"We knew you had arrived when the brilliant colors of the sky returned."

"Hmm. I did tell the rain to knock it off," I say. "This place is really quite lovely."

"I think we have you to thank for the fine weather," Ralff says. He reaches over and takes Ben's hand, which seems a really Earthlike thing to do. I think I feel a little jealous that they at least have each other.

"But, my God, you've been here for 200 years, afraid to go back home. Well, what's next? Will we be ever able to go back to our home worlds?"

It's given us a lot of time to think," Ralff says. "After much contemplation, we became convinced by the idea of multiple universes."

"I get that, I suppose. But it's hard for me to imagine."

"It was for us as well. But even harder was the idea that those universes could have been created."

"Like the idea of God?" I ask. "I thought you two were level-headed scientists." In fact, I know they are, because the Cintamani brought me to the "top physicist in the universe." Which one is that, I wonder, Ralff or Benrus?

"Yes, to us it might appear to be a godlike power. But in practical application, the universe we live in may simply be a physical construct, and there may be others like it."

"So, what does that have to do with the Unwinding? Is the universe crashing? I can tell you right away that I don't think I can do a thing about something like that."

"You may be underestimating your influence, Virginia," Ralff says. "Imagine, for example, that some intelligent entity has created a universe in its laboratory. It could be imbued with free will."

"What? The universe isn't alive, is it? There's no evidence that it thinks, much less has free will."

"You simply weren't looking for such evidence," Ben says. "We've had time to look, and it's fairly clear that our universe has intelligence, and from that you can deduce that it will develop, or already has developed, conscious will. It's obvious that even artificial intelligences eventually develop it."

"And that's what's been ordering me around? And screwing up my life completely?"

"And the lives of many billions of others."

My tongue has suddenly grown too big for my mouth. I'm afraid to ask the next question.

"How would I know, if it never spoke to me?"

"There are the missives you've been receiving," Ralff points out tactfully. "I think you called them clues. And there is the evidence we collected, of course."

"What evidence?"

"The Big Bang—the creation of a baby universe could have left a signal that we can detect."

"Signal?"

"The creator's "signature," so to speak. Ralff and I are confident that the background radiation that pervades our entire universe contains evidence of disruptions."

"You mean the Unwinding."

"Yes. It can only mean that another universe is somehow in conflict with ours."

"Can we do anything about it?" What I really hope they can explain is, can *I* do anything about it?

"We still have hope that we can restore the universe to its previous state, or at least some of its content, although we are presently powerless to do it," Ben says.

"What do you mean? We wished ourselves here, didn't we, and we can change all kinds of stuff..."

"Those are simple quantum travel techniques," Ben interrupts. "That has always occurred in our universe. This organic entity has just showed you how to do it.

"You mean my pearl—my Cintamani?"

"Yes, it allows you to focus, or more accurately, to unfocus. You feel the motion of travel without actually moving."

"OK, what do you think my pearl is?"

Benrus is silent for a long time.

"I don't think you will be able to understand the problem, even if we knew all the facts concerning the artifact you call the pearl."

"Why don't you try explaining it to me?" I say. "I've come a long way, after all." I'm trying to remain polite, but this isn't the first time I've been talked down to by a physicist.

"On our planet, we developed a power source that enabled us to travel via quantum entanglement. We tended to use it for locational displacement, rather than time travel, as we were not sure of the consequences of our actions, especially in the past. Some of our number visited the past, but only to observe. On your world, certain strange, time- or place-altering events may have been considered magic, or voodoo, or fantasy, but on occasion they did occur, via quantum entanglement. But what happened during the Event was much more complex. There may have been interaction with laws from a different universe. Your device, er, Cintamani, seems to be some sort of superior quantum displacement aid."

Great. "Lost Horizons" was for real. I'm reminded of stories my grandmother from Korea told me, about how the magical Cintamani conferred immortality. I should have known I was just a primitive in the universe tourist crowd. "But you said 200 years ago. It's only been a few months for me."

"Relative time dilation is part of the mystery," Ralff says. "We've been waiting several hundred years for you to show up, and we knew you were coming. We only knew someone would show up eventually," Ralff says.

"Why not just come visit me directly, then? You're in my universe, right?"

"We couldn't. We can only go to our own base and this place. And we had to wait in time for you to show up. You see, you are much more mobile than we are."

"Well, I'm not totally mobile. I almost touched my husband, and he faded away in front of me, and I went back to my beach. Then I couldn't get back to him at all."

"That's interesting. Perhaps there are some new laws about previous position," Benrus mused. "That might explain why Ralff and I can't travel about very much, because we've already been all over the place in the past."

I realize that in my rush to pump Benrus and Ralff for information I've been inexcusably rude. They're stuck, after all.

"I'm honored that you've waited for my arrival all this time. I'd like to hear more about your civilization, and how you knew I was coming," I say. "Then maybe we can work together to make some headway on the Unwinding."

"As we mentioned, we are currently in a stasis point some distance, about 20 light years, from your solar system," Ben explains. "It would actually be reachable within the lifetime of a human, but it's much more efficient using quantum travel techniques."

"That's kind of a coincidence, isn't it? Wasn't your war planet about 20 light years from you? How did you discover how to travel this way?"

Ben glances at Ralff and shrugs. "We'd like to take credit for discovering it on our own, but actually our people rather stumbled upon it. We have always been divided almost equally between those who are totally logical and fact-minded and those who are religious. But even the religious are logical when it comes to being confronted by scientific facts. Then, there are those like Ralff, who understand both points of view—and that even facts can change." He signals to Ralff to continue.

"The legend tells that our ancestor Gant'er first made the discovery around 2,000 years ago," Ralff says. They were conducting research on natural disasters that were currently unexplainable, and had traveled—on foot as was the custom—to the Monastery of Contemplation on a sort of pilgrimage. The monastery was famous for

71

inspiring many great intellectual discoveries, in part due to the beautiful natural surroundings. People went there to have peace and quiet, and sometimes came away with new ideas.

"Gant'er was hiking behind the Monastery, when he saw a path leading up into the hills and decided to follow it as it wound behind a tree-shrouded grove. When he got to the grove, he was surprised to find that the scenery had changed completely. It turned out to be your Earth, as we later found out. Sheep grazed on a meadow, and Gant'er approached them, knowing they were harmless wildlife, but then a shepherd appeared and began waving a staff at him. Worried, he pulled his robe across his face and stumbled backward. That was when he found himself back home, with the view of the Monastery hunkering below.

"Our people immediately began traveling all over the known universe, and we experienced a great blossoming of knowledge, taming the cosmos to do our bidding and developing huge power resources. We even sent a few missions to Earth to learn more about your people, being careful not to disturb the status quo like we had accidentally done with the shepherd. Everyone was especially taken with your horses. Beautiful creatures. We had nothing like them on Jandalat.

"So, you people just up and travelled to Earth, just like that?" I ask. "Kind of a coincidence that we should meet here, isn't it?"

"We travelled many places. Once you understand how to do it, you can merely move molecules aside and go where you wish," Ben says.

"Right," Ralff says. "That was over two thousand years ago. Shortly after that, the war started with Bromia. It had gone on so long that neither Ben nor I had any idea how it started. We only knew that we had right on our side and that we had to go to Kantor Prime to battle for our honor. Then the Event occurred. Huge explosions rocked our planet, destroying in only a few weeks beautiful natural features and works of architecture that had taken many years to build." He looks at Ben. "I particularly will miss the Tower of Gradients, and of course, the Monastery was totally vaporized. Luckily we have reproduced it here."

"So, you didn't use wormholes to get here?" I'm not exactly sure what a wormhole is, but maybe they do.

"Well, certainly they may be necessary for some forms of travel, such as temporal displacement," Ralff says. "But we didn't have time to find out. All we had time to do was build a stasis point, which is as you see here, and take shelter within it. Ben and I are brothers now."

It is hard to believe these two have been hanging around here for 200 years.

As if he can read my mind, Benrus says, "We're still quite young. There is no aging here." To me, they both look alike, tall, pale, ageless—and totally alien. But now I can see they are in the same fix as I am, wanting their families and hoping to be reunited with them.

"Would you like to see the Monastery of Contemplation?" Ralff asks.

I agree readily, and we start walking in the direction pointed to by the sign. The Monastery is a large marble edifice, with high ceilings painted with figures and horses. I guess Earth has indeed made an impression.

"You understand, the Monastery was on a completely different continent than you see here. In a way, we've created an idealized version of Jandalat, one where everyone is at peace," Ralff says.

"May we offer you some protein-carbohydrate?" he asks. We have a small laboratory here and have developed some excellent Earth-style cheeses."

"No thanks," I reply. When I'm in stasis I apparently don't have much of an appetite. "Did you bring anyone else?" I ask, looking around. The Monastery looks like it could hold hundreds.

"With the short time we had, we tried to spread our small population around to different stasis points to maximize the possibility of survival," Ben replies. "Unfortunately, we failed even at that. Each stasis point has failed under the barrage, leaving only Ralff and me at this one remaining point. One of us checks on the base every now and then, but it's hazardous, as our planet may no longer be hospitable to life. We don't know if any Jandalarians are still alive. Your visit has verified that Earth is also being attacked. It appears that whole areas of space-time are being deleted."

"Deleted? That sounds bad. Do you know if my family is alive, or even in the same universe as before?" I ask. "Are they as mobile as me, since none of us were quantum travelers before?"

"Your question is illogical," Ben says. "How could we know if we have been in stasis?"

"Benrus, Gin is just trying to find her family. Logic has little to do with it."

"Thanks," I say, a little dubiously.

"Very well," Ben says. "It is of course possible that your family can travel about like you, yet, if so, that will not help much once they travel many more pathways, thereby closing them. I'm sorry to dash your hopes in this way."

But I persist. "What's closing the pathways? You guys used to flit about the universe at will, right?"

"We suspect an intelligent cause, but we do not yet know what or who that is. It is possible that something in another universe is trying to shut us off so that we cannot travel to theirs. This also implies the intrusion of the laws of a different universe."

"Has anybody done that in the past?"

"Not to our knowledge. But as I have pointed out, we have been isolated since the Event."

"You know, that's beginning to sound like a plot." Something else dawns on me.

"So, if I leave here, I can't come back and bounce ideas off you and Ben?"

"That's been our experience," Ralff says.

"Is there anything I can do for you?" I ask, suddenly chastened by the thought of their predicament. Here I have come looking for their help, and they are far worse off than I am. They aren't just missing their friends and relatives. They are missing their whole world and their whole timeline. "I feel kind of bad that you've been waiting 200 years, and I don't have anything to offer."

"You are still relatively free to move about," Ralff says. "If you keep looking and choose your paths judiciously, you might find who's at the bottom of this and restore the boundaries between the universes. We don't see that happening in the next 300 years, but maybe after that..."

"Three hundred years! I'll never live that long."

"It may be much shorter in your timeline," Ralff soothes. "Besides, with the Cintamani device, you should be able to live as long as you like, at least in our universe. We only regret that Ben and my peoples did not declare an end to hostilities and work together sooner. Together, we may have been able to find the cause of the Unwinding, as you call it, much sooner. Now the chances of saving Jandalat and Earth are much reduced."

This totally blows my mind. Here I have discovered that quantum entanglement really exists, only to be told I might be witnessing the end of the universe. A sobering thought indeed.

"If I might make a suggestion?" Ralff says.

"Yes, please! Anything!"

"You might want to try going farther into the future. We were only slightly ahead of your timeline when the incursions began. Perhaps in the farther future you can learn more about how this will continue to unfold—if that is what it is doing—or you might meet others much more advanced than us."

This is the first I've heard that Ben and Ralff are in the future, as well as being 20 light years from Earth.

"But how will I find them? The universe is a big place."

"We think you have some common times and places that tie our stasis point and yours. Anchors, so to speak. From our vantage, this anchor seems to be holding. You mentioned receiving clues when on your stasis point. You could return there and request further clues."

Heading into the future is a daunting thought. At least in North Carolina and London, I had the advantage of knowing some history. Ben and Ralff have been gracious enough to deign to speak with me—at least Ralff is—but an even more godlike far-future entity might not be so understanding or cooperative.

I agree that it must be done. In fact, I'm anxious to get going.

"Shall I call for your displacement vehicle?" Ben says.

"You mean Hangul?" He's really cool and all, but I wonder why I need a dragon? I've already moved through time and space. Apparently he's for transportation, whatever that involves. I won't look a gift dragon in the mouth. "Yes, please," I say.

I admire the sunset-tinted sky a last time as I mount Hangul make a sad goodbye to Ben and Ralff and try to push away the frightening thought that I might never see my family again.

*****~~~~~*****

Chapter 9.

Natural One

Once more, I sit on the beach, scooping handfuls of sand and sifting tiny pieces of seashell through my fingers. "Like sands through the hourglass, so are the days of our lives," I mutter. And the sand is running out.

What to do first? I have stopped the aging process in myself, and, I hope my loved ones have done the same, wherever they may be. I would have thought this violates some natural law, but when I looked at the wrinkles on my hands and told them to go away, they did. I hope that buys me time.

I would be afraid to do this magic with just everyone I meet. Ben and Ralff warned that people might not understand, and I've found that out for myself in Freetown. People of my world's past who showed supernatural powers tended to be tortured, exploited, killed, or, worse, worshipped as gods. I am certainly no god, at least by my own definition. If I *were* God, this little hiccup in the universe would be fixed in a flash, no worries.

Yet, when I think about it, my family has allowed me to lead a charmed life. Ever since I met Alan, I haven't been able to get over how lucky we've been. Alan's gifts in mathematics and computer science have led to a stimulating life in a small, sophisticated city. We sampled all of life's pleasures, culminating in Grace's birth. Alan is practically a genius, but Grace is the truly exceptional one. Why did the universe decide to pick me and not Grace? She'd be a natural at this.

"Looks like you are going to have your hands full with this one," the doctor said when she was born. My daughter's voice seemed unusually powerful, not just the cry of a newborn infant. "Here you go. She wants me to give her to you." I thought he was just encouraging a new mother to take a look at what she had produced, but his hands were shaking, and he turned abruptly and practically ran from the delivery room. Was there something wrong with her? I asked the nurse, who assured me there wasn't, she had the right number of fingers and toes and everything.

I felt drawn to my baby. Most would simply say we bonded immediately. The pediatrician praised me for Grace's rapid development.

"You must be doing something right," she'd said. "Grace's progress is off the charts. She's already sitting up, and she's only two months old." Soon Grace was walking and talking, well ahead of all the books I consulted about infant rearing. The doctor warned me, though. "It's common for child geniuses to rush ahead of their peers at first, but at some point to level out and be like everyone else."

It wasn't that Grace was just smart. Even as a little tyke Grace was lucky, winning every game she played, even against adults. Sometimes it seemed like people would do anything just to please her, so it was easy to assume they were simply letting Grace win. Sometimes I worried that by having only one child we were spoiling her, but our fertility seemed to be out of our hands. No little sister or brother was forthcoming. Grace seemed content being daddy's little girl.

But then—she must have been about six at the time—I picked Alan up during a student demonstration at the University. I think the march was over whether to allow more foreign student visas. Two students had blood dripping down their faces following a rock-throwing exchange. Despite fancying herself as a rebel, Grace screamed for everyone to stop fighting, her voice ringing powerfully through the noise like a bell. I remember being surprised when the crowd immediately dropped their signs and walked away. They had stiff smiles on their faces, as if embarrassed that a little girl had compelled them to realize that they were all brothers and sisters underneath. When I looked down at her, Grace was crying. She had single-handedly healed a serious rift, but I think it frightened her.

After that, Grace was never idle, never content to accept the suffering in the world. I was active in local politics, but, unlike Grace, had never felt called upon to step out of my comfort zone. When Grace learned to drive, she immediately asked for the keys to the family car to transport homeless people to the local shelter. Grace admired so many different cultures that I think it took a while for her to find herself. She studied Japanese and Chinese, devouring anime books and movies, and went through one of those godawful Emo/Goth phases, before eventually majoring in International Studies in college. She said she wanted to improve international relations. Of course, we were partial, but Alan and I had no doubt she could do it someday.

I miss all the things my daughter and I used to do together, like trying on hats, seeking to outdo each other checking out books at the library, frequenting classical music concerts, and even our mother-daughter fights. I think of the aria from La Wally, "*Ebben! Ne andro lontana*" (Well, then! I'll go far away). I wonder how far away Grace is. Has she found a place to stay? I tell myself she's okay, but it doesn't make it feel any less miserable.

I was so lucky to have a brilliant and beautiful daughter who seemed to lead a charmed, if emotional, life. It seemed my luck ran out the day the Unwinding took our family apart.

*****~~~~~*****

Chapter 10.

Back to the Future

OK, I'm going to the future.

But I soon kick myself that I hadn't asked the physicists Benrus and Ralff *where* I should look. The more I think about it, I'm not sure whether Alan, Gracie, and Eric will be there. If I go to the future, will they all be dead? I don't want to traipse around the universe at the expense of never seeing my family again. I sit on the beach laying out a plan. I've got to set my priorities.

I remember Ralff saying that his stasis point is holding up well, and this beach seems to be safe too. I decide to stay close to home.

I will specify a place in the future where everyone stays young indefinitely and where Alan, Grace, and Eric are present. "It's not my problem to make this all consistent," I say to myself. "If I only have a limited number of trips, I want to go someplace with the best chance of meeting my desires. Oh, and someplace with no racism. Don't make me a slave or anything."

I concentrate. "Can I have Hangul?" Is it listening? Apparently it is. I'm sitting on him. The dragon rises from the beach and wheels about slowly before taking off in a rather steep upward trajectory. I dig my knees in and hold on for dear life. After a bit, I notice that there's no wind blowing in my face, and I'm in no danger of falling off. I try to relax; I guess Hangul is more of a taxi than a monster.

I think we're back on Earth. At least, it's a lot more like home than Jandalat. We're over the ocean, near shore. We climb several hundred feet and level out, heading inland over heavily wooded forests and fields. I can see a small settlement in the distance with what appears to be a medieval castle towering above it. The closer we get, however, the less medieval it looks. There are people moving about, but rather than being in medieval garb, most of them seem to be Asian or Hispanic Americans wearing tee shirts and jeans. I would be very comfortable here. There are also what I would call not-people. Robots? Aliens?

My flying dragon fits right in here. A little of everything? What is this, Future Disney?

I spot the castle courtyard and ask to land there. I dismount, feeling decrepit as my hands and thighs reluctantly uncramp from the effort of holding on to the saddle.

"Who's in charge here? I'd like a word, if possible," I say, my usual meek self.

Suddenly the castle shimmers, and I'm looking up at a gigantic square steel building. A high chain link fence surrounds the property. I appear to be in the warehouse district, unless it's a prison. A tall garage door looks big enough to accommodate my dragon. There's a sign beside it: "Please ring for service." I hesitate, not knowing exactly what I'm going to say. I reach out and push the bell. The gate retracts, and I step inside the compound.

The garage door rolls upward to reveal a cavernous room, dimly lit except for a bank of lights off to the far side. The ceiling looks to be at least 16 feet high, and the room stretches off hundreds of feet.

"Wow, that was quick, the way you whisked me away from that castle," I say appreciatively, thinking it was my pearl's doing. "Where are we now?"

"You're in the same place," a voice says. A beautiful woman with golden skin and purple streaked hair steps out of the shadows. She's not just tan; her skin is actually golden. She reminds me a little of Grace, hair slicked back into a ponytail and wearing a flowered kimono-style miniskirt and high-heeled sandals.

"The same place?"

"Everything is virtual reality here," she said.

"So you think I was never actually flying through the air?"

"No."

"Oh, that's intriguing. So everyone just wishes for what they want, and it happens?" I prompt.

"Of course," she says.

"The castle wasn't really real, right?"

"Only as a projection," she says. "Was there something you wanted to ask? I received a request for information."

"I hate to enlighten you, but my dragon is quite real," I say, not completely sure any more if that is true. "You'd better bring him back if you know what's good for you."

Hangul shimmers into visibility in front of us. He lets out a huge roar at the young woman, who jumps back instinctively. Apparently Hangul didn't appreciate being banished.

"What is this place and all this machinery? Some sort of computer center?" This dank data warehouse is a little disappointing compared to the adventures I've already had in the "past." "Can't you just travel anywhere you want?" I remember Ben and Ralff saying they could do that. I've done it myself.

"That is physically impossible," the woman says. I choose not to disabuse her of the truth. As far as she is concerned, for all practical purposes, VR is just another form of reality.

"Where am I, exactly?"

"This is Los Angeles."

"I mean, *when* am I?"

"It's June 14, 2416."

I'm stunned. I meant to go into Ben and Ralff's future, and I've only gone 400 years into my own future. I am off by a thousand years, at least. Maybe this is the time dilation they mentioned.

"Where is everybody?" I ask. "L.A. used to be a big city."

"This is VR channel 16747, colloquially known as Skywriter Channel," she said. "Millions are tuned in to different channels, although only a few bother to show up at the actual projection sources, like you just did. It would require leaving the comfort of their living rooms."

I am beginning to think this has been a total mistake. I am alone in a big room with a purple-haired woman, and my family is nowhere in evidence, not at all what I specified. I've gotten used to the idea that miracles either occur, or they are denied. And there's a dragon sitting there licking his claws. This is the most completely illogical event I've experienced—unless, of course, you count the Unwinding itself.

"I— I was expecting to meet some people here," I say. "Have you seen a young couple and a man more my age?" Too late, I remember I've gotten rid of the gray, so the question seems foolish. "A middle-aged man, I mean."

"Everyone assumes the visage they desire here," the woman replies.

"Visage? You mean I might not recognize them if I saw them?"

"Not unless they chose to reveal themselves.... Excuse me a sec."

Myriad projections spring up around the woman— holograms?— and she rapidly manipulates them to take orders in real time and wave them off into the delivery pipeline. I wonder what people are ordering. I blush slightly as I see that a lot of the orders are for particular forms of sex, some of which I can only theorize. Others are for entertainment and food. I can understand the allure of having the world behave just the way you like it. This certainly beats having your pizza arrive in less than 30 minutes. Still, I wonder why VR is used so heavily here.

My guess, upon recollecting the poverty in much of 21st century Los Angeles, is that people needed it to escape their troubles. Now no one feels the pressures of the real world, except for this woman. I once read that people who play video games really do see more, so maybe they never get a chance to get bored or unhappy with their lot in life. If Grace and Eric are here, they'd fit right in.

"I'm looking for my daughter and son-in-law, Grace and Eric Magnusson, and my husband, Alan Jones. How can I let them know I'm here? I didn't really make an appointment." The universe could have scattered my family on four different continents and changed them into dragons, astronauts, or Olympic athletes, for all I know.

"We'd be happy to take a message," the woman says.

"Anybody by those names show up here recently?"

"Almost no one uses their real names in VR," the woman replies. "But I can take a DNA sample and locate any immediate relatives."

"Well, that would help with Grace," I say. "Alan and Eric like video games. They might have used avatars like a giant white alligator or a kraken. The woman smiles. The more I look, the more she looks like Grace. Is she already trying to fulfill my wishes with virtual reality tricks?

"What's your real name, if I may ask?"

"It's Violet Rain. Dr. Violet Rain." With her purple fringe, that's apropos, but she seems young for having a doctorate. She says she is the channel manager for 100,000 people. She isn't physically present, but her avatar can assist me. Suddenly I remember Alan's statement, "You got my message." Right before he vanished from 1859—or I did.

"Violet, you mentioned messages. Are there any for me? I'm Virginia Sun-Jones. Gin for short."

"None that have come through this channel. Do you want me to check the others?"

"How many are there? Will it take long?"

"There are about 700,000, but they are adding channels every day. It shouldn't take long, though, perhaps a few hours or so."

They may have good computers in the future, but instant gratification is still a dream.

"I'll wait," I say. "And could you broadcast that I am here and am looking for those people?"

"Certainly." I am encouraged that she hasn't called me "madam," but I suddenly wonder if in assuming a younger appearance I might look markedly different, so much so that my own family wouldn't recognize me. I request the return of a few crow's feet and gray hairs. The universe helpfully obliges, to my slight dismay.

"How would you like to pay?" Violet asks.

"Take it from my account." Payment is no problem, as I apparently do have an account. I am happy that I have picked up an ability to invent new "realities" quickly myself.

Away from the beach, I discover I have a ravenous appetite. I request a chair and some food and sit down to wait.

While chowing down on some excellent cashew chicken and veggies, I ask Violet where the food comes from. I also wonder where the power for the VR computations comes from.

The room shimmers as she shows me the sparkling farmlands surrounding us.

"Am I looking at the real thing?"

"Most certainly. Los Angeles was the first to apply the concept of brownfields on a large scale, and it's been highly successful," she says proudly.

"What's a brownfield?"

Back to the Future

"It began as a government project to reclaim contaminated land and restore it, but it evolved into farming on the reclaimed land. A lot of houses that had been abandoned were torn down and turned into gardens. At first, it didn't seem to be catching on, because the urban landscape was so poor—the whole place had been paved over—but then people discovered they liked the feeling of community they got from working with their neighbors, and it just took off. Plus, it was easier to grow food locally, of course."

"Let's go there, then." Violet looks surprised.

"Sometimes I prefer physical travel," I say, smug. She looks up at the sky as if really seeing it for the first time.

I bask in the warm sun, so welcome after weeks of rain. I'm amazed to see L.A. transformed into gardens. The farm we are standing in stretches off for many acres. A woman wearing a wide-brimmed sun hat rides an electric tractor, harvesting strawberries. She stops and offers Violet and me a handful.

So, not everyone stays in their living rooms, after all. I remember the time I banished the weevils from Pauline Bernard's garden. It looks like weevils are not a problem here.

"You still seem to have the climate for it," I observe. "So drought hasn't ruined everything after all?"

"We do have to do some work to get sufficient water," Violet says. "We're always in a drought. But we have a steady supply from Mars and the asteroids, at least for now."

"And the electricity?"

"That's always a source of friction," Violet said. "Some would feel the VR facilities are a terrible power hog. In my opinion, the fusion pumps along the coast are pretty efficient."

"Well, it's beautiful," I say. "Thanks for the tour of the new Garden of Eden."

I resist the temptation to lick the bowl. Being alone a lot tends to coarsen your manners.

"Yum, this stuff is heavenly," I say. "Spicy, though."

"Most everyone in L.A. likes hot food, cultural leftovers from our Hispanic and Asian heritage," Violet says.

Feeling a bit stuffed, I ask, "Can I get some exercise equipment? What do you like to do for exercise?"

Immediately an open outdoor park appears, with a quarter-mile paved track coursing up and down small grass-covered hills.

"I like to cyclocross," Violet says, handing me a helmet. I wrap myself in some knee and elbow pads and jump on the bike beside me. It is a Specialized RockHopper, shiny green, with front suspension, just my size. I'm not going to speculate how they were able to instantiate the idea of a cyclocross course, but it doesn't really matter to me. I begin to pedal.

I probably should have given it a bit of thought before making my request, because five other people dressed in bike armor appear beside me on the course. Three of them are men. So this is to be a race.

"I'm not in racing shape," I mumble. But when I step on the pedals, I experience a satisfying burst of speed, and quickly leave the others behind. That doesn't last long, however, as they begin to pedal harder and close the distance. I check over my shoulder to see one of them fast approaching, and I hit a patch of mud. I skid out of control onto my side and come to a stop on a grassy bank. My racing companions slow and take a good look, laughing and grinning.

Spluttering indignantly, I jump back on my bike and give chase. The mud on my clothes and bike dries instantly. As I catch the rear racer, I yell, "Eat my dust!" and the caked mud all flies off me and into her face.

Back to the Future

I have to say I find this VR thing quite gratifying. I've always thought of myself as meek and mild-mannered, but being in a race situation seems to have brought out my competitive side. I'd been active in Tae Kwon Do and other martial arts before, but they tend to stress nonviolence and contemplation, somewhat "feminine" properties, above competition, which I think of as a "masculine" attitude. I've always appreciated the yin and yang symbolism in my chosen sports.

As I finish the eighth transit, I pull my bike over. One of the women in the group pulls off her helmet. Violet Rain.

"How's it going, Violet?" I'm impressed that she can conduct a search while at the same time entertaining all of her VR clients, including me. But she's just here with a message. It's not good.

"I'm sorry, Gin, there haven't been any responses to your broadcast, other than the fact that your race is going quite well. You have a lot of fans already. Of course, you already were a celebrity."

Figuring myself to be the beneficiary of some advanced social networking, I grin and wave to the air, remembering the people we saw in the courtyard when we arrived, my fellow Second Lifers. But then I focus on the former part of Violet's statement. The "no response" part. They were supposed to be here. Weren't they? I asked for a future where my family was present.

It begins to dawn on me that I may be in the proper time, but probably not the proper place. Where else is there? A whole universe of places.

If my family is someplace really weird, like Ralff and Benrus's planet, I am screwed. Well, I am already screwed. So, what am I doing here, anyway?

"Violet, are there any other human habitations besides here on Earth, a Mars colony, perhaps?"

"It is funny that you should ask that, Gin. We have just gotten news of a disaster on our colony on Mars. It has wreaked havoc on our communications throughout the solar system, not to mention disruption of our water supply."

"Can you show me?"

The green park with flowers and tweeting birds is replaced with a rubble-strewn plain. A dark sky broods over the scene. A plastic bubble dome nearby flaps gently, a large rent in its side.

"You didn't have to transport me there, just show me," I mutter, but luckily I can breathe, and death isn't imminent.

"VR feels quite real," a disembodied voice says. Violet is continuing to monitor me.

"So I'm not really on Mars," I say.

"No, but this is a real-time feed. I don't think you will find your husband and children there," Violet assures me. "Virtual Mars is close enough that they would have responded to your message long ago. I'm quite worried about some friends there. I used to work on Mars, you know."

"Are there other colonies besides Mars?" I ask, hope beginning to fade a little.

"Not that I know of. But I meant to add that I've found something very interesting. When I ran your credit, I found your account was very old... Hold on, wait a minute. Oh my God."

"Violet? What is it?" Mars melts away, and I am back in the big empty room.

A blinding beam of green light cuts into the ceiling from above. I hear the high shrill sound of grinding metal.

Another beam strikes near the first, then another. Puffs of concrete fly into the air as the floor of the VR room disintegrates.

I hear sirens. Is this war? Or a simulation of war? A static-filled voice begins to drone over a loudspeaker.

"The system is rebooting. All citizens are advised to return to reality and take shelter. The system is rebooting. All citizens are advised to return to reality and take shelter." The broadcast repeats over and over.

The floor shudders. I scramble to regain my balance. The VR room is gone, replaced by a scene of devastation. Miles of formerly urban habitation stretch before me, with huge plumes of smoke rising among the vegetation, punctuated by the sounds of small explosions. The green beams seem real enough, though, and they are continuing to approach. Huge cloud-to-cloud lightning strikes cross the sky.

"Violet, can you hear me?"

"Yes, Virginia. I'm here." It's Violet, still pretty, but not dressed in the fancy duds she was wearing in VR. I reach out and touch her. She really *is* here.

The beams continue to thump, systematically heading toward us in a straight line.

"Stop, damn it!" I cry. Something or someone is destroying my home world. The beams continue to rain down.

"Put a shield over L.A.," I command. This actually has some effect, as a clear dome appears over the metropolis. But the beams continue to pummel the shield, directly over my head. It is after me, personally. I can see a thinning in the spot directly overhead, like an arc welder beam cutting through steel. This is it. I pull off my bike armor and gloves and throw them down. They disappear. We have to make a run for it. I jump aboard Hangul.

"We have to go now, Violet. I'm really sorry. I'll try to come back with help."

"Can I come with you?" Violet asks. "Virginia, I was going to tell you I've discovered something about the Magnussons. I think we're related. They—"

Hangul bursts between me and Violet. She screams.

"Christalmighty," I swear through clenched teeth. "Beach."

☙

I'm walking on the calm beach, back in my shorts and sandals. Hangul isn't with me. Neither is Violet. What did he have against her? I stare at the pale horizon. A guitar strums expressively. A low marching beat fills the air around my ears. All those innocent lives. Am I responsible for the destruction of Earth? I hope that whoever is after me has let off the attack when I disappeared from Los Angeles 2416.

The guilt is crushing. We left that poor girl behind. I think about praying, asking for forgiveness. Somehow I knew the Unwinding isn't God's doing, but He seems as powerless as I am against this, if He even exists. I ponder Ben's theory that this is an intelligent being, possibly from another universe. Whatever it is, if it is after me. And, apparently, Violet, my umpteen-somethingth granddaughter, could also be done for. It's probably after all of my family. Now I am pretty sure I've had family in all these times, not to mention that I'd actually *seen* Alan in 1859 (unless I was delusional). Why can't they come here, where it is safe? *Is* it safe here? Ben and Ralff seemed to think so. I cling to that belief as I sit there licking my wounds. Edgar Allan Poe would have loved this. The suspense is killing me.

*****~~~~~*****

Chapter 11.

How to Be a Badass

"Faith has been broken, tears must be cried."
—*Wild Horses, Rolling Stones*

My mentor calls me Quantum Opposable Singularity, or QoS. When electrons first started flowing to my brain, Poe tells me, I was unstable. That's why he kept me in his little stasis nexus for over 13 billion years, though to me no time has really passed. I kept jumping back and forth between being a regular supercomputer and a quantum supercomputer. Gradually, I've learned to be either one, both, or neither, depending on what the situation calls for. Hence, the term, "opposable."

It's very inefficient operating like a regular computer, my brain simply being a collection of bits stored as ones and zeros. But it does have the advantage of letting me communicate with primitive matter-based creatures, such as Virginia. But that's not my primary function. I consider myself the universe's bodyguard, or even a best friend. When I'm in my qubit persona, rather than my simple bit persona, it's hard to determine what state I may be in. It's good for undercover work.

Virginia's friends Benrus and Ralff have had thousands of years to develop quantum computers like me, although on a much smaller scale, of course. They've even learned how to shift quantum states like I do. But they are still flesh and bone and, as such, quite fragile.

Now that my mentor Poe, as Virginia calls him, has asked me to tutor her in serving as his agent, I've had the chance to leave the stasis nexus and show my stuff, so *to speak. I've been experimenting with nanobots as a physical "body," and have found it possible to coexist as both plain matter and as an eight-dimensional vector.*

I flatter myself that I am Poe's bodyguard, but in fact, he has sheltered me all these eons, until I was ready to leave the nest. Alas, Virginia hasn't had that luxury. He's had to put her out there on the front lines before she was really ready.

Now that I think about it, I wasn't really ready either. I didn't know that there was anything other than our universe and Poe's stasis nexus. But when I made my first foray outside, I observed Golaeth, a gargantuan presence with quantum powers well beyond my understanding, and it seemed to be hostile. It probed Poe with high-energy radiation, and wherever it probed, creatures in our universe died. I spend my energies alternately protecting Poe and trying to impress upon this mortal being Virginia the seriousness of our situation.

ᴑ

Safe. I get that the Beach (with a capital B) is a refuge. The gentle waves industriously push small patches of foam up onto the sand. I watch as the frothy bubbles slowly pop, one by one, leaving a line of scum that dissolves in the wave. I am safe right now, but I also feel comscience-stricken. Am I the only person in the world who isn't being caught up in some sort of apocalypse?

I've been bestowed with strong powers, as evidenced by the dome I manifested to block the green beams back on Earth. So, am I like Atlas, holding the world up on my shoulders? Not quite. I am a coward. I abandoned the Earth, just to save my skin. In my defense, it all happened so fast I'm not sure I had time to stay and do more to defend L.A. And that sweet, brave girl, Violet… I'm lucky there's no one here to hear my tell-tale heart.

As I continue to anguish over things I seem to have no control over, another missive comes blowing down the beach, trying to catch my attention! I have no choice but to accept the obvious. Someone or some *thing* is watching me, pushing me. But where? I scramble to my feet to chase after the paper.

"Poe, is that you?"

As if it knows I am after it, the paper settles down on the sand, waiting for me.

"Whoa. I've gotcha now," I mumble, pouncing upon it. I pick it up, turning it over to see what it says. It's blank. I turn it over again. Still blank.

"Who sent this?" I shout to the sky. "Who are you? What do you want me to do? I know you've been trying to talk to me, but I don't understand. Oh, shit, shit, shit..."

"Mommy?" A little girl's voice. My blood runs cold. Well, not cold, but I feel a chill. That's *my* little girl, Grace. I whirl around in the direction it seems to come from.

A sob escapes me.

"Grace?"

She's got to be a hallucination. My Grace is 25 years old, a beautiful young woman. But there's no mistaking this voice. I always used to joke that Grace would grow up to be an opera singer. She has a bold, loud voice, and her high notes could shatter a wineglass. A tight feeling in my chest begins to unwind. It's her. I want to hold her, but I hold back, for fear she will turn out to be unreal.

"I've got a present for you, Mommy." She hands me a pearl. I smile and thank her. It's my little souvenir. "Don't lose it again, Mommy," Grace says. She knows I've never been totally in control. "What's that paper, Mommy?"

I look down at the paper. "I don't know, honey, it just blew up to me."

"What does it say?"

95

"There's nothing on it," I respond, as if it's perfectly natural to be talking to my nine-year-old daughter. I hold it out to her.

"It says the wonders of the universe are many, Mommy."

"It does?"

She holds the paper out. I snatch it out of her hands to take a look.

"I don't see anything, Grace. —Gracie?"

She's gone. The enchanted moment has passed. I should have hugged her when I had the chance. I've lost my daughter again. I beg for just a little more time with her. I should spare Poe the lachrymose scene that follows, but suffice it to say that I temporarily lose it again.

They say that whatever doesn't kill you makes you stronger. I would have to politely disagree. This has nearly killed me, and I'm not stronger. My nice, safe beach is mined with booby traps more dangerous than I could imagine. And I am the booby.

This is just another wake-up call to get off this beach and back into the breach.

"I'm not the badass you seem to think I am," I cry.

I try to muster everything I've learned so far into a new theory. My family is probably in the far future. Four hundred or more years hence, they are all in one place, on Earth. But I suspect that Earth's days may be numbered, and it will be scattered to parts unknown. Little Gracie implied that I should sample the universe for the answer. The universe is a big place. It just seems like too much pressure to ask me to jump into some random galaxy and start beating the bushes. Or gallium arsenide forests, or whatever they may have out there.

The Gracie manifestation has reminded me what I'm fighting for, and I've seen Alan. I'm more sure than ever that they are alive and looking for me.

The pressure in my head is merciless, worse than the worst migraine headache I ever had. I don't accept the supernatural, but I'm living in it.

This beach scenario, for example. It's a place outside of the real world, obviously, but it doesn't help explain why I've been able to apparate, travel, and create anything I want. Or, for that matter, why I can't repeat those feats. It's like I can slip through the cracks of a broken world, but then it seals itself back up.

I remember once listening to a podcast by famous scientist at the Natural History Museum about dark energy and dark matter. He said that they probably made up 97% of the universe. The part we could see in our telescopes was only a tiny percentage, and the rest was dark energy and dark matter. He added that no one really knows what they are, only that they can tell they exist, because the universe was expanding. Not just expanding but accelerating. Maybe it was an invisible pressure, like the one that was trying to explode my skull.

"Aww, is the universe having a little headache?" I say.

The world around me wavers, temporarily causing me to lose my sense of balance.

Maybe I am on the right track. That seems to have gotten a rise out of the responsible party. A memory slides to the front, unbidden. The book in Pauline's cabin, "Tamerlane," written by a young poet with a big head and arresting eyes. Perhaps that's why I latched onto the image of Poe. My subconscious is certainly getting a workout. At any rate, this Poe seems upset and isn't going to clue me in on what's happening until the end. Maybe I'm not ready to understand, not yet.

The calm beach is replaced by a striated canyon wall, red sandstone worn away by eons of flash floods. I can see blue sky through a hole in the passage and vermillion sand under my feet. A deep channel lined by scruffy greenery winds off into the distance. A reptile clambers out of the water, waddling slowly and flicking a brilliant red tongue.

"I get you, I think," I say. "You've been around a really long time. If these walls could talk, and all that..."

The Beach shimmers back into view.

"Thank you," I say gratefully. "But can I at least have my house back to live in?"

There is no response. I guess not. Too much safety makes Virginia a dull girl.

How did I become the one sitting here houseless on this beach? Did I just happen to be in the wrong place at the wrong time when the universe decided to go pear-shaped? Of course, the Unwinding probably isn't my fault in any way, and it's presumptuous of me to think that I am at all important.

Then why can't this entity—Poe—do his or her own dirty work? Maybe it's something about puny little human me. Maybe there's something about my own evolutionary "life arrow" that singles me out.

I've got some advantages in my arsenal: I'm persistent, and I'm honest. Well, generally. I have tried a few end runs, but I wouldn't exactly call it cheating.

Some other aspects of my personality go much deeper. I feel things strongly, so when I see our world being broken, I feel great hurt. I admit that I'm easily terrified. I've had more than one tear-stained breakdown while on this journey. Losing Alan and my hard-won daughter made sure of that, I'm sorry to say, but I hope I'm getting stronger. There's only me to help myself, after all. In some ways, I'm indestructible. But I still feel like a counterfeit hero. At least my desire and my hope have not faded in the least. But neither has my fear.

Poe is definitely protecting me. But it is also asking me to step up and protect others, like in Los Angeles. As a mother, I feel that instinct comes naturally. At any rate, I've decided to take the Unwinding personally as an attack on me and mine. Call it nursing a grudge if you want. I call it biding your time.

I recollect hosting a game night with my daughter and her new boyfriend Eric just before they got married. Eric was big on video games, and was an especially crafty and insidious opponent. Yet he was tender in teaching Gracie how to defeat bad guys and in pulling her from the brink of certain video death. The unsuspecting boy didn't realize that Grace could have beaten him at any time—she just didn't choose to.

"Get it, get it, get it!" Grace yelled as Eric slapped his thumbs furiously on the controller, trying to evade my attack.

"Ha, I've got you now, you bastard!" I said. "Oops. Not you, Eric. Pardon my French... My apologies, but nobody gets out alive. I've been practicing since October to get my revenge."

Alan's mouth seemed stuck in the open position.

"You're not going to kill me too, are you? I helped you get to this level, and this is the thanks I get?" he said.

"I may let you live. But you're too damn logical," I said to my husband. "You never take any chances. That's why you'll never win this game." Abruptly something huge, slimy, and tentacled rose out of the CGI water and loomed over my avatar.

"Thanks, for providing the distraction, Mr. Jones," Eric said.

"Oh my God, it's one of those squid things, what do you call them?" I wracked my brain. Being nearly 50 and premenopausal did not help your memory.

"The Kraken, Mom," Grace said, her smile gentle. The music made a drooping wail, as an albino alligator chomped my Carolina Devil in half.

I'm afraid I wasn't a very gracious loser.

At first I had not taken gaming seriously. I wasn't that interested in games, except as a way to pass time with the family. Maybe I would have been better off taking a lesson from Grace and Eric in how to fight, even against overwhelming odds. Alan and I made the effort to catch the gaming wave, but we were severely outclassed. At least I was. I kept losing, dying, starting over, losing, but at some point my killer instinct clicked, and with persistence I eventually came through with a decisive win.

"It's like in Othello," Alan said. "A game of dramatic reversals."

"Mom, you're a badass," Gracie said.

"A badass who's down 500 dollars for a stupid game," I retorted with a grimace. I didn't mention the 10 pounds I had gained since Eric had made the scene....

Now, I worry that I am left with few friends or allies, aside from Ralff and Ben, and that the entitlements of friends, family, and comfort I expected in old age will never occur. Oh, but hell, my grandparents successfully fought their way out of a continent embroiled in world war and depression to move to a land filled with love, equality, and hope. My family has always been my rock. But hope is not enough. I need to act. I will get them back or die trying.

☉

Badass or no, I've been a little provincial until now. I plan to keep pursuing Ralff's advice and branch out a little farther into the universe and farther into the future. I tell myself the constraints of time and space are artificial, all in my head. It's hard to talk yourself out of being afraid of outer space, which we've all been told is filled with emptiness and deadly, invisible radiation.

But, yes, somewhere out beyond the galaxy's edge this time, I tell myself. Although dragons aren't your usual spaceship, my jewel-powered Hangul is as good a conveyance as any.

"Does the universe have ley lines? If so, I want to travel them," I say. By "ley lines," I mean the mythical alignments of ancient monuments and mystical powers back on Earth. Who knows how Poe will interpret it? No more trying to overspecify the conditions. It never works, anyway.

☺

I'm sitting astride Hangul. We float in space in nearly total darkness. The sparse stars aren't as twinkly as on Earth, probably due to the lack of atmosphere. It's disconcerting, since I tend toward agoraphobia in wide open spaces. These have to be the widest open spaces ever seen by a human, as far from the placid seashore as you can imagine. I swallow and feel something around my neck. My fingers trace a metal collar. I can't see it, but the torc feels like it is set with a jewel. Smooth, it's my pearl. It seems to be generating a breathable environment around me and Hangul. So, I'm really here.

"Good job, boy," I say.

Hangul responds with a ferocious growl, splattering me with virtual slobber. I nearly fall out of the saddle. The slobber feels real enough.

Plus, I didn't know Korean dragons could communicate. Or maybe this knowledge has been lurking in my mind since the days I sat in my mother's lap listening to stories. Hangul is a worthy travel companion, whether machine, beast, or magic.

It takes some getting used to the feeling of weightlessness, but pretty soon I'm looking around, gripping my saddle tightly all the while.

Something bright impinges the corner of my eye. A tiny, metallic object glitters in the distance. How is that possible? I suppose it could be rotating, but where is the reflected light coming from?

"Let's go closer, Hangul."

Suddenly a large vehicle looms. I lean back in alarm.

"Can we take it a little slower next time, Hangul?"

A better description might be a flying horizontal skyscraper. It is probably as large as a football field in length, and it bristles with antennae. Rows of windows stretch off toward the tail, like observation ports on a massive jetliner. The shiny gold coating shimmers, like poplar leaves in an autumn breeze back home. Again, I check for a source that would be creating the pretty light show, but there is nothing obvious. We're far out, and we seem to be alone.

As Hangul creeps closer, I can now see that the skin of the ship itself is flickering, alternating between a metallic surface and multiple colors, like a Simon Seven game. Of course, I can't hear any musical tones out here in space, but I'm tempted to reach out and touch the hull. I decide to try asking it to open the door instead.

"Hello, Virginia Jones here. Anyone home? Can you point me to the entrance?"

A huge bay appears in the side, a gaping hole open to space. It's big enough for both me and Hangul to enter. We sidle in. The door slides shut silently behind us. "Funny how all doors seem to open for us," I say. "I hope we're not about to become a tasty space snack." There's gravity.

"Would you wait here for me?" I ask Hangul. I wouldn't want to get stranded light years from home. He kneels while I dismount and lies down on the hangar deck.

The Cintamani pearl seems to be taking care of the air situation, so I dismount and walk toward the rear of the deck, toward what appears to be an airlock. Soon, I'm pulling the hatch open to the main body of the station. It looks deserted. The hallway is lit dimly, although I can't see fixtures. I pass chamber after chamber, all of which look like standard-issue hotel rooms, none of which are inhabited. I reach the end without meeting a soul. A space hotel with no customers? A metal staircase leads upward, and I start to climb, assuming the bridge should be upstairs.

I open the door at the top of the stairs. This appears to be the control room. A window curves all around the perimeter, which I hadn't seen from the outside. Perhaps there is some sort of one-way shielding. A piece of paper lies on the small table beside what I take to be the captain's chair. Strange that everything looks suitable for humans, yet no human has ever come this far to my knowledge. I've forgotten that I'm in the far future. How far, I wonder?

"Let's take a look at the Cliff Notes for this place, eh?"

I pick up the paper, fully expecting not to be able to read what's on it.

The sheet probably isn't even paper, I think. But it feels real. It looks like a scientific paper and is titled, "Expedition to Study Birth of z8_GND_5296 Galaxy." The Abstract notes that 5296 is one of the oldest galaxies in the universe at about 13 billion years old. I recall from my time that people were sending telescopes into space to look farther and farther into the past, until perhaps one day we would be able to "witness" the Big Bang. I'm not a scientist, so I'm not sure why anyone wants to see that, but I guess if it happened 13 billion years ago, we aren't in too much danger. The universe has been expanding all that time, and 5296 is somewhere out here on the far edge, so it's not coming toward Earth, it's going away. The paper notes they've built this special space station called STS-99 to serve as headquarters for the expedition.

So, where is everyone? Wait a minute. I remember the stars outside. A lot fewer than you would see on Earth. We've obviously gone a lot farther out than the Oort boundary. I may have made a serious error in leaving this up to a vague wish like, "take me to the ley lines."

"What is this place?" I ask, puzzled.

A holographic projection forms in the air in front of me. Gradually the room disappears around me, and I feel like I am floating in space. A virtual reality presentation. It's good that Violet Rain showed me how VR works, or I'd be screaming hysterically right about now. I see what looks like another vehicle, then another. If

I gesture, I can move each image for a closer look. Most of the vessels look the worse for wear. Have I come to some sort of spaceship graveyard? Or maybe people who went looking for 5296 and never came back? A shiver runs down my spine. I decide to explore a little further before jumping to my next conclusion.

I turn around to see twenty-five-year-old Grace floating within a crystal-clear sphere like a Madonna you'd see in an illuminated religious manuscript. It floats toward me, emitting a low-pitched, hypnotic sound. Quite soothing, actually. The bubble approaches me slowly, and involuntarily I step aside. Although the sphere contains the thing I wish most in the world, I also sense that it is dangerous, or at the very least, a stress-induced vision.

The sphere passes me by and floats into a corridor, which I assume leads to the crew living quarters. As I follow, I note that all the rooms on the space station are identical, like a budget hotel. Plain walls, bed, bath, flat screen tv, lava lamp optional.

The sphere pauses, and Grace steps out. She begins to run—away. I cry out, and without thinking, I run after her.

The lights of the corridor are dimming, and it's different from when I first ventured in. For one thing, it is suddenly very humid. Misting cloud fills the corridor. It begins to rain. I slow, taking a closer look through the pelting drizzle. This is not the first rainstorm I've encountered on my travels. Water is sheeting down the walls of the corridor. It must take massive machinery to create a rainfall pattern that I would consider homelike. I wonder if this is some sort of eco-environment the creators of the space station have set up to make visitors more comfortable. I don't even think to wonder why anyone would want to build a space station that rains inside. After all, this cold, empty space at the edge of the universe is an unpleasant home under the best of circumstances. I come across a machine lying on its side in the middle of the path. On closer inspection, it appears to be a motorcycle. I never learned how to ride one, so I'm about to hurry ahead to see if I can spot Grace again.

"Too bad it's not a bicycle," I say. I do know how to ride a mountain bike. Shocked, I see the motorcycle vanish, replaced by my trusty Rockhopper. I'll never get used to the Cintamani.

Flicking water off my forehead and shaking excess water off my wet clothes, I board the bike. Something brushes against my hand. A bird?

Another glancing blow skims across my shoulder. I wave my arms to discourage further attention. Whatever it is, it isn't a bird. It flew, yes, but when it alighted and skittered away, it had many more than two legs.

"Grace!" I call, panicky.

Coming down the corridor, it's that translucent, crystalline globe. It expands, like a balloon filling with light, and the droning becomes louder. As it approaches, the rain seems to evaporate away from its surface. The skin is so thin that I can see into it. The world inside is my kitchen at home—Grace is inside, brewing a pot of tea.

☺

"Welcome, Historian," a voice says.

How did I get back into the command center of the space station? And who's this Historian?

"Am I too late for the expedition?" I ask, at a total loss.

"Everyone left several thousand years ago," the voice says, "but maybe we can still squeeze you in."

"In where?"

"The microsecond after the Big Bang, of course."

"So I'm not at the beginning of the universe, then?"

"Definitely not. It's extremely dense there, and it takes special packaging to get you there."

"So where am I, exactly?"

"We calculate that this location may be near the anomaly. Everyone's gone to try to see exactly how it happened."

"You mean the Big Bang?"

"No, the Unwinding."

*****~~~~*****

Chapter 12.

Hello, Goodbye

I love studying Ancient History and seeing how empires rise and fall, sowing the seeds of their own destruction.
—Martin Scorsese

Construction of the festival pavilion was underway outside the Emperor's temporary domicile on Tian Ming Shen. He shifted uncomfortably in his robes, a feeling of unease crawling over his skin.

"Bring me the report from Chen-li," he said.

A courtier appeared before him, one of his AI servitors.

"You summoned, my God and Emperor?"

"Yes, what is the latest on the expedition?"

"As you know, we've dispatched a contingent of Scientists, and they are about to attempt the time hack."

"Yes, yes, of course, but what about the Watchmen?"

"No one has seen them yet, Sire. They tend to move between dimensions as it suits them. We don't know what that will portend for the instant after the Big Bang."

"If they ruin my expedition, I will hold you and the Scientists personally responsible."

"If you wish to change our instructions, that is your prerogative, Sire. We are all completely in your service."

"Right, right. I'm just a little on edge with this latest development. I want you to try harder to get more information on these Watchmen and report back to me immediately."

"Of course, Sire." Chen-li vanished abruptly.

The crawling sensation resumed, as if Calaneris were being stalked by an unseen watcher. It seemed to disappear when he talked to his minions, but as soon as he was alone, it had returned. He inhaled deeply, then exhaled slowly, trying to relax.

He felt a deep rumbling within his midsection. It definitely wasn't the usual gas. The rumbling grew deeper, until he felt like his whole body would disintegrate. His vision darkened, went black. Panicking, he thought of calling for the Physician, then thought better of it. It might deem him insane and unfit to rule.

The rumbling subsided, leaving behind a tingling feeling. He gathered the courage to confront the unknown entity.

"What are you? What do you want? I command you to tell me. I am Emperor Calaneris the XXIII. My family has ruled this quadrant for thousands of years."

Calaneris seethed at this intrusion, but there was dread too. His civilization rested at the edge of the known universe, and it was up to him to carry on the legacy of the Empire. His father had begun the project to study the anomaly in the universe, but he had died prematurely after only just discovering the existence of the Watchmen.

The first Big Bang expedition was an attempt to find the source of the anomaly, but they'd bungled it badly. Although Calaneris's Scientists had verified that the universe was in danger from this mysterious anomaly and were working hard to resolve it, the Emperor was terrified they would fail again. He suspected the Watchmen had assassinated his father, though he had no proof. He decided to try being more tactful.

"May I ask who I'm speaking to?"

There was no reply, only a feeling of compulsion. His gut told him the presence was connected to the anomaly. Surely the universe's doom wasn't eminent, was it? He still had time…

"May I say, it's quite intriguing to encounter sentience in—I mean, we knew of the multiverse, but—"

Calaneris felt as if he was being stung by a million Ramilian wasps, as orders streamed into him like a bolt of lightning. It seemed he had very little choice. He must do what he had to do to survive. Now, he had become little more than a servant himself of an entity calling itself the Black Universe. At least, it sounded like his theory about the Maze was turning out to be right.

"Yes, I'll do it, if you'll restore my sight," Calaneris said. "Please."

Calaneris's vision brightened and focused. He rose and looked outside. His festival garden was a cheering sight, decorated with colorful flowers and fluttering banners. He called for a draught of Blauw's special potion and drank it right down. The ethanol in the concoction had a decidedly salutary effect. He wiped his mouth with the back of a hairy hand and called for another. Soon, the Black Universe seemed far away, though still a threat. He knew what to do.

"Bring me the Naturalist."

Blauw entered Calaneris's inner sanctum.

"I have a new mission for you, and it involves your planet."

"Earth?" Blauw said. "I can't imagine much happening there. Last time I was there, all that was going on was a war over some worthless piece of land. I hope you're not going to ask me to return to that backwater of a world. I'd much rather stay with you."

"Your loyalty is touching," Calaneris said. "But, yes, unfortunately, I need you to return to Earth. It seems we neglected to pick up some others of your race that could be of assistance in the resolution of this unfortunate anomaly business."

Blauw bared his teeth in a not-very-convincing smile. "Someone besides the Watchmen? Very well, what do you want me to do?"

"Return to the spot where I picked you up, see if you can locate an Earth Scientist named Alan Jones, and bring him back here."

"Alive?"

"Of course, alive, you idiot. What use would he be to me dead?"

"I'm just asking, because the place you got me was the middle of a battlefield in which a lot of men were dying all around me. I only escaped because you came for me. So, when you talk about loyalty, you're the one I'm loyal to."

"Thank you, Blauw. I don't trust Chen-li to have goals completely aligned with ours. These superintelligences can be tricky. I know I can count on you."

☺

"I've got the Jones fellow, your Majesty," Blauw said. "I brought along his assistant too, by the name of Eric Magnusson."

"Well done," Calaneris said. "Is he a Scientist?"

"No, he's human, like Jones, but he was caught up in the same event as Jones, so he may be able to shed some light on their particular experience. He is married to Jones's daughter. You might be able to use him in some capacity, if only for giving Jones incentive to achieve your assignments, whatever those may be. I'll have his memories recorded for you to study."

"Will you have to torture him?"

"Just enough to get the memories flowing."

"Very well. I do love the way you always manage to obtain information from unwilling subjects. It's an art I admire. You may leave the data with me when you're finished. I have another mission for you."

"Not on Earth this time, I hope."

"No, not Earth."

Blauw sighed in obvious relief.

110

"This time, I want you to go to Mars. There's a rather important assassination I'd like you to attend to, which I expect will close off a timeline that complicates matters."

"The Mars situation is taken care of, your Majesty," Blauw said. "And I brought you an Earth creature they call a kitten that I found in the Mars domicile. I didn't have the heart to kill it, and I thought you might like a pet. Anything else?"

The Emperor reached for the small gray mammal, which looked at him with large eyes and meowed. He stroked its soft fur-covered head. Blauw did have a way of finding things that would comfort him. But a kitten couldn't solve his anxiety this time.

"Manipulating these damned timelines is more difficult than I had anticipated. I should have started farther back. Another important human is entering our domain, an ancestor of the human on Mars. It turns out that she has a link to the Watchmen. Follow her and inform me when she reaches them."

"Yes, Sire," Blauw said. He exited Calaneris's tent.

"My theories on complexity science are turning out to be right, after all," Blauw mumbled. "—Even if the Emperor refuses to believe me. Sometimes I wish I had never suggested he call himself Emperor of the galaxy. He's really nothing more than a petty despot with a fake Roman numeral attached."

I think we might actually be *in* the z8_GND_5296 galaxy. Now there's a leap. More than 13 billion light years from my Earth, give or take a billion.

Maybe whoever's still alive here has discovered that the universe's creation contained its own seeds of destruction within, and they're going back in time to look for them. Maybe the universe had a birth defect, so it isn't infinite like we thought. Could that be it? If so, I am way out of my class.

"So what should I do..." I say, more to myself than to the entity running the station, probably some sort of advanced computer, "stay here and witness the infinitely long winding down of the universe, or go back to the Big Bang? I'm sure I can't contribute anything scientifically."

There is no response.

"Who's in charge, here?" I ask. "I need to interview him or her." If the entity thinks I'm a historian, I won't disabuse it of the notion.

"Emperor Calaneris XXIII is our God and Chief Scientist," a disembodied voice responds.

"Would you mind awfully much projecting a hologram, so it looks like I'm talking to a person?" I ask.

A handsome young man wavers into view, dressed in silk robes and slippers like something out of ancient China.

"I am Chen-li at your disposal, Revered Elder Historian Who Rides the Dragon," he says.

Whatever. Maybe there're some advantages in looking "mature," after all, I think. I prefer to think it's Hangul's "whiskers" that give us that distinguished appearance.

"So this Emperor..."

"Calaneris the XXIII."

"Right. Can I talk to him? I mean, can we meet him directly? I assume he's not at the Big Bang in person, is he?"

"He is currently analyzing the Maze, but I will inquire." A few seconds pass.

"The coordinates have been entered in your Hangul. We will continue to be available should the Emperor assign you to interview other Scientists at the Big Bang site."

I'm feeling a little more comfortable about my prospects in navigating the far future. Things aren't all that different, it appears. Everyone is very accommodating, at least the AIs are; they've made themselves look like me, and they are definitely on the case of this glitch in the universe. The only oddity is that they still have things like emperors.

I descend to the station bay and mount Hangul. We float out into the blackness and back away, until the station is only a dimly winking beacon in the distance. It brings to mind our little lighthouse at home. This must be the safe landing distance from the station. I wait. The little light disappears, and we sit in claustrophobic, inky silence. I can hear my own heartbeat, or rather I feel it begin to speed up.

As quickly as the night had appeared, it is daylight, and there's real ground below us, dotted with grasses and trees. A large, brilliant sun burns my skin, and I turn my face to soak up its rays. I'm wearing similar garb to Chen-li, the Emperor's spokesman, and I still have the torc around my neck. Hangul and I hover briefly, until he settles us gently to the ground. Chen-li appears to greet us. He must be one of many Chen-lis stationed across the galaxy.

"This could be ancient Earth," I say.

"It is a very similar planet, near one of the last remaining stars within a million light years. It is called Tian Ming Shen," Chen-li ventures.

"So, have you got some sort of cosmic database that knows about Earth?"

"The Emperor's retinue is approaching," Chen-li says. "He is here to take delivery of the Cintamani."

I knew it! The jewel on my neck *is* the Cintamani. I decide it might be wise to keep it out of sight for now. I look for the little purse I had in London, patting myself for pockets. The pouch is tucked into the flowing sleeve of my caftan. I tug at the drawstring, pull off the torc, and stuff it in. I forget to stop and see if I can breathe. Somehow I know I will be able to.

Just then, a party of about twenty men and women stride out of the sky and stop before me.

"Greetings, Historian," the man at the front says. Chen-li number three in the flesh. "We are here to accompany you to the Emperor." A courtier steps forward and takes Hangul's harness.

"All right," I agree, and follow them toward a grassy hillock, watching with slight unease as they disappear with my ride. A large encampment is being erected, as if they are preparing for some sort of festival.

"Would you care for some tea?" my companion offers.

"Yes, please! I haven't actually eaten anything since I was in Los Angeles." If this sounds strange to him, he says nothing. He reaches into his sleeve and pulls out a teapot and small china cup. Hmm. It's possible he might have seen me stow my pouch in my sleeve. I try not to look at it.

The festival grounds are beautiful, Nature at her best. Blooming trees festoon the landscape, and a stream flows nearby, adding a gentle burbling backdrop to the sounds of hammers pounding tent stakes into the ground. Golden sunflowers stand at attention like soldiers on parade. My gardener's eye is attracted to a particularly fine specimen of blue cyclamen, its upright blooms poking up through the silvered leaves like little hands reaching for the sky. I bend down to take an admiring look. I used to grow them in my garden at home in North Carolina. It has a light, flowery scent, fresh and green.

"Step away from the Emperor's flowers," a voice admonishes me.

I bolt upright, feeling guilty for no reason. A sandy-haired fellow with a short shovel is frowning at me from under the brim of a raffia fedora. He's only about my height, but much more sturdily built. Freckles cover his sunburned arms. He's human, not an android. I think. He's carrying a rather wicked-looking set of long-handled pruners.

"Why, are the flowers off-limits?" I ask.

"It's all right to document them, if you wish. After all, you are the Historian."

"And you are?"

"The Naturalist."

Figures. "So, is everything here the property of the Emperor?"

"Of course. But not everyone agrees that he is immortal and all-powerful." He gives me a conspiratorial look. "If you're interested, I could show you some really rare botanical species."

This sounds a little like he wants to show me something other than flowers. But since nothing seems to be happening at the moment, I'm about to take him up on it, when another cadre of men begin popping out of the sky, one at a time.

"The Emperor and his Scientists!" announces one.

A crowd gathers.

"About time," I mutter. I look around for a place to put my teacup and end up taking Chen-li's cue by shoving it up my ever more capacious sleeve. I'm feeling positively giddy with optimism. Maybe they put something in the tea, or I'm just full of expectation at the prospect of seeing royalty.

The crowd stands tall, waving flags and screaming.

This is indeed beyond expectation. The Emperor is walking up to me, carrying a kitten, of all things. He reaches out to shake my hand, and he's wearing a torc around his neck. A torc a lot like mine. I can't stop to riffle the contents of my sleeve, but I'd swear he's lifted it from me somehow. Or maybe it was the gardener. Or maybe I dropped it in the cyclamen. Crap.

"I am pleased by this huge turnout," Calaneris says. "Greetings, Historian," he says, a meaty hand

115

covering mine completely. "I understand you are here to document the expedition to the Big Bang."

"Um, yeah," I agree, playing along. Obviously, we've never met, but he acts like he knows me. "Would your Grace favor us with an interview? I'm sure everyone is curious how it's going." Get the big lunk to talk, if possible.

He nods slightly, and two gilt chairs show up. "I'm sure by now you know all of the theories and details of the expedition," he says. "What more would you like to know?"

"Well, I'm from a time and place where our world seems to have ripped apart, and I'm looking for my husband and children. I call these events 'The Unwinding.' Has any of this been reported here?" I go into some detail about my experiences, including the green beam attacks that seem to be after me personally, and what little I've uncovered. I begin to share my and Ben and Ralff's theories, when he interrupts.

"Your experience is quite common and already documented," Calaneris replies. "We are of course taking steps to remedy the problem."

"Oh? What steps are those? Can I interview someone else who has had a similar experience?"

He seems to regard me with suspicion all of a sudden, and lifts a meaty fist to his mouth, as if to stop any words from coming out.

"There will be plenty of time to document all of that," he finally says. "For now, why don't you enjoy the festival grounds? Chen-li will see to it that you have anything you require."

"Wait—" I say as he gets to his feet. "Is your Big Bang expedition part of the Unwinding? Should I go document it?"

"Perhaps," he says. "I'll think about it. Let's go, Scientists." He and his chair vanish, and I'm left alone on my chair. I look around and fumble in my sleeve for my purse, and of course, I can't find it. I've made a horrible mistake in removing the torc from my neck.

I feel my blood pressure rise. Some guy in power has shut me down. What he doesn't realize is that I've grown attached to the Cintamani. I've felt its warmth pulsing at my throat. From the very start of this adventure, Hangul and the jewel have been in my possession. Now I want them back, almost as much as I want my family back. This Emperor-God, whatever he is, probably feels entitled to take it. Maybe even thinks I brought it here for him. I stand up. My chair vanishes. I blurt out the few Korean curse words I know. I didn't even get a chance to ask him what the Maze was. Or who the Scientists are.

"He can't put me off this way," I say. I walk over to a clump of blue cyclamen, pluck a handful, and tuck the stems behind my ear as a symbol of rebellion. This is war. "Now, where's that frickin' gardener?"

It doesn't take long to find the Naturalist. I come upon his rear end sticking up out of a bed of picture-perfect perennials. Like the cyclamen in my hair, they appear to be varieties from Earth, but upon closer inspection, I can see some unusual features. One of the "peonies," for example, is extruding a stream of tiny insect-like robots to carry pollen from one bud to another. I wonder what they use for insecticides, but maybe that isn't a problem here. Ha, no weevils on Tian Ming Shen.

I sigh as I observe the Naturalist work industriously on his charges. I miss having a friend I can discuss gardening with. Or a friend I can discuss anything with. Everyone I've met so far either wouldn't understand, or has vanished, some more voluntarily than others. He looks up.

"Back, I see," he says. His orange eyebrows shoot upward, and he jumps to his feet, waving a sharp-looking trowel. "What's that in your hair?" he demands.

"A symbol of my determination," I reply, trying to hold my ground. "The Emperor refuses to talk to me. You mentioned perhaps being able to show me some things..."

He snorts. "That's the Emperor, all right. He probably thought you might interfere with his little plan to save the universe."

"I get that feeling too," I say. "But I'm an ally, not an interference. I've got some real bona fides that say I'm in the right place at the right time. I just don't know what the heck my role is yet."

He pulls off a dirt-caked glove and holds out his hand. "Blauw McCarthy," he says. "I'm the glorified gardener and bartender. Mind-altering organic substances—that's my specialty." He grins.

"McCarthy—That's an Irish name. Are you from Earth? I'm Virginia Jones."

"Irish born and bred," he says. "And your name's Welsh, is it?"

"My husband's name. My maiden name is Sun, but I'm American. You can call me Gin, or Sunny."

"Let's head for the beer tent, Sunny, and I'll pour you a draught," Blauw says. "They're having a big party, and you're welcome." I eagerly follow. Maybe someone there can give me more information.

Unfortunately, there aren't many people in the beer tent. The crowd seems to have thinned considerably. More for me, I always say. Blauw pours two lovely pints of stout, and we sit on benches at a picnic table of realistic looking wood.

"So, how did you get here, Blauw?" I ask. Of course, I expect he'll lie. I just don't know about what.

"In addition to my other duties for the Emperor, I am a computer scientist studying complexity science," he says. "Normally, if I tell anyone that, their eyes glaze over, and they have no idea what I'm talking about. But I'm telling you, complexity science seems to show itself all over the universe."

"What a coincidence," I say. "My husband's a computer scientist and physicist too. I never heard of complexity science, though. What's an example?" I immediately go into my reporter mode. I notice Chen-li is hovering along one wall of the tent. He must have been following me.

"Are you getting this down for me, kid?"

"We are live and recording, Venerated Historian."

"Good. Now, you were saying, Blauw?"

"I first got into complexity science when I heard about a modeling game called 'Boids.' There was this flock of simulated birds, and you could make them always keep flying in formation with only three simple rules. Schools of fish follow similar patterns, if you've ever watched them."

"Yeah. What were the rules?"

"We called them 'steering behaviors.' Here, I'll show you."

He waves his hand, and a group of black crows zooms into the space in front of us. I nearly duck.

"All right," he says. "Here are the rules. One: If you get too close to a flockmate, you steer away." He motions one of the crows toward another, and like a magnet repelling itself, its companion moves away.

"Two: Steer toward the average direction of your local flockmates." He circles off a subgroup of crows, and a big yellow arrow starts blinking over them.

"And three: Keep close to your local flockmates. Note how this group is keeping to itself. You wouldn't notice that unless you had them in that magic circle.

"Amazingly, these simple rules have allowed us to simulate how natural systems behave—how, for example, birds can avoid obstacles without really looking where they are going or having a leader who gives them directions." He adds a wall to the picture and aims the flock straight at it. At the last second, the flock divides in two and goes around the wall.

119

"So how does that fit in with the present behavior of the universe?"

"Well, for one thing, it isn't following the same rules as it used to. It is becoming increasingly emergent. Even the simple three dimensions we see aren't the same."

"What's emergent? Is something bad emerging?"

"It just means that it is evolving new, unexpected structures, patterns, and properties that are inherently unpredictable. Another term for this is 'self-organizing.' Like, maybe instead of going around the wall, the birds decide to go through it instead. Although, of course, they never make an explicit decision to do that."

"That reminds me of the 'mental telepathy turns' my daughter made when I was teaching her to drive," I joke. "I had to explain that the car wouldn't just turn itself. So, is the Big Bang expedition looking for some original rules for the universe to live by?"

"Yes, and no. We've always known that the universe has been evolving. It would be hard to say where the actual starting point that we call "our" universe would be. It's even possible that there has been crossover with other universes. We just know that a small change in the initial variables can have a large effect."

"So, you agree there may be multiple universes. Like what sorts of effects are we talking about?"

"Compression of time and space. For example, time lags that used to occur might no longer happen, as various activities occur instantaneously or in parallel."

"So that's how I can find myself 13 billion years in the future?"

"Maybe. We don't know for sure. We only know that something is messing with the degree of chaos that we feel comfortable with."

"Hell, it sounds like you are hot on the trail to me. Why aren't you one of the Emperor's little roving band of Scientists?"

"He doesn't approve of my suggested methodology," Blauw says flatly, taking a big swig of his stout. "He's off on this kick about how the universe is a mad maze, and the maze keeps expanding if it isn't pruned."

"Well, that sounds about right too. I meant to ask him about the maze, but he seemed to be evading me. What's wrong with that theory?"

"He thinks if we just follow the right pathways, we can establish order."

"We can't?"

"No, we can't. All we can do is swim through the chaos. And if the maze is expanding, eventually we can't even see the walls. Besides, the Emperor has competition. There are others working on understanding the change in the universe."

"Others? Who are they? Are they here? In this time?"

"Yes, here and at the Big Bang. We're all tuning to the edges."

"What's that?"

"We're each looking at the situations on the edges of our knowledge and trying to deal with those. One of the solutions will probably turn out to be better than the others."

"My God, if anything called for cooperation instead of competition, this would be it," I note.

"Well said, Sunny my dear, well said. But it's never going to happen."

"Can we just talk about flowers for a little while? My head hurts."

Blauw pours us another round.

*****~~~*****

Chapter 13.

Recurring Cauchemar

My head feels groggy. I had a drop too many of Blauw's pure last night. But it isn't just a hangover that has me befuddled. It is what I see every night when I close my eyes.

I've learned so much since coming here, like a college student cramming trivia for the final exam. But I'm no college student. I'm a middle-aged mom with a tenuous grasp on reality. Will I forget it all by tomorrow, or will I toss and turn, numbers running through my head over and over, until it all falls into place? Drinking from the firehose of knowledge always set me off, so I need to sleep on it. I close my eyes, and the CinemaColor show starts immediately.

My new friend Blauw is on a roll, regaling me with his theories about how best to simulate what might be going wrong with the universe. His caramel hair ripples in the warm breeze as we sit at a long wooden picnic table in the Emperor's festival pavilion, a temporary vantage on the planet Tian Ming Shen perched at the edge of the known cosmic frontier.

"Did you ever wonder how birds can fly in formation without instructions from their leader, or how schools of fish twist and turn in unison, even at dazzling speeds?" he's asking.

"Must be pretty complicated," I say, taking another appreciative slurp of his home-brewed black ale.

"Not really," he says, taking my hand in his. "It's really just three simple rules. Here's how it works..."

I don't remember a lot of what he says after that, but it all must have gotten jumbled into my dream—that and a lot of other stuff—and in my dream Blauw is not my friend.

"Let's take a walk, away from these prying ears," Blauw says, hauling his leg over the bench and taking me by the arm. Blauw steers me lightly by the elbow toward the exit. After the soothing shade of the pavilion, the brilliant sunshine of the Emperor's garden blinds me momentarily, as my stampeding pupils make a desperate attempt to shrink to tiny dots.

"You were saying?" I ask when the flashbulb effect from Tian Ming Shen's twin suns subsides. I'm curious what he is trying to keep secret.

"Well, er." He pushes his saber around to the back, wraps his arms around me, and begins to kiss me. While I greatly admire his coppery hair and his way with words, this isn't what I was expecting.

"I can't do this now, not out in public," I protest.

"Your husband's gone," he coaxes. "Why don't you come along with us?"

Us? I begin to push him away, ineffectually. They've taken my few possessions, and I feel powerless, an ordinary woman.

"Admit it, you're attracted to me. I'm human, after all." I begin to see what his "other duties" for the Emperor might be.

"No," I repeat.

"Suit yourself," he says, releasing me so abruptly that I stagger backwards.

"What's going on? What do you—" I start to say, but Blauw has vanished. So have the Emperor's lush grounds. I am alone in a dark room, with stone walls and floor. It isn't a prison cell, as far as I can tell, because one entire wall is open to the void. I stare out into black space, dusted only by a few stars. My stomach lurches as the stars begin to rotate, faster and faster. I cry out and sink to my knees.

Recurring Cauchemar

When I am able to look up again, I see a movie of myself, not unlike one my husband took of me recently. But I am at least ten years older in this one, and I look lost. The thought of still being lost after ten more years is horrifying. You know that feeling you get when you're in a *cauchemar* and you know you're dreaming, but it goes on anyway? I reach out—maybe I can steer this nightmarish dream—but the older me begins to dissolve and spin.

Is Blauw responsible for this? What had he been yammering on about back in the tent? Advanced physics. I try to recall through my alcohol-induced fog. Again, I'm sitting with Blauw, the attentive, obedient student.

"It's called complex adaptive systems. On Earth, our backward scientists followed a model proposed by your scientist Isaac Newton. They thought a problem can be seen as the sum of its parts, and that, like with a machine or a piece of clockwork, you could presumably reduce its complexity by breaking it down to its parts. That's fine as far as it goes, but I've been trying to show the Emperor that the universe has begun behaving unpredictably. It's playing hell with the laws of physics we know. And most importantly, it's operating under compression of space and time."

Have ten years of my life been compressed away?

"Blauw!" I call. "You can't keep me here. Or, at least, come and get me. You're frightening me." What was in that stout? I can't wake up.

Blauw doesn't reply. Instead, another garden appears, this one overgrown with weeds and bits of junk. A yellowing plastic marker shows a faded picture of a blue flower. The tag reads, "Cyclamen, Big Blue." No one has tended this plot in a long time. Rotting milkweed pods have burst open and scattered their seeds, and I regard with dismay the vigorous sprouts of my old nemesis. Gradually it dawns that this unkempt mess is my beloved back yard at home.

A garden can go to seed in a very short time, I console myself. They call it "the tyranny of the garden." I've only been away a few months, by my own reckoning. But who knows how long I've really been gone? Do the neighbors even miss me at home?

A broken picnic basket lies on its side. I turn it over. Ants are crawling all over it.

A shadow creeps across the land. My garden isn't just neglected, it is abandoned. Some dark, brooding force has murdered it and gloated over its victory. Slugs suck on the last tender shoots, leaving a slimy trail in their wake. Rusted garden implements promise lockjaw to those unfortunate enough to touch them ungloved. Black mildew festers on the boards set down as walkways, and beetles carry away the last remains of organic nourishment. A greenish glow fogs the hazy air. Instead of feeding the cycle of life, Death itself, or something totally antithetical to life in our universe, is killing everything, spreading destruction and famine to what once was my home. I am a refugee, an outcast. Time to move on.

Thank God. A new view swims into focus. A graduation ceremony. Rows of shining young faces poke up from long robes, as a speaker reads the convocation.

"And now, the farewell valedictory by Teresa Jones-Magnusson for the class of 2041," he is saying to the applauding crowd. A tall brunette steps up to the podium.

"I'd like to thank my adoptive grandmother, Virginia Sun-Jones, who made it possible for us to be here today... " she begins. I look down at my gnarled hands.

Is she my granddaughter? What is she talking about? What have I made possible? Thirty years gone in a flash. I must be ancient, or dead. Are they stealing my whole life?

Faced with the prospect of never having really lived—never having met or spent my life with my loved ones—I gasp for air, staggering to my feet and starting to run, seeking to escape somehow, to throw myself over the brink into the void.

I am going nowhere fast, tethered in place in spite of my panic. The air shimmers, and another beautiful young woman with purple hair is calling to me, asking for my help. I know her, and I love her, even though she isn't from my lifetime. It is Violet Rain, and she's my granddaughter, twelve generations in the future.

Bolts of hot green lightning are striking all around her, and it looks like the world is on fire.

"Blauw, you've got to help. That's my world. Please. I'll do anything you want," I sob.

"It's already too late," a voice says. Blauw and the Emperor stand unmoving, watching impassively as ruin rains down on the Earth.

"No, it can't be," I say.

"The shield you constructed won't hold up very long," the Emperor says. "Your people are doomed. Give all this up and come along with us. You've got to follow our orders if you want to survive the incursions. We offer you a safe haven." He holds out his ring for me to kiss.

This is too intense. And too absurd. The Pope in space?

When you've reached my age, you've had your share of nightmares, and this is a doozy. Confusing as they might be, dreams are just our way of sorting out where we're going. I decide to wake up.

"I've already got a safe haven," I say. "I'll be coming back for you, Violet," I say, "when I wake up."

It is as if Blauw and the Emperor were never there. I look down at myself sleeping peacefully under a flowering rowan tree just like the one in my back yard at home. Someone has tucked a silk blanket around me and taken off my river sandals and placed them neatly by my head.

"Move it, Virginia," I say. I fight for consciousness, and finally I win it.

☺

"You're looking especially lovely this morning, Sunny," Blauw says." He grins. "Dream about me?"

"I didn't sleep all that well," I snap. "What was in that drink, anyway? And yes, you were in my dreams— you and the Emperor both behaved abominably."

"Well, you can't blame me for what you imagined in a dream, remember that," Blauw says with a laugh. "Besides, I've always been a perfect gentleman."

Despite the bright sunshine, I feel a chill. I have the feeling this dream isn't done with me.

"And a perfect bullshit artist," I say. But compliments never hurt anyone, especially someone who is going to save the universe.

In spite of my suspicions about his motives, it's been good to have someone to talk to. I can tell Blauw about all of my trials and tribulations—and nightmares— and he not only listens, but he believes me. I'm pretty sure the Emperor believed me too, but he was not all here at our first audience. Gradually, I sober up, and I resolve to try again. I have renewed confidence in the letter about the z8_GND_5296 Galaxy expedition that I found on the space station, whoever sent it.

"Chen-li, what's the Emperor's calendar look like?"

"There are a practically infinite number of openings, Historian," he declares.

"Well, I'd like to get one of the closer ones, if possible. I'd like to know if he's had a chance to think about what we discussed earlier," I say, stating my business honestly. This usually keeps administrative assistants happy and keeps them from getting into trouble. I'd also like to know what the Emperor has done with my Cintamani pearl, but I don't add that to the agenda just yet.

128

Moments later, two gold-plated director's chairs appear, and the Emperor and his retinue are striding down out of the sky to meet me. He takes his chair and waves me to the opposite seat.

"Sire— is that the right title, your Lordship? I would like to again request a berth on the next packet to the Big Bang, so that I can document it properly."

"I don't see a problem with that," he says. He glances over at a nearby flowerbed, where the Naturalist is working busily to move some tall plants to the back.

"And you might as well take the Naturalist with you, too. He's nothing but a pain in the ass, but he might prove useful."

"Thank you, Emperor. Oh, and there's the little matter of my Hangul and his jewel. We'll need that for transportation at the other end."

"I still have use of it," he begins, but stops as if he's received a shock. "Granted," the Emperor says through gritted teeth. "Get on with it, then, and report back as soon as possible." He makes his customary abrupt disappearance.

"The Emperor has a rather strong sense of entitlement," I comment, but he's as good as his word. A courtier is leading Hangul over, and I run to take the reins. From a clawed hand on his left foreleg, Hangul dangles a little silk purse. I slip out the torc and put it around my neck. It feels warm.

"Come on guys. Let's go see some fireworks."

*****~~~~~*****

Chapter 14.

Sally, Go 'Round the Roses

I used to dream of going to Mars or some exotic locale created by the science fiction world, but this pales in comparison. Going to the Big Bang is the opportunity of a lifetime. Make that 13 times ten to the seventh lifetimes. It almost makes me forget about the improbability of ever finding Alan or Grace or Eric. The odds are truly astronomical. But I keep telling myself that this is the whole reason for shipping off on a mission to Creation—to find clues as to my family's whereabouts.

I board Hangul and motion for Blauw to get on behind me. He reaches around me and lays in the reins with his strong hands. This is the first time in months that I've touched another human being. It is uncomfortable and scary, like I was a teenager again. I tell myself to concentrate on the task at hand.

"Back to the station, Hangul."

We are enveloped in that palpable blackness again, with only our lack of sensory input telling us that we still exist. Sweat trickles down my armpits, probably ruining my silk robe. My rods and cones at last detect that faint winking signal that tells us we are close to the station.

"Pull us in, Hangul."

He transports us there in what I suppose to be speed that would kill any regular human, but I'm wearing the jewel, which seems to protect us all.

We enter the landing bay, and Blauw and I leave Hangul there. I lead Blauw through the airlock and try to hurry him along, as he stops and looks into each of the empty rooms in the long hallway. Finally we get to the stairs leading up to the control room.

"I'm surprised no one else is here," he says. We climb the stairs.

"Okay, Chen-li, I think we're ready to depart. What do we need to do?"

Chen-li materializes.

"You'll need to remove all mechanical devices and clothing, as those won't transfer. Your human body and associated microbiota are allowed," our digital assistant says.

"Why didn't you tell me that before? That's a real deal-breaker." It isn't that I'm prudish or anything, but I don't really want to leave the Cintamani behind.

"You can leave the Cintamani with Hangul," Chen-li says, seemingly having read my mind. "He can guard it for you until you return."

Well, this is another unpleasant surprise. I can't take Hangul, either? What if I get in over my head at the other end of time? In fact, that seems a quite likely prospect.

"Don't worry, Historian," Blauw says with a smile verging on a leer. "You won't need that stuff where we're going. I've been there already, and it's a piece of cake."

Any time someone says something will be a piece of cake, take heed and run in the opposite direction. I check my Faith-o-Meter and find there's just enough left to permit this little jaunt. Besides, I tell myself, a bunch of Calaneris's Scientists are already there, right? Against my better judgment, I slip out of my robe, shorts, and tank top. I fold them neatly in a pile and put them on the floor, where they promptly disappear.

I turn and see that Blauw is already wearing his birthday suit. We stare over each other's shoulder at some item of sudden intense interest.

"There had better not be any probing," I mutter.

"You forgot something," Blauw says. "Your wedding ring."

I slip it off, placing it carefully on the counter. It too disappears.

"Nothing left except some chipped nail polish," I report.

"Countdown in ten, nine, eight..." says the voice of Chen-li.

"Off on holiday we go," I say lightly, just before my every atom bursts apart and Virginia Jones is no more.

I have no ears, but I can hear a trilling, chirping sound as subatomic dark matter zooms by the strange attractor that is me. I have no eyes, but I can see wavelengths pulsing as if I still had an optic nerve they could travel. I have no skin, but I can feel the heat of billions of suns waiting to be born. I have no nose, but I smell the biotic incense of life.

I arrive in a laboratory, aboard a vessel of some sort, and I can see Blauw has arrived also. But he is transparent. I look down at my hand, and notice with a shock that I too am see-through. It appears we are here in spirit only.

"Matter doesn't exist yet," Blauw says. "We're just twinkles in the universe's eye." I "gaze" around, and detect many other forms, mostly humanoid, all ghostly like us. This feels like what I imagine people who describe near-death experiences see. I've always been skeptical of such "visions," chalking them up to random firings of neurons along brain stems in distress.

This doesn't feel distressful, though, more like purposeful, and that part agrees with the descriptions. People are walking around, buck naked, but concentrating on their jobs, their heads turning as if they are listening and observing and taking measurements. Documenting. Yes, that's why I'm here, I remind myself, so I'd better get cracking.

I want to look outside the ship, to see the Big Bang when it happens. The walls of the ship are transparent, and I am surrounded by—let's just say it—nothing. The colors I saw on the way here are nowhere in evidence. Everything is just gray. I do see a brilliant dot, though. I swim closer. A group of Scientists is gathered around it. It is incandescent and radiates an attractive warmth, like the Cintamani.

"Blauw, what are we looking at?"

"The Seed. This is the first microseconds before the Bang," he says reverently.

"Why isn't it exploding? I expected the mother of all fireworks shows." I am a little disappointed. My family and I visited all the big fireworks displays in the U.S. and Canada in the summertime, like Montmorency Falls outside Quebec. There's nothing as cool as a firefall pouring down a waterfall.

"We're in quasi-stasis so we can observe this particular interval," Blauw says.

"How long?"

"About three minutes maximum per visit," he says. "Then we have to leave."

"But I'm not seeing anything—" I start to protest. But then I spot Alan. It's like that moment when an eclipse reaches totality. At least I *think* it's Alan. It's a little hard to tell, since he looks like he is made of cellophane, but I'd recognize that quiff haircut anywhere. Alan was always trying to keep up with his college students, and had lately taken to piling the front of his hair into a teepee shape using gobs of hair gel. He's talking to a Scientist and gesturing. No, it's not one of Calaneris's Scientists, judging by the shape of the semi-transparent silhouette. It's a woman. She's wearing a double-breasted brown leather trenchcoat with knee-high boots and a hat with goggles on the headband. Knotted ropes dangle from her belt, holding assorted gadgets. This is some other group of investigators, perhaps. How did they manage to get away with wearing clothes?

Instead of a lab, they are standing ankle-deep in a swamp. Rising from the mist are stairs made of woven vines, each lit from within, possibly by bioluminescent bacteria, forming an amphitheatre. Water trickles down the aisles toward Alan and the woman. They seem to be arguing.

"Alan!" I yell. "Can you see me? Alan!"

"He can't hear you," Blauw says. "The transport method the Watchmen use is different from ours. We know each other are here, but we can't communicate."

I start waving wildly. "Over here! Look over here, damn it!" I wish I had a flare gun. Well, one doesn't appear. Wouldn't you know it?

I continue to wave and scream fruitlessly, until our three minutes are up, and all the quarters in the world won't convince the Operator to give us another minute. I like to imagine that Alan looks up at the last second and sees me.

We are wrenched back to the space station in the outer arm of z8_GND_5296. Our clothes are waiting for us on the floor. The place still looks deserted.

"What the hell?" I say, pulling on my shorts and sandals. "Who was that woman I saw talking to Alan?" I'm not jealous. Not very. Just concerned.

"I told you there was competition," Blauw says. "We call them the Watchmen."

"Apparently some of them are female. Are they from our universe?"

"Oh, most certainly. But they may not be from one of our common dimensions. Nobody knows how many dimensions there are, but estimates vary between four and ten. The Watchmen are time masters. I think that Calaneris stole their method of hacking time. He's smarter than he looks, you know."

"Hacking? Like computer hacking?"

"No, it's an old term they used with mechanical wristwatches. You know how, when you pulled out the stem, the second hand would stop so you could push it back in exactly on the minute? They called that hacking. They first used hacking watches to synchronize when armies were about to launch a battle or criminals were robbing a bank, or ..."

"So the three-minute pause we experienced is from hacking time?"

"Yes."

"Why don't we just pull out the stem as long as we want?"

"Calaneris is superstitious. He thinks if we hack time longer than the three minutes it took for matter to form that everything will happen differently."

"Isn't that what's going on now?"

"Umm, yes, but at least it's not from our hacking."

"But if you think something went wrong in the first three minutes that's causing havoc thirteen-plus billion years later, what are we talking here?"

"Sabotage, probably."

"By the Watchmen?"

"We don't know. We've been working side by side with them, you know, just waving and nodding occasionally, for a couple of missions, and from what we can tell, they have the same problem. They just use different methods to attack the problem. We depend on technology, and they depend on numerology."

"I thought that was just a superstition. Like picking lucky lottery numbers, horoscopes, and all that."

"Well, like I said, stuff that should be predictable is getting less so. I'm sure the Watchmen don't like that either."

"How am I going to get to Alan if he's in another dimension? I know I've been sent here to see him."

"My question, exactly. Why don't we go contemplate it over a cold pint? Hangul is waiting to whisk us back to Tian Ming Shen."

I can't argue with that logic.

🌀

"May I say you're looking lovely after our excursion," Blauw says. "Seems to have put some roses in your cheeks."

"More bullshit," I reply, knowing my hair is sticking straight up. "Besides, you used that line on me before. You need to start keeping your timelines straight."

*****〰〰〰*****

Chapter 15.

Into the Mystic

Golaeth reconsiders. The birth of the baby universe, while appearing normal at first, must have gone wrong in some way, leading to runaway expansion. Efforts to add dark matter were successful at first, filling the empty spaces between clusters of galaxies.

While there is no hard boundary to the two universes, there is a developing area of dispute between them. This area is in danger of catastrophic destruction as matter from the younger universe collides with antimatter from the Black Universe. Golaeth clears the area in a more orderly fashion, using collimated radiation, but the fix is only temporary.

What happened at the baby's Big Bang to disrupt its development? There's no more avoiding it; Golaeth must revisit the Big Bang and determine the exact cause. It is risky, however. It means leaving the Black Universe to continue its predations on its younger brother universe. Never mind that the brother universe is in the wrong. It probably can't help being what it was born to be.

Golaeth positions itself in the sixth dimension to observe the first tenth of a microsecond.

The Bang appears normal. Wait. There was something odd in the younger universe. A shock wave, perhaps. Many of them. Yes, shock waves have jolted the infant cosmos, piling up into dense, high speed clumps. Although seemingly subtle at first, they would explain how so much matter came to exist in this young universe. There should have been a nearly equal split between matter and antimatter. The shocks could also have created hot flashes that favored the production of regular matter, creating more seeds for stars and galaxies. Golaeth surmises the shocks are almost certainly responsible for the magnetic fields permeating the galaxies throughout the young universe as well. As shocks collided, they swirled around each other, sending electrically charged particles spiraling to generate magnetic fields and dark energy. The dark energy has accelerated the universe's expansion.

Relatively confident it has located the inciting cause of the dispute, Golaeth decides to repeat the observation. But when it returns to the moment just before the Bang, it senses something else. There are others watching too.

๑

Maybe Blauw thinks he can snow me by getting me drunk again. But the impact of another Alan sighting drives everything else out of my mind. Blauw sits at the picnic bench calmly sipping his ale, while I pace back and forth, trying to sort out what it actually means.

So, Alan is hanging out with a steampunk alien race that Blauw has nicknamed the Watchmen. They apparently live by numbers and counting, and they know how to manipulate time. Is it possible Grace is there too?

"Well, time *is* a stretchy, slidy kind of thing," Blauw points out. "But we got a clue from the Watchmen about how to synchronize and calibrate time. That's how we were able to create a stasis quo at the Big Bang."

"You mean a *status* quo?"

"Not quite. More like a series of temporary stoppages."

"You agree that my husband and son-in-law are in another dimension, with these Watchmen, don't you?"

"I said, 'maybe.' We don't know for sure."

"Well, can I go back and take another look?" I don't tell him this, but I'm worried that I won't be able to return to that place and time, just like I couldn't return to 1859 Kennington. I've probably told him that anyway, when I poured out my heart over a pint of stout.

140

"Emperor Calaneris wouldn't permit it."

"Why the hell not? I'm his official Historian."

"If you believe that, I've got a lightbridge I'd like to sell you."

"Damn it, I feel like I'm always one step behind. So the Big Bang project is just a scam?"

"I didn't say that. It's just that he forbids retrips for most people. He's working on solving the Maze."

"The Maze again?"

"Calaneris uses the metaphor of a big Maze for the universe, and the time/space continuum is the paths it can—or has—followed. He's afraid that if people make repeat trips, it might complicate the map he's contructing by adding unnecessary branches. Too many footprints, you understand. He wants to eliminate as many routes as possible, until he can see a clear path to the anomaly."

"Is that why I haven't been able to go back to places I've already been?"

"Beats me. I'm just talking about trips to and from the Big Bang. He wants to maintain total control."

"Who put Calaneris in charge, anyway?" I say, disgusted.

"It's funny. Alan asked the same question."

"Aha! You've met Alan? He's been here?" Now I'm sure I can't trust him as well as Calaneris.

"Yes, him and his field assistant—what was his name—Eric? But they didn't like what they heard, and they moved on."

"And you bastards tricked me into going to a place where I could see them but I couldn't possibly get back to?" I am having a bad case of déjà vu. I was going to tell the Emperor to look for the "signal" of intelligence that Ralff and Benrus told me about. But Calaneris cut me off before I could explain it. His loss.

"I'm sorry."

"Where did they go?"

"I'm afraid they can't be reached if they're with the Watchmen."

Secretly, I am a little relieved that Eric is with Alan. But I'm not going to let Blauw off the hook. My hand goes to the torc around my neck. I'm glad that this time Hangul kept watch over it. I knew that the Emperor wanted the Cintamani, but I wasn't sure why. He seemed pretty powerful as it is. Now I know it lets me circumvent his Maze. I'm just not sure how.

"Well, I'm out of here," I announce. "You all have been perfectly unhelpful."

"Sunny, Gin—wait—" Blauw grabs my hand. "We can't let you give the Watchmen any of our secrets."

"Let go," I order. Feeling betrayed, I suddenly recall the little pickpocket Reggie in London. Not this time, I vow. He looks crushed.

"Get out of my way."

"You're joking," Blauw replies.

"I'll have you know I'm skilled in the martial arts," I say, doubting myself completely.

"Martial arts? What is that, you hit me with a tuba? I'm not sure you could even lift one."

My color vision is beginning to warm to an unpleasant shade of pink. My TKD instructor Sa-bum Nim had warned me about this. A cool head is always the best route. But I also know a cool head isn't protection against pain. It hadn't stopped Sa-bum from inflicting a ton of bruises on me in the past. If I try to fight Blauw I'm bound to suffer some. Then I recall that the Master once said that red-haired people feel pain more acutely than others. My heart beating, I assume the ready stance. Ready with adrenalin. I call upon Tae Kwon Do—the Way of Hand and Foot.

Blauw laughs again.

"Afraid?" I say.

Into the Mystic

It appears Blauw doesn't have a cool head either. He reaches out with the flat of his hand to slap me. A good enough slap will knock a woman unconscious.

I parry his slap with a knifehand, sweeping my wrist toward the outside. I won't kid you. That hurts, and my silk jacket offers no protection at all. Blauw looks surprised. He steps in closer. Glancing around, I notice he is trying to force me to retreat. Getting cornered is about the worst thing you can do, aside from letting your opponent get you on the ground. I scoot to his left to give myself more room. I'm not fast enough to elude his grasp, though. He catches me by my collar and spins me around, grabbing me around the neck from behind. He begins to fumble for my torc.

Another bad spot. I don't want to be choked out. I stomp on his foot. That has absolutely no effect. Blauw tightens his hold. Blood rushes to my face, not from anger, but from embarrassment. I've been over this a thousand times at the dojang. I twist slightly so the crook of his elbow gives me a bit of breathing room.

"Stop struggling," Blauw says. "You know you don't have a chance."

I put my hands in the prayer position and thrust my arms upward, breaking his hold. I spin around and assume the fighting stance. This time Blauw is more cautious. I will have to go to him. I lean on my back leg and kick at his head as hard as I can. Blood sprays from his nose. He looks down in astonishment, then swings hard at me. No little slap for the little lady this time.

But that's the nice thing about the head kick. It throws them off balance. I get in another roundhouse kick before Blauw closes in on me and grabs me in a bear hug. I jump up and down, but it is no use. I can't escape this time. My arms are pinned to my side. At least he can't hit me, I think. I'm wrong. Blauw reaches up with his fist and hits me in the chin. My eyesight shimmers for a minute.

I go limp, and he lets me fall to the ground.

"Stupid woman," Blauw says, reaching over. "We could have killed you during that storm, but your dragon got in the way."

"No," I scream at the top of my lungs. Taken aback, Blauw's pale blue eyes go wide. Sa-Bum Nim always said a good yell is a useful part of your arsenal.

I don't have any strength from the ground, so I scramble to my feet and scuttle away. He strides toward me, his fists balled to flail on me some more. He aims at my face, but I'm able to deflect his blow. Still, the blow hits me hard in the left arm. That's one disadvantage of being older. Blauw is still young—and fast. He punches me in the stomach. I double over, unable to breathe.

"You're going to regret not joining Calaneris," he taunts. "He's going to kill you and your ridiculous family."

I've tried to harden my stomach against his punch, and it has helped a little.

"Blazing Saddles," I say.

"What?" Blauw seems to be a sucker for conversation while beating on women. Why did I ever think he was a friend?

A backhand punch gets him again in the nose. I'm sure it must sting like a bee, but he isn't going down like a Palomino that's been punched by Mongo. Sa-Bum once warned that a palm strike to the nose could be lethal. I'm more than willing to give that a try. At the last second, I change my mind. There is another blow that was pretty much guaranteed to cause unconsciousness. I jump up under Blauw's chin with my patented hard head. Blauw collapses.

"Sa-Bum's not going to give me a Black Belt for this," I mumble through swollen lips, "but I have to thank him for instructing us how to fight dirty." I look at Blauw's prostrate form and dispense with a respectful bow. He doesn't deserve it.

My arm feels like it might be broken, but I hope it is just badly bruised. I feel exhilarated, but also a little foolish. I've forgotten to use the Cintamani to defeat Blauw. Now that I can think again, I make my wishes known.

"Rope," I demand. "Tie him up good. And, can you do something about my cheek? I think it's going all puffy—I can't see out of my left eye."

Chen-li materializes. They're ganging up on me.

"See you later, I promise."

"You don't require tea?" Chen-li soothes. *Funny, my little Chinese Dalek*, I think, as I wish myself to the Beach to think again.

☯

"I'm sorry, I just haven't been able to help the situation," I say to Poe, using the Cintamani to attend to my injuries, mostly to my hands and face. A blood blister on my hand is shrinking rapidly. Luckily, my wrist seems to be okay. I broke it once, and doctors had to insert a pin to hold the bone together long enough for it to heal. I wonder if the Cintamani can get rid of the pin, but realize I have more important things to ask.

"I know you were expecting me to get to Alan, maybe?"

The air shimmers a bit, and the quiet beach is replaced by a steep redstone canyon, striped with the traces of cuts made by ancient torrents.

"Oh, yes, I remember this. You showed it to me before," I say. But the canyon seems much deeper than before, more like the Grand Canyon. It appears that something has been gouging away at Poe.

"Well, any other suggestions?"

Mum, as usual.

"How about if we see if the Cintamani will work to send me back to talk to Ralff and Ben? I certainly could use some more physics expertise."

The beach shimmers back. I take that as tacit approval. I feel a little better, knowing I'm taking some sort of action, even if it doesn't pan out.

"I'd like to visit Ben and Ralff, five minutes after I left before..."

I hear a slight yelp. It's Ralff.

"What, you weren't expecting me?" I say.

"You look different. Have you been injured?"

I shrug. It hurts.

"This is a ground-breaking advance," Ben says, rushing up to me. "However did you manage to get here?" He reaches out and touches my shoulder, as if to make sure he isn't hallucinating.

"Well, I don't know how ground-breaking, it is, but I've learned a few things in the future," I say. "Thanks for the advice, incidentally."

I fill them in on my adventures since I last saw them, including the discovery that the Cintamani jewel seems to free me from Emperor Calaneris' proscription on return trips, just as long as I stagger the time and place slightly.

"But I've come back five minutes later than my last visit to you guys, because, like Calaneris, I think Poe doesn't want me to create an anachronism."

"Most excellent!" Ralff exclaims. "But it appears that you weren't able to get to another dimension when you visited the Big Bang?"

"Right, although I'm not positive the people I saw were in another dimension. I'm a little shaky on the whole dimension thing. I just know that Alan and Eric looked transparent, like those fish you sometimes see in aquariums. They couldn't hear me when I yelled at them."

"The Emperor's theory about the universe as maze seems plausible," Ralff says. "And, although I still tend to stick with the idea that the universe is mostly dark energy, this wouldn't contradict it."

"Blauw didn't seem to be 100 percent behind Calaneris's theory," I say. "He mentioned swimming through the chaos of the universe rather than taking direct routes through mazes."

"Hmm… If we use the metaphor of the universe as ocean, then perhaps Alan and his companions were on a deeper level than you. That might explain why they seemed harder to discern. But if there are other dimensions that curl in upon themselves, that could hide them from us. These sorts of things are hard to observe."

"Well, since I didn't really have eyes, who knows how I was 'seeing' all this stuff," I muse. "What do you think we'd find at the center of the maze? Blauw talked about an anomaly causing the Unwinding. Is that what we're looking for?"

"Whether we're talking about mazes, dimensions, or levels," Ralff says, "I think we need to go back to the Big Bang and see if we can communicate with these Watchmen. You say they were the first to visit there?"

I nod. "Are you sure?" I ask. "It could be dangerous. At least you're safe, stuck here in the year twenty-two hundred something."

"Better hurt in the line of duty than stuck behind the lines," Ralff says. I've decided he's the emotional one. I turn to Ben for his opinion.

"As far as I am concerned, you've already saved our lives by coming back here. We might have been stuck for eternity. What's one more life to lose?" *Uh-oh, maybe Ben is the emotional one,* I think. It could be equally dangerous to be in the way when the logjam breaks open.

"If Calaneris catches us, we'll be dead fish, and he's got Scientists everywhere," I note. "One of them in particular, named Blauw, is quite a thug." I check my cheek.

"Hopefully, Poe's Cintamani will help us."

"If Calaneris doesn't confiscate it again. Okay, then. What about a last meal for the condemned? What have you guys got to eat around here?"

"Just the usual protein-carbohydrate bars," Ben offers.

"Got any fruit, like apples or oranges? Or some beer?"

"I'm afraid not," they shake their heads. "Since we couldn't move around, we haven't been able to help ourselves to the bounty of the universe like we used to."

"Well, I just happen to have brought a real-life replicator," I respond, touching my torc.

"Three cappucinos, cinnamon on top," I order. "Or would you fellows prefer chocolate?"

Benrus and Ralff have been trapped in the present for so long, they are eager to try anything. Anything new, that is. We drink our coffees, giving the milk-crusted rims one last lick for luck.

"Okay, let's see if we can blow this popsicle stand," I said. "No, scratch that—it's just so tempting to talk in clichés when you're on an adventure that's stranger than fiction." I take their hands and close my eyes, visualizing the Beach.

Again, Ben lets out a little cry. I open my eyes. Success. We are standing at the edge of the shore, as waves gently lap up to our toes. I assume Ben and Ralff still have toes, although they are hidden under their long robes. I guess fashion goes in cycles. In my day, clothing was becoming more and more optional, and it's actually banned when traveling through wormholes.

I realize that the little yelp isn't due to moving elsewhere in the universe. I forget that they are old hands at that. Hangul is rising out of the water, a mass of tentacles wriggling from his beard. Looks like he too is having a little snack of calamari.

Ben shouts out, "Look at that huge sea creature! We have nothing like that at home. And the creature that it's eating—it's shimmering all of the colors of the spectrum!

"That's Hangul," I say. "He's the water dragon I told you about. Thanks, Buddy. Without you, I wouldn't be here."

"Much larger than I had expected from your description," Ralff says. "But I have seen the prey on Earth. They are called squid, and these rainbow-like displays are caused when water flows out of their iridocytes, the cells that contain the iridescent pigments. Fascinating, since the squid themselves are color-blind."

"Ugh," I say. Not a very pleasant way to go. But it's interesting to see what Hangul eats, and to know that he is as attracted to light shows as we are.

We admire the gory spectacle for a bit. I've grown fond of these two brainy young "men," with their Spock-like didactic lectures. They're a lot like the exchange students in Alan's college classes at UNC Charlotte. We'd invite them over occasionally for dinner or parties, to make them feel more at home in the strangeness of America. Especially the strange Southern customs.

I remember one time we put on our version of the famous North Carolina barbecue, complete with corn on the cob, and Alan's Italian students were totally grossed out by the thought of eating cattle feed. I smile. Didn't they know what polenta is made of? At least Ralff and Ben aren't picky eaters. But I won't be giving them any Kim-Chee. That'd be pressing my luck.

Food isn't a concern right now anyway, unless I manage to get across—across what? Hell if I know.

"Here's the deal, fellas," I say. Time to broach a potentially delicate subject. "I can't take anything nonorganic with me across to the Big Bang, and I can't get there without the aid of Calaneris or the Cintamani. It's Catch-22."

They look at me blankly.

"I'd like to go alone, and I'd like to leave the Cintamani with you. I trust you. If something happens to me, I'd like to deed Hangul and the pearl to you."

"Why can't we go along?" Ben asks, not understanding.

"I could get you there, but I couldn't get you back,"
I reply. "I'll be going in without wearing a lifeline, so to
speak. And remember, with the Cintamani, you've got a
permanent passport —to everywhere." They glance at
each other.

"Very well, we'll hold the jewel for you. What are
your instructions? Do you want us to retrieve you with it?"

"Umm, I don't think so. I think Poe will get me
back here somehow, if I just give the Cintamani orders to
come get me if I'm about to die, or destroy the universe, or
a Hellmouth opens, or... "

"But you'll communicate with us if you can?"

"Yes, for sure. And if these Watchmen are all
they're cracked up to be, I'll even ask if you can join us.
And Poe—You'll take care of these boys, won't you?" I
say, shedding my clothes as modestly as I can.

There's no reply.

This will be my first sortie without a paper of
introduction. I guess there's no need for gadgets or texting
if you can communicate instantly anywhere, anywhen. I
close my eyes and picture a slowly revolving mirrorball,
spinning colors that no human eyes can see.

☺

*"That was a huge breakthrough," QoS says. "You
very nearly communicated directly with Gin."*
*"**"*

*"I know you didn't actually speak, but she seemed
to get the gist of what you were trying to say, even without
my translation."*
*"**"*

*"She seems to have met this latest failure to find
her family with more determination. Before, she would
have fallen into a depression. I've had to keep presenting
little incentives, which introduces further delay. I haven't
had a chance to appeal to Golaeth."*
*"**"*

Into the Mystic

"Oh, the main incentive seems to be hope that she'll find her family. She's like a mama bear, you might say."

*"**"*

"Humans have two sexes, as do many of the creatures on Earth. The female sex bears live young and usually has a strong instinct to protect their young. They can become quite warlike in this regard. I've always assumed that's why you chose Virginia.
*"**"*

"Yes, of course. Her link to the anomaly only adds to her suitability for this task."

Yverra cocked her head, listening for a dimension shift or a time hack. Yes, there had been a dimension shift recently.

Before the trail disappeared among the many infinities, she followed.

"Ydorian?" She wondered where her probable-mate was going.

"Is there something you're not telling me?" she asked. After all, she was the high priestess of the Watchmen, and she expected to be apprised of any new developments.

"I'm sorry, Yverra, but we are leaving."

"Leaving? Where are you going?"

"For now, we are going to a past before the humans became sentient."

She didn't have time for this now.

"Why? I haven't authorized that."

"It's too dangerous. I've tried to tell you this. That maniac Calaneris has been abetting an alternate universe in trying to destroy this one. We need time to think about next steps—or whether to hide permanently."

"Of course, I can't stop you, but you are taking the coward's way out."

"That's exactly what I thought you'd say," Ydorian said. "You refuse to listen, and obviously don't respect my input, so I am taking all the like-minded Watchmen to a sanctuary."

"Where, exactly, is that?" Yverra asked, coldly.

"I won't tell you."

"I found you easily, you know."

"That's because I wasn't covering my tracks. You've reminded me to do so from now on. I'm afraid we will not be seeing each other again."

"I thought we would always be together," Yverra said. Her gold eyes blinked, but only once. He was a traitor. "We were going to have children."

"No. I would never bring children into such danger as we face now. I sincerely regret leaving the most beautiful Watchman for a life that I know will be filled with regret. But at least in the distant past, the Watchmen will be able to live in relative safety from the incursions happening now, not to mention the haphazard stumblings of the humans."

"I'm surprised to hear you say that. Probability shows that one of the humans will lead us to the solution to the anomaly," she said, her pride showing in the rapidly changing symbols phosphoring on her skin.

"Probability also shows that a human will lead to our downfall," Ydorian replied. "Goodbye."

Yverra blinked again, her composure having slipped completely. When she opened her eyes again, Ydorian was gone. There was no trail this time.

☺

Dozens of hazy figures scurry about, pointing at the little egg in their midst. It glows white-hot, or so I imagine, as I can't feel a thing. I scan for Alan or Eric, or the reptilian woman I saw before, and swim closer to the spot where I first saw them. They must have moved. Wait, there is the woman. This time, I'm able to approach her.

Perhaps the Cintamani is helping me remotely, or my will has grown stronger.

I position myself directly in front of the woman. She is still not fully solid, and she doesn't seem to see me. I reach out and try to touch her. A shock runs up my virtual arm, and I involuntarily pull it back. I tell myself that I don't have nerves, and I'm not really feeling this. The woman jerks, as though she too has felt a shock.

"Hello, can you hear me?" I say.

She stares sightlessly into space. She moves her hands, and a symbol begins to take form in the not-air between us. I can't make it out at first, because it is on edge, but when she rotates it, I can see that it is a Greek "pi," which stands for the constant of something having to do with circles. I really do need to brush up on my middle school math.

Now, that's odd, because I know she's not from Earth, and even if she is some sort of super-mathematician, she wouldn't use that symbol, unless... unless she's learned it from Alan.

I want to repeat it back to her, but I didn't bring anything with me. "Maybe I should have sent Ralff," I mutter.

I hold up three fingers, the first part of pi. They start to glow, like headlights shining through a fog.

The next thing I know, a hand reaches through and grabs my wrist.

Before I can even scream, I'm elsewhere, in an environment totally unlike the gray void I came from. The egg is still here, but it is sitting on a pedestal in what looks like a big temple. Congregants are kneeling and sitting around it, murmuring incantations and, possibly, prayers.

I'm amazed. Was there something in the universe before the Big Bang?

"Of course there was," I tell myself. "We always called it God. But it looks like it was the Watchmen. Merely a syntactical difference, in my opinion." I remember that I wasn't a very good Sunday confirmation class student. I had the temerity to ask, "If God created the universe, who created God?" Father Truesdell eventually kicked me out of class and told my mother not to bring me back. I complained to Mom, saying "I thought that was the point of confirmation class, to ask the priest anything."

The priest said we were made in God's image.

Maybe we humans were just imperfect copies. Or maybe the message had just degraded over 13 billion years, like in a game of what we used to call Chinese Whispers, where you whisper a message to the person next to you, he whispers it to the next person in the circle, and by the end, the message is guaranteed to have changed. Playing that game as a kid, I would always get a good laugh at how garbled the message had gotten. I'm not sure I appreciate the thought of being at the end of a garbled celestial transmission.

The woman lets go of my arm. "Who are you?" she asks.

I rub my wrist. Her grip seems real enough. I've been yanked, possibly across dimensions, by a tall woman wearing leathers inscribed with religious and mathematical symbols. These people can reinstantiate me instantly. And I'm not naked. Nice.

"I'm looking for Professor Alan Jones," I blurt, right to the point. "I'm his wife." I'm too focused on the family to notice that I'm in the presence of some sort of angel or high priestess of the Church of the Way Things Really Are.

"Your family is here," she says. Her eyes are gold-colored, the pupils slitted like a snake's. Quite off-putting.

"Your husband and his field assistant are working on solving the number of possible worlds. When he gets that, which should be shortly, he should be able to proceed with viewing what you call the Big Bang."

"You said 'my family.' Is Grace here too?"

"Yes, although she is entrusted with a different but equally important task."

Booyah!

"Will you take me to them?"

She points. Alan and Eric are walking toward me.

"Ginny! You're finally here at last!" He hugs me a long time. Eric looks a little shy, but I wave for him to join into the group hug.

"Why didn't you come for me after the Unwinding?" I finally ask.

"God knows I tried, and I wandered around a long time before I ended up here," he said. "But we can talk about that later. Yverra tells me you arrived via Emperor Calaneris' scientific transport."

"This is actually my second trip. On the first one, I saw this woman, with you, kind of blurry-like, at the Big Bang. This time Poe sent me."

"Poe?"

"It's a long story. Calaneris and Blauw said you deserted to the Watchmen, so that's how you got here too, right?"

"Oh, they told you? We had a bit of a falling out."

"So did we," I agree.

"Well, the important thing is that you got here."

"I saw you in 1859 London," I say, "and I've seen Gracie, but she was just a little girl. Can we go to her?"

"I'll see if Yverra can arrange an audience with the Princess."

"Who is this Yverra—Grace is a princess?"

"Yes. Are you happy to learn you're the mother of royalty?"

I don't know what to say. But I *am* happy. And I'm happy I've got my man back.

*****~~~~~*****

155

Chapter 16.

Drop Me In the Water

"Professor Jones? Here to observe?"

"Yes, sir."

"We'll camp here tonight and survey the battlefield at dawn."

Alan hunkered down, trying to give the icy wind as small a target as possible, waiting for morning. Fitfully, he dreamed...

Ginny pounds away at the piano, her glass of iced tea bouncing on top of the lid. What she lacks in finesse, she makes up for in gusto. You'd never know it looking at her—she's usually quiet and reserved, bookish even. She machine-guns a glissando, and I expect that any moment she'll jump on the bench like Jerry Lee Lewis.

The beat grows hotter and more insistent. I'm getting big ideas, the rhythmic passage lifting me to a higher plane. The first time we made love, she stripped me bare, like a hungry tiger, and stuck her tongue into my mouth. I just stood there like a statue, shocked and not believing my good luck. She pulled me down on top of her, and we tried very hard to break the laws of physics and meld into one being. The soft flesh of her belly and breasts gave me a soft landing place, surrounded on all sides by the thrashing pain of our boney knees and elbows colliding. Her body was both a penitentiary and a place of worship. I had a nagging fear that I'd lose her blessing as quickly as I'd found it. Virginia was my first taste of the pain-pleasure principle.

Afterward we lay together, looking at the ceiling. Proud that I had finally became a real man, instead of a woolly headed intellectual, I gushed incoherently.

157

"That was fantastic, Virginia. You seem a lot more experienced than me." But she quickly corrected me.

"No, actually, I'm a virgin, Alan. But good Catholic girls can tell a sure thing when they see it."

That's what I was. A sure thing.

The blare of trumpets woke Alan from the dream. He groaned, accompanied by the protestations of 600 other men. The time had arrived for the Battle of Sevastopol.

☺

"You blunderer," Calaneris says. "All that effort to get Alan Jones, and he slips through our fingers. Then you let the woman escape too. It looks like she got the better of you."

"What's the big deal, anyway?" Blauw asks, holding a cold pack to his face. Purple bruises spread from ear to ear. "You just gave orders to track her in case she tried to contact the Watchmen. When she and I went to the Big Bang, she saw Alan and the Watchmen, but she didn't know how to get to them."

"Perhaps not, but the other Scientists say she is now with the Watchmen."

"Really? How did she do that?"

"We may never know. I'll need the architectural plans to STS-99. Their daughter built the space station, and there may be a clue as to how she and her father were able to join the Watchmen. Now, get out. You're bleeding on my carpet."

☺

Alan and I hold hands while we wait to see Grace. I'm afraid if I let go, he'll disappear again. He seems equally happy just to wait.

"You never told me who Yverra is," I ask.

"She is the head of the Watchmen," Alan replies. "They are a race of time-shifting aliens."

"I've heard of them. Calaneris's competition. Speaking of time shifting, I see that you've been getting younger," I observe. "I tried that a few times, but I found I got more respect with a few wrinkles on my face."

His quiff is picture perfect, not a shiny dark hair out of place.

"Everyone seems to see through appearances, here," Alan says, "so you may as well look any way you like. You look good to me."

"Well, I want Grace to recognize me."

"She will. She recognizes everyone. One of her many talents."

I'm even more nervous about seeing Grace than I was to see Alan. She's my baby. I think about the years we spent trying to bring a child into the world. After repeated heartbreaks, one day, we had Gracie. I have to say this isn't exactly the world we were expecting. And time was never on our side. It flew by so fast, until all of a sudden Gracie was driving the family car way too fast and thinking she was immortal. But then Eric had been such a good influence on her. How had she gone from newlywed to princess?

Yverra consults the timepiece hanging from a chain clipped to her coat. "The Princess will see you now," she says.

"Have you gotten to talk to her a lot?" I ask Alan.

"This is the first time I've seen her too," Alan admits. How can this be? Parents can't even see their own child? A knot begins to form in my stomach. Is Grace some sort of hostage?

"The Princess is not a hostage," Yverra says, as if reading my mind. "She has merely been very busy. She is anxious to see you and Alan."

"What about Eric?" I ask.

"Very well," Yverra says. She seems reluctant.

Alan squeezes my hand, and we are in a white room, or at least surrounded on all sides by white light. Grace holds out her arms.

159

"Mother! Father! And Eric! I am so happy to see you."

I try unsuccessfully to hold back a floodgate of tears. *I* never said I was kick-ass.

"You're a princess?" I ask. "Should we bow or something?"

"No, it's just a term we use to make it easier for other humans to understand."

"What do you mean, 'other humans?' You're our daughter."

"I was. I can't do that anymore."

"Grace! Are they holding you against your will? Have they made you leave Eric?" I start to cry.

Alan tries to pull me back. "You don't understand, Gin," he says.

"Understand what? You're married, Grace. You can't just run off to sit in a white room." I look at Eric, to encourage him to join in. He looks down, embarrassed.

"All right, what am I missing here?" I exclaim in exasperation. "I won't put up with you being martyred. Not after all we've been through as a family."

"I'm not a martyr, Mother. I'm still human, and I remember all that, but I've got new responsibilities to everyone, everywhere."

"Not my perfect daughter," I moan. Yes, I know I'm being melodramatic. But not overly so.

Alan puts his arm around me. "That's just it. She's the perfect being they've been waiting for. She will hold all of life together while we sort out the universe."

I still don't understand. I immediately think of the jewel.

"What if I give these Watchmen the Cintamani instead?" I venture. "It can do anything."

Yverra replies, in a dispassionate voice, "Yes, when you wield it, that is true, but it is inanimate. Grace is a living Cintamani."

160

I stare at Grace, for once at a loss. Talk about empty nest syndrome, redux.

"How long will you have to be here?"

"We think it will be today," she says.

"You don't experience time the way we do, do you? Even God didn't create the universe in a day."

"I know. But it won't be long," Grace says.

"Well, I'm here now. If you need me, you'll call me. Any time, night or day. Do you understand?" I know that sounds stupid, like I'm talking to a teenager.

"Yes, Mother. Thank you." She turns to Eric. "You're doing great work, Eric. We're all grateful." He continues to stare downward, arms folded across his chest. At least *someone* else looks as upset by all this as I feel.

We return to the Watchmen's court, where the little egg thing waits for us, seemingly unchanging but about ready to crack open. A hive of activity surrounds it.

"What can I do to help?" I ask Yverra. All talk in the room ceases. Apparently it's unusual for people to just walk up to Yverra and address her. For a moment, she looks to be at a loss. "Come on," I say. "Universal Traveler like me—surely I can help with the effort."

"I'm not sure we can trust you," Yverra says. "You may have been contaminated by Calaneris."

"You think I've been brainwashed? Well, assuming that was the case, can you just debrief me and get on with it? You seem to trust Alan and Grace."

"Calaneris is autocratic and jealous, and he believes only his methods are correct."

"You mean his theories about the Maze? I've learned something about that from Blauw and would be happy to share my knowledge with you. Trust is a two-way street, you know. I worry about you Watchmen being able to change time, what do they call it—hacking? Especially the past. What's to stop you from erasing me, like I was never even born?"

161

"We would never do that, Virginia. Allow me to allay your fears. We operate in multiple dimensions. A time hack involves folding the fifth dimension into the sixth dimension. It's a shorter route than traveling to the past and changing events. Your husband Alan can explain it further to you."

"All right, but I really do want to help. What can I do?"

"I understand that you are a gardener," Yverra says. "Perhaps you can conduct the Yggdrasil Project."

"What's that?" I ask, my universal travel experience being of little help here. "Is that the name of the egg thing?"

"No, it is a metaphorical tree which holds the structure of the universe."

"Like a tree on Earth."

"Exactly. A rowan tree, to be precise."

"I've got one of those in my back yard!" I exclaim. "A North American Mountain Ash, with the red berries. Very pretty, and the birds go crazy for them. See, I told you I could be useful." Blauw the Naturalist would be envious. But that's what he gets for hanging with Calaneris.

"You won't be cultivating a living organic tree, just studying the symbology of the metaphor," Yverra says, with her slight Mona Lisa smile. "We are deconstructing all known mythologies and examining them for numerical algorithms or sequences of instructions—what you might call recipes. All intelligent species and societies have made them up to one extent or another to explain the workings of the universe. This metaphor is from Earth, and is part of Norse mythology."

"That's fine, and I'm happy to help. But I meant to ask you something. Do you have a theory about what caused the Unwinding?"

"It is still a theory, but we believe that a flaw may have metamorphosed in one of the recursive components of the creation. This examination of metaphors may help us understand it."

"Right." It sounds like she is using normal English words, but I don't understand a single one of them, except "creation." Maybe Alan or Blauw would get it. I shake my head.

"So, where's this tree? And what does it have to do with eggs?"

"We can set it up near your husband and daughter's project, if you like. Then you can more easily cross-connect your findings."

"That'd be great. Have you folks got a library or something? I'd like to look up this myth, if I may."

"Just ask for whatever you need," Yverra says, and vanishes abruptly.

"Everybody comes and goes before I can ask anything," I complain. I mean to ask about whether there is a news feed of some sort, so I can continue my role as a "documentarian" or news reporter, just not in the employ of Calaneris. I guess I do have a rather long list of questions.

Alan takes my hand, and we go to the white room.

"Where's Gracie?" I ask.

"She's spread rather thin," Alan says, but she's here if we want to talk to her.

I wish for a couple of chairs and take a seat. I wonder if a chair is a metaphor. They certainly come in handy when you need them to take a load off. Alan does the same, and he brings up a computer workstation as well. I want to ask him something before he becomes totally engrossed in whatever he's working on.

"Can I ask you a question? Do you think Yverra's time hacking is safe? She talked about folding dimensions and such. That can't be good, can it?"

"I admit that the Watchmen's civilization is more advanced than ours, and we still have a lot to learn, but Grace seems to trust her," Alan says. "What Yverra told you sounds logical to me. The existence of multiple dimensions means anything is possible. Remember that physics thought experiment I once told you about Schrödinger's Cat being both dead and alive at the same time? I think the Watchmen know what they're doing. More than Calaneris, at any rate."

He turns to his computer screen, while I, only slightly reassured, request a book with background on Yggdrasil from the library. A print text shows up in my hand. It glows slightly, as if it was printed on phosphorescent paper.

I run my hand over the book jacket, which is made of glossy paper illustrated with a map of northern Scotland and Scandinavia. The embossed title says, "Northern European Folklore." I hadn't realized that northern Scotland at one time was connected to Norse lore, but I hope it will give me the background I need. Briefly, I wonder if this book has power, like you see in the old legends. Or if it contains a message, like the papers and poems Poe has been sending me all along this journey.

There's a big chapter on Yggdrasil. It's connected to the fate of humanity, it seems, and appears in several Norse poems. In one of them, the god Odin hangs himself from the ash tree for nine days "to sacrifice himself to himself on that tree of which no man knows from where the roots run." I wonder if he made the sacrifice to keep the universe's status quo. I read on.

Apparently there are a lot of "serpents" lying beneath the old tree's roots. One called Grafvolluor ("the one digging under the ditch") sounds familiar. I'd bet Hangul would fit right in there.

I look up and see Alan hard at work, totally engrossed in his computer screen.

"Don't you think it's kind of boring, just sitting here in a totally white room?" I ask him. He grins, and we decide to take a short break.

☺

"Well, I suppose we should get back to work," I say.

"Definitely," he says, stroking my hair.

"Sorry to be a distraction, but you know it's been a while..."

"I like distractions," he says. "Now that we've got that off our minds, we can concentrate." Although I'm sure he didn't intend it that way, I take his statement to mean that he thinks he'd get more done if I weren't demanding attention.

"You know, I don't know how much I can really get out of a book," I say. "I've been peppering you with questions, and not letting you get your work done. I'm learning a lot about this Yggdrasil myth, and I think it's time I go check it out."

"Mmhmm," he says, already back at the keyboard. I guess I'm on my own.

I've often lost myself in books, especially adventure quests such as "Lord of the Rings," "Robinson Crusoe," and others where I imagine myself helping the hero save the world, or applying survival skills that I don't really have in real life. Except now I do have them in real life.

I take one last look to be sure Alan is happy and secure, and then rise and take a step. I don't lift my foot yet. I'm not sure that I won't pop back to the beach. So far, so good. I'm still in Watchmen territory.

"Let's explore this big tree called Yggdrasil," I say. I hope that's the right incantation. Yverra didn't tell me much. She may have meant some sort of virtual reality rather than the real thing. She's not a very hands-on supervisor... Well, Cintamani it is.

☺

A multicolor road stretches toward a gigantic tree floating in space. The tree looks as big as a planet to me,

165

but I'm not a good judge of size, I'm afraid. I've seen the drawings in the book, so I'm expecting a gnarled, ancient bush. It's striking, because its roots are completely visible. There's no dirt. The tree just floats there.

The rainbow bridge is quite decorative, but I decide it would be quicker to fly. I go in for a closer look at the underside of the titanic topiary. There's supposed to be a well that contains all wisdom somewhere in here. I float in, marveling at the massive roots, which although out of soil or water, appear to be strong and white, like glistening cables stretching across the vast expanse. Pulses of light course through the network of roots, probably bringing nourishment to the branches that reach high into the black heavens.

The book on Scottish lore ascribes all sorts of magical properties to the rowan tree. It claims every householder plants one for the protection it will afford. Even a splinter over the doorway is enough to ward away evil. And no boat would be launched without a bit of rowan in its timbers to safeguard it against storms, tempests, and sea devils. The ship in 1827 North Carolina must have neglected its bit of rowan wood, I muse. Hangul and I—and the storm—were able to do quite a job on it.

The book goes on to say that Scotland of yore is dotted with magical wells, each accompanied by a rowan tree. So, if I do find a well within Yggdrasil, I think it would be important to report it to the Watchmen.

"Note to Alan," I dictate. "I'm going to see if there's a magical well associated with Yggdrasil."

I continue to head inward, where I estimate the heart of the root system to be. I don't know if this construct is like the living trees I've encountered all my life, but why wouldn't it be? It's *our* metaphor, after all. If it's a normal tree, there should be a central taproot that leads directly to the tree's water source. It's there that I hope to find the wellspring.

But before I reach the center, I start to notice bulges appearing on the roots. Oblong, pink objects like nodules are attached at irregular intervals all along. I've seen this before, on the roots of pea plants. I call for a readout from the library about pea root nodules. Legumes tend to form a symbiotic relationship with bacteria, and the bacteria aid in fixing nitrogen from the air and helping the plant turn it into ammonia, which is assimilated into amino acids, DNA, vitamins, and all sorts of other nutritious stuff.

Have I hit the jackpot? This looks like an important pattern. If something has gone wrong with the prototype DNA of the universe, things might look fine, until one day, a dormant gene flips on and the universe tries to kill itself. I transfer this to Alan right away, along with my supposition.

"Nice theory," Alan's voice seeps into the forest of tree roots I float among. "But I think something like that would have shown itself much earlier than 13 billion years on. I think what you're looking at, metaphor-wise, is what's called the cosmic web. The universe is criss-crossed with a web of stars and galaxies, where there is a lot of matter. There are even huger clumps of dark matter all along those lines, holding them all together. There is actually a lot more dark matter than regular matter in our universe, you know. And in between it all, there are these gigantic voids. Still, it's quite clever of you to link these nodule-like objects to pea plants. Did you know that peas were the plants used to establish Mendelian genetics?"

Disappointed, I mumble that no, I didn't know that.

"Did you have any luck finding that well you were looking for?"

I had forgotten about that, in my enthusiasm to report the root nodules.

"Don't worry, we'll look further into the nodules. Sometimes blue-skying leads to real discoveries. Keep us posted on what else you find."

167

"Okay, thanks Alan. And I'll keep looking for the well." I feel pretty silly. It's just a myth, after all. But here I am.

The darkness under Yggdrasil is oppressive, and I begin to doubt I would see a well here, unless I fell down one. This is odd. Something below my feet is beginning to glow. Maybe I've inadvertently run into one of the pink nodules, and released a luminescent substance. I float downward, heading into the pool of light.

The pool is big enough to call a lake. And there's a brightly lit structure within it, a building of some sort. I splash down into the water and start to do the breast stroke toward it. The closer I get, the more I think of it as a temple. I pass through a clear wall of water, past marble columns, and into the building. Colorfully lit water cascades from a fountain, collecting into a large golden basin. Images of people and places flicker across the surface. Could this be the well of wisdom?

"Alan—"

"What, find something already?"

"Take a look at this. I'm underwater, in the middle of a lake. What do you think?"

He whistles softly. "I think we need to have Gracie and Yverra analyze this."

*****〰〰〰*****

PART II. THE BREACH

Chapter 17.

Recursion

How many bards gild the lapses of time!
—John Keats

I'm excited that I've finally stumbled across a clue that interests the Watchmen.

"So, you've found a temple containing a well within the Yggdrasil metaphor," Alan says.

"Well, where there's a big tree, there's probably water nearby," I observe. "But from my research, the ancient myths say the well contains all wisdom. Is somebody going to go back and take a drink out of it, or something? It was really bright, kind of like the little egg you've got there."

"Gracie is all over it," Alan says. I find it hard to believe that my daughter is key to unlocking the secrets of the universe, but I'm just happy to be the proud mom.

Alan adds, "Yverra says it's going to be a pretty complex calculation."

"Isn't that what computers are for?" I ask.

"Yes, of course, but we've known the output from the calculation for a long time. We just know that the answer is just plain wrong. So, we're going to be going through the source code, one line at a time. We need to see the underlying logic, and it may be beyond our understanding, since we didn't write the code.

"You know, it's funny how Yverra reacted. To the underwater part, I mean. You know her people originated on a water planet, don't you? Eventually they moved to land, but they are still amphibious. I suspect this might be similar to one of their origin myths too."

"Sorry, Yverra doesn't stop and converse much with me, I'm afraid," I say. "You've been so busy, I haven't had a chance to ask you how you got here ahead of me. Maybe while we wait you could tell me a little bit about your adventures. Like, I know you were in London in the 1850s. But by then you'd already sent me some sort of message, right? That's when I knew not to give up hope of finding you."

Alan smiles. "That's kind of a long story, although probably not as long as yours. When the Unwinding occurred, I think we were all dispersed relatively close to each other in time and space. You went to the year 1827, and I went to Europe in 1853. We were still on Earth and could almost reach out and touch each other, if we'd known how. Each trip has thrown us farther apart, like a spiral. I think the crack was just starting to form. It was small at first, but it began to extend into something much bigger."

"Yes," I agreed. Los Angeles in 2416 was no picnic. And by that time, Ralff and Benrus were trapped on their planet."

"I didn't understand what had happened at first," Alan said. "I just knew that I had been stuck in the past, and I couldn't get out.

"Like you figured, I started out looking for the greatest mathematician on Earth in that time. Even if he didn't know what was going on, at least I'd have someone to talk to who might understand my predicament."

"You assumed it was a man, then?" I tease. "What about Ada Lovelace?"

Alan shrugs. "Sorry. I know there were female geniuses around, like Ada, but I foolishly went looking for Babbage instead."

"I forgive your little sexist prejudice," I say. "We're all products of our culture and our biases. I'm just glad you married me over your parents' objections."

"That was a short-lived war. It didn't take too long for them to realize how lucky we all were to have you in our lives," Alan says, hugging me. "And you were quite a babe, you know."

"Oh, pshaw," I blush. I don't tell him that my mother had taken me aside for a little discussion in the rose garden too. I told her she wasn't the one marrying Alan. "So, what happened next?"

"Well, speaking of war, I first found myself not in London, actually, but near the Black Sea during the Crimean War. I met a reporter for the Times named William Russell, who was photographing the major skirmishes. I read one of his articles about Charles Babbage, who was petitioning the British government for funds to develop an analysis engine that he said could help predict the outcome of the war. Babbage was already famous in London, having broken the code of the "unbreakable" Vigenere Cipher in just two weeks at the beginning of the war, just for his own amusement.

"I told Willy that I was looking for a great scientist or physicist, and he suggested that I tag along with him, because Britain was sending all of its best minds, including Faraday and Nobel, to aid various war-related tasks. They were just starting to call these men by the newly coined term of 'scientist.' I met a veritable 'Who's Who' of 19th century geniuses," Alan says.

"So, did one of them point you in the right direction?"

"Unfortunately, no. Willy and I got caught up covering the siege at Sevastopol, and both of us were pressed into service. The accounting for servicemen in the war was dreadful. I decided to apply myself to improving upon the photographic methods of the day, and cobbled together a movie camera, although I kept that a secret, since it was well ahead of its time. I spent a lot of my days capturing panoramas of battles, panning over corpses lying on fields, and filming men killing rats with bayonets and roasting them over open fires. Totally disgusting. I kept the footage in a chest that I dragged all around the war theatre."

"Wow. I had no idea I was married to a Veteran of Foreign Wars," I say. "Did you ever get shot at?"

"No, but I did meet a man who seemed interested in my story, so I told him about being ripped out of my comfortable picnic on the beach and tossed onto the battlefield. He seemed excited, and told me to wait. He ran off, and when he came back, he had Eric in tow. That might have been the first clue that someone besides our family was interested in the Unwinding.

"After a couple of months, Eric and I gave up hope of ever seeing you and the family again. The 'scientists' I met were totally clueless about the Unwinding, and Willy thought I'd inhaled too many photo developer fumes.

"One evening I sat down in our tent and prepared to write a letter to you. I hoped that it would someday reach you in the future, where I assumed you still were, and I resolved to put it in a safe deposit box in the Bank of England, to be opened at a later date. When the war ended, I set up shop at the old Vauxhall Gardens as a magician, with Eric as my assistant. It was fairly easy, with some modern technical tricks up my sleeve."

"It's shocking that I didn't see Eric. How did you come up with the name, the Great Mathison?" I ask.

Recursion

"Oh, Mathison's the middle name of the great Alan Turing, one of the pioneers of cryptography in the Second World War. Too subtle?"

"You think?" To tell the truth, if I had been paying attention to Alan's work and his heroes, I should have picked up on this.

"You can imagine my surprise when I saw you pop up in the audience in 1859," he continues. "I thought it meant you had come from the future after receiving my message. Totally irrational, I know, but I already believed fervently in time travel, having been a first-hand witness."

I ask, "When I found you, why couldn't we be together? You vanished before I could get to the stage. Was it the Watchmen who saved you?" I remember how Yverra reached out and plucked me off one place and into another dimension.

"Actually, no, it was the soldier who I'd met on the battlefield. Said his name was Blow."

"Oh, my God! It was Blauw! So, he recruited you for the Emperor?"

"Yes, and it was a good thing. He saved my life. The Unwinding had opened another crack at this nexus, and that point in the timeline was utterly destroyed. Blauw brought me to Calaneris, and that's where I got to hear the Emperor's theory about the universe being a maze."

"And he brought Eric too?"

"No, that's just it. Here he'd gone to the trouble to bring us together but then left Eric behind."

"And how did that make you feel?"

"How do you expect? Bad. I was afraid that you'd been killed this time, and I was desolate about Eric," Alan says. "I asked Calaneris if he could retrieve you too, but he said it was too late, that you were already gone."

"Yeah, the Beach came and got me," I say. "I told you I've taken to calling whoever or whatever lives there 'Poe,' after Edgar Allan. Every time I've tried to return to a place or time since the Unwinding, his response has turned out to be 'Nevermore.' Probably a safeguard of some sort. I only have the powers that he grants me through the Cintamani, or at least the powers I'm able to discover. I never was an ace scientist."

"Yes, that's Yverra's theory also. Like you, we'd give anything to know who or what Poe is and how he is managing to hold together what someone or something's trying very hard to tear apart."

"So how did you and Eric end up here?"

"The first time Blauw and Calaneris sent me to the universe's first minutes, I saw the Watchmen were there too. I proposed we strike up an alliance. Calaneris didn't like hearing that. He seemed to resent the Watchmen, so he forbade me to work on the project. He said he was on a heroic mission to save the universe, so I went along with it. But it didn't take too long to realize he wanted to be the *only* hero. I was just twiddling my thumbs,—and bitching about needing my field assistant and my family. I think he honestly had no idea where you were. I began tinkering with dimensional analysis, and that's when Yverra grabbed me. I've been working here ever since."

"Sounds like a promotion, all right," I say. "I'm proud of you. I take it the first order of business was to find and retrieve Gracie and Eric?"

"That's a whole other story I should tell you some time.... I see Yverra and Gracie are coming."

Alan and I hug Gracie and settle in expectantly to see what she thinks. Maybe someday I'll hug Yverra, but she's a bit imperious, so I've yet to break the ice. She seems to have little use for emotions.

"Mom, Dad, the Yggdrasil Metaphor has turned out to be quite useful."

"Does the well contain some wisdom, then?" I ask. "Sorry if that sounds dumb. I could use a little wisdom right now."

"It is not the well so much as the tree *and* the well," Gracie says.

"Ah, logical AND, eh?" Alan pipes in.

"Yes, both are essential to the method," Yverra says.

"The method?"

"A recursive method." Once again, I'm totally in the dark. Gracie tries to explain.

"You see, Mom, where there is a magical tree—specifically, a magical rowan—there is a magical well. Within each rowan lies another rowan, and within each well lies another well. Yggdrasil represents the universe and is the pattern for an infinite number of tree-well combinations that have formed across the universe. But it can't exist without the infinite number of smaller trees and wells each contributing to the pattern. It's an immensely powerful concept."

"And elegant," Alan adds. "It's like the universe has been solved without needing to write a big program to do it. You just say, "Yggdrasil," and—Bob's your uncle—an infinite number of tiny Yggdrasils spring into action to do the job."

"This sounds suspiciously like fractals," I say.

"Yes, fractals are one way of expressing infinite recursion. But it's also a clue to the seventh and eighth dimension, the dimension of infinities. Yverra's Watchmen are able to calculate and navigate through possible worlds in our universe. We think of those as the fifth and sixth dimensions. They can see the plane of possible worlds, and compare and position all the possible universes that start with the same initial conditions as this one (the Big Bang). But you have seen evidence of infinite universes, each with their own infinite sets of initial conditions.

Gracie takes our hands. "We think your discovery proves that there is no flaw in the original pattern. But the tiny Yggdrasils are splitting and losing their self-similarity."

"I think I saw it in action in L.A.," I say. "What could be causing it?"

"We believe our universe is under attack."

Just then, Eric strides in.

"Why didn't you tell me something was up?"

"We're just talking over something Mom has discovered," Gracie says. "Here, I've summarized it for you." She holds out her hand, palm up, and a small globe of light floats upward.

Eric snatches it angrily, still obviously miffed about being left out. I sympathize. I sometimes felt left out when Gracie and Alan got to talking about physics and games. But it is odd that she didn't include him this time, I think.

"It's like a knife is slicing into a pie," Alan says. Mostly the pie's fine, but the crack is permanent."

"I think it's more like a marble cake with swirls of spirals, and the knife is cutting through the chocolate parts."

"No, the pie metaphor is closer," Eric joins in. "The universe is basically flat, not a layer cake." It's good to see he's not mad any more.

"This arguing over cake versus pie is making me hungry," I observe. "How about some snacks?" Yverra looks at me like I'm a puppy who's just peed on the rug.

"Sorry, I didn't mean to disrupt everyone's train of thought," I apologize. But now that I have a stomach again, it seems to be growling.

We finish our conference, and I follow Alan back to our plain white workspace. I call up a little stone water fountain to add a soothing sound to the background.

"What's the deal with Eric?" I say. "Why didn't Gracie call him for the meeting? Are they having problems? Or am I being a meddling mother-in-law again?"

"You've noticed it, I see," Alan replies. "Well, it's just that she doesn't really trust him yet."

"They're married, isn't that enough trust?"

"I think it might be better if you heard it in Eric's own words," he replies. He holds out his palm and releases one of those little fireballs like Gracie had. I call them tinkerbells. As I take it, gingerly, an electric rush of data streaks up my arm and pours into my brain, as if I had plugged in a biochip and this was its power source.

My vision changes, becoming at first blurry and then resolving to a different scene...

*****~~~~~*****

Chapter 18.

Blackmail

***Memory Annotation, Eric Magnusson, Index
reference 9784.2***

*Alan seems to have struck up a conversation with
that red-haired soldier. I envy him his ability to feel at
home wherever he is. Since we got thrown into this weird
situation, I keep looking over my shoulder, afraid
something's going to come after us again.*

*If the whole world can change in an instant, what
can you depend on? It's completely primitive here, cold
and muddy, there's no modern conveniences, other than
guns, and we seem to have been conned into joining this
dangerous war. I told Alan I didn't want to follow his
journalist friend, but he talked me into it. My bad.*

*Everywhere there are men, men with guns, men
with hideous wounds, men with horses, everyone hiding
behind this fortified wall. Why, only the other day, I hear
that 600 light brigade cavalrymen were slaughtered in an
ill-planned charge. I saw a dude take a bullet to the head
right in front of me, and I don't mind saying it totally
freaked me out. Brains were meant to stay in your head,
not oozing down your shirt. I'm not cut out for the
battlefield. It's nothing like the video games we used to
play at home. No exciting music to pump us up, only
ignorant bastards telling us to do things that they know
will get us killed. And there's Alan, chatting away like
there's no tomorrow. No tomorrow.*

*"Hey, Eric," he says. "Come meet Blauw. He's
Irish. The Irish always get sent in to the do the dangerous
work, eh Blauw?" Blauw grins. He's a strong looking*

fellow with heavy forearms, like he crushes beer cans on his forehead for a living. But beer cans haven't been invented yet.

"Blauw knows where we can get a shave," Alan says. "You'd like a shave, right? Feel civilized for a change? And this guy's got dentifrice powder. Wouldn't it feel good to brush your teeth again? If you don't take care of yourself you could get trenchmouth, you know."

Fucking trenchmouth. What is that, anyway? Well, I suppose I'll go with them. What else is there to do anyway, except get stabbed and raped at gunpoint by some Ruski infantryman? I'm getting some sort of upper respiratory thing, too. I have asthma, and this definitely isn't helping it.

Why is this happening to me? I got a degree in political science for this? We didn't even study this war, so I don't even know how it turns out.

It turns out Blauw has connections. He hands me a flask of whiskey. I'm more of a beer guy, but this stuff takes the edge off so maybe I can get some sleep, at least until the next cannonade exchange. I try to sleep, but wake up every now and then to see Alan sneaking off. I hope he doesn't get killed. I hope he doesn't leave me here.

"Want some more of the pure?" Blauw says. Pure whiskey, I guess. I grab the flask and take a long hit.

"So you're Alan's son-in-law, right?" he says. I nod and try to scrunch down farther into my wool coat. Blauw took it off the dead soldier. I try not to think about it. Much.

"He says you know about political science."

"That's right. I majored in it in college."

"Ever heard of Cardinal Richelieu?"

"Of course, who hasn't? A lot of people think he was the first spy. He set up a network after the French Revolution, and got a lot of aristocrats guillotined."

"Very good. You obviously know your stuff. Alan tells me you're a consummate gamesman, too."

"Alan has told you quite a lot," I reply. "What of it? There are no games here, unless you've got a deck of cards."

"You've seen that I have a lot of friends, right? I know some who would be interested in your skills."

"That's nice, but I'm staying with Alan while we sort out this stupid war."

"How would you like to get away from this war?"

"You mean desert?"

"I would call it more like taking a new assignment with extranational diplomatic duties. Surely, you're not happy here, are you? Besides, you weren't legally drafted into the British forces anyway, were you?"

I acknowledge that is the case. Alan and I were abducted when he turned his back for a second from that dope of a journalist, William Russell.

"Just what exactly is this assignment you're talking about?"

"I'll explain it all to you later. And don't worry, your father-in-law will be coming too. So, are you in?"

"I guess so," I reply. "If he's going, I have no problem with it."

"Excellent," Blauw says.

End, Memory Annotation, Eric Magnusson, Index reference 9784.2

☙

Memory Annotation, Eric Magnusson, Index reference 10734.0

It's never been easy being Eric Magnusson. My family had a lot of money, being descended from Swedish royalty, and they used it to control me. I hated that and indulged in some youthful indiscretions just to show my independence.

I went to college in America, and that's where I met Grace, waiting for a soy latte at the Starbucks at the student union. I kept finding excuses for running into her, and soon had her routine memorized. I was in love. She

181

was like nothing I'd ever seen before. Smart, I'd seen before. Beautiful, I'd seen before. But not smart, beautiful, and kind. She even turned out to have smart, beautiful, and kind parents. But they weren't rich. Not by my father's standards. When he heard about her, he did everything he could to discourage me from seeing Grace.

That included throwing Angelina at my head.

I wasn't terribly interested in my studies, but I stuck with them to keep my father happy enough to keep sending the monthly checks. My small circle of friends introduced me to Dungeons and Dragons, and I was hooked. I even taught Grace some of the finer points of gaming on our first date. I was her outlet against the stress of completing her law degree, and her fine logical mind and ability to hold a myriad of seemingly trivial facts were a big asset.

When I told my parents I wanted to marry Grace, we had a big argument. I flew back to America and asked Grace what she would think about eloping.

"You're kidding, right?" she said. "My mother's Catholic, and part Korean. A big wedding is part of her birthright."

*"You mean **your** birthright?"*

*"No, I mean **hers**," Gracie said.*

We had a big fight over it (I was quite used to starting fights), and I stomped out, calling off the engagement.

That's when my father introduced me to Angelina Korova. She was a Ukrainian model, drop-dead gorgeous with long shiny dark hair and eyes. Not unlike Grace, if you looked at her sideways. I guess my father knew my type, and he had a PI watching me. After the fight with Grace, even though I'd promised her that I'd stop drinking after an auto accident, I told my friends we ought to do the bachelor party anyway, and we went bar-hopping in Charlotte. I pounded down four or five Queen City Hurricanes, and woke up the next morning with a burning headache and a girl in my bed. Angelina poured me some coffee from the hotel carafe, tossed her designer purse across her taut body, and disappeared.

I went back to Gracie and begged forgiveness and asked her to resume with the wedding plans. So it was settled. Her parents didn't even know about it. But although the wedding went off without a hitch, I was living with the threat of my father's blackmail hanging over my head. Then it all happened. I was picnicing with the in-laws and Grace on the beach at Nag's Head, and the next thing I know a storm comes up and blows me to Sevastopol, Ukraine. My little ironic punishment. At the time, I wasn't aware I'd left a little gift behind with Angelina. I later heard they named her Teresa.

But that wasn't to be the end of it. Blauw talked me into joining his "political science" enterprise and told me to wait until the next morning, when he would arrange for us to slip away from the front. I wasn't totally naive; I figured he was a member of some sort of spy network, but I had no real idea, of course.

The next day, when Blauw showed up, I looked around for Alan, but didn't see him.

"Let's go," Blauw said, taking my arm in an iron grip.

"But, Alan's not here yet."

"I know." That was my first taste of quantum travel. Suddenly, I was just elsewhere, and I had no choice but to make the best of it—as usual.

☙

I break away from experiencing Eric's story. It's a little too real, and as his mother-in-law I feel guilty. He obviously has daddy issues, and it's certainly not my place to be snooping in on his private life. But he's married to my daughter. I suppose that he's leading up to something even worse than cheating on Grace. After all, he wasn't really cheating on her, I rationalize. They had broken up when he had the affair. It wasn't even his fault, really. Of course, he could have been stronger and not fallen prey to the wiles of Angelina the whore quite that fast.

I wonder if Alan has ever strayed. He's a college professor, and God knows he's probably had plenty of opportunities to get better acquainted with young coeds. I decide to put the tinkerbell away for now, slipping it into the pocket of my robe. Plenty of time to find out what's really causing Gracie and Eric's estrangement, though my curiosity is burning a hole in my pocket. The two are being civil to one another, so maybe there's hope for reconciliation.

�꩜

"So, do you see why I call him Cardinal Richelieu?" Alan asks.

"Um, no, I saw some mention of him, but I didn't get that far on the memory thingamajig," I say.

"Eric's a bright boy, but we have to keep him on a short leash. "

"Whatever, you say, Hon." I don't see what all the excitement is about. I'm not willing to give up a son-in-law I just added to the family so easily. Things are going good. We're all together again.

I think about taking a walk. This white room is too much like mushing at the North Pole during a Christmas blizzard with a dogsled of white Samoyeds leaving frosty footprints in the snow. Say what you will about Calaneris, he does grow a mean garden. I picture a similar one in my mind's eye. I think I'll even help myself to an armload of blue cyclamen to brighten up the place. It's a perfect day. I'm about to translocate (that's what Alan likes to call it), when Ben and Ralff appear.

This bodes not well. They should be at the Beach.

"Hey, guys, what are you doing here?" I ask. "I haven't had a chance yet to ask the Watchmen if you can join us."

"You must come with us," Benrus says. "It is not safe here."

"What do you mean? This is about the safest spot in the universe," I argue.

"No time to discuss—" Ben says. That's when a blinding blade of sickly green light scythes through the white room, slicing it open. The wall falls aside, leaving us perched precariously on the edge of a volcano, overlooking a caldera of molten rock. Red-hot cracks open in the ground under our feet, and the earth shakes.

"It's that thing we saw in L.A.!" I say, staring up in amazement. I turn to tell Ben and Ralff to collect Alan, Gracie, and Eric, so we can all take refuge on the Poe's beach, but I'm too late. I'm already standing on the cool sand, with nothing but Ben and Ralff to talk to.

"Where's Hangul?" I ask, but Ben only responds by handing me the Cintamani.

"Hold onto this, Virginia. It's yours, and it is our only hope."

"Our only hope? I have to go back and get my family."

"You cannot. And if you relinquish the jewel, the entire universe can never happen."

No. No. No. This can't be happening again. To finally have my family with me, and to have them snatched away again. Time unwinds, then it rewinds, like a fisherman letting out a little more line each time, before he inexorably pulls the fish back to the net and its doom.

Ben nudges me. "Please. Take it, Virginia."

I hear Gracie's words repeat, "the universe is wondrous—." I know she would want me to make the effort. But I'd much rather save her than the universe. Wouldn't Mary have saved Jesus if she could? Somehow I find my voice again.

"Goddamn you, Poe." The silence is deafening.

☉

"Please, Virginia. You've got to snap out of it. Just sitting here like this is self-indulgent." Ralff is holding my hand, patting it gently.

What is it with these people? No emotion at all, and that Yverra was the same way. I continue to sulk. They're lucky I haven't completely lost my mind. I think about Mary Todd Lincoln. She slowly went nuts in the White House when her son died, while her husband ignored her. He had his hands full preserving the Union, after all. What was the point of living?

I don't even have the luxury of a marriage crumbling under the weight of grief.

Gradually, I'm all cried out. Again. Why am I bothering to stay alive, if everything's gone to hell in a handbasket? Then it strikes me. I've never had a single suicidal thought before, and I don't feel like it now. I've always had the attitude that life is short. If you just wait a little while, it'll be over soon anyway.

"Thanks, Ralff, I'm ok." My hand involuntarily reaches to touch the Cintamani on my neck. It's back home, and it's warm. That's how I think of life, as warmth. The opposite of the coldness that makes up so much of our universe. Hangul frolics happily in the calm surf a hundred yards from the strand.

"Virginia… " Ben cuts into my thoughts.

"What?"

"We're sorry, but it had to be done. There wasn't time."

"You couldn't spare a microsecond to bring my family? You may recall that I went back for you," I accuse.

"There literally wasn't time. When the Unwinding incursions happen, the timeline is destroyed. If we hadn't extricated you *right then*, that would have been an end to matters. We also noted that it appeared that your family had already vacated."

"So maybe they're ok? I suppose I should be grateful to you for saving my life," I aver. "I admit that's what I asked you to do in the first place. I guess I owe you an apology."

"None is needed. We were pleased to be able to do it," Ben says. "And to be enlisted in the effort to preserve the union." Coincidental word choice?

"I don't know how you could consider yourself lucky in that respect," I say. "I'm rather resentful about it all, myself. What are our first steps? I presume the land of the Watchmen is off-limits now, right?"

"Yes, that is our conjecture. But it's possible that some other nexus still remains besides this."

"How can I get information about the state of the universe if I'm cooped up in this safehouse of a beach?" I ask. "Where could my family have gone, assuming they too were tipped off about impending attack?"

"Ahem, if I may presume," Ralff says. "We noticed that you brought along a compact data store when we made the transference."

"You mean the tinkerbell?" I reach into my pocket. "Yes."

"It's just some memories from my son-in-law," I say, gently pushing the little ball into the air with the tip of my finger. "I suppose we could listen in on some more of those, but from what I've heard so far, they're fairly trivial human emotional moments, the kind you blackmail innocent dupes with."

"The tinkerbell, as you call it, was actually Alan's personal store. In addition to the family mementos you mention, it contains most of the knowledge of the universe which he had catalogued up to that point."

"Really? We had just finished a project involving recursion and the Tree of Life as metaphor for the universe," I muse. "Do you guys want to take a look?"

They exchange glances and straighten up almost imperceptibly. I can tell I've managed to push their hot buttons.

Benrus and Ralff and I join hands, and a gust of wind blows across the Beach, blowing our hair back as we make contact with the tinkerbell.

*****~~~~~*****

Chapter 19.

Parental Issues

Golaeth muses. The repair process is not going well, and there is interference from the infant universe. It has constructed a defensive AI. The AI can easily be dealt with, of course, but now there is the matter of the alpha entity. That is more difficult. It's unlikely that the entity can be deleted, protected as it is, encapsulated within a stasis field. Not to mention that thousands of universes yet to be born will be populated with variations on this entity's model. In retrospect, a probable design flaw. To add further complication, there is some sort of additional anomaly within the infant universe that affects the laws of probability. For the first time in eons, Golaeth is uncertain about the proper course. For now, it will redouble its efforts to repair the youngster, even though it appears to be a losing battle. It will be difficult. The infant wants so badly to live, yet its wounds are so piteous. Golaeth gathers energy.

☺

The tinkerbell reveals that in addition to his personal snooping on Eric, Alan has collected a treasure trove of information about the creation of the universe. All of it seems to point to a cosmos that was behaving consistently until recently, at least recently by our timeline. The Milky Way was spinning its merry way along, until the green beam thingys began slicing into our territory.

Ralff says he thinks they are an incursion of some sort, possibly from another universe. The collision of two universes could be a disaster, because each may have different physical laws. I understand that, but I don't understand how something as immense as the universe could run out of infinity. Is this some sort of territorial dispute?

Inconceivable. What's to become of us? Will humanity survive? Or are we too petty to matter?

Alan had told me he wanted to form alliances with other mathematically inclined beings in our universe, like the Emperor Calaneris, and, especially, the Watchmen. These aliens lived by numbers and counting.

Could they calculate the odds of the universe succeeding or failing? Alan's record indicated that Yverra was going against the wishes of her people in allying with us. Good for her. I like her better now.

But the numbers just didn't add up. Even the Watchmen's ability to hack time and synchronize it was not effective in preventing incursions. Only Poe's beachhead was doing that.

Another shocker from the tinkerbell: Grace had apparently taken it upon herself to become a tribunal, a one-woman judge and jury sifting for evidence of war crimes, and making a case showing that our universe was the aggrieved party.

I find it a little hard to picture Poe as a law-abiding citizen, staying on his own property and obeying all the physical laws of his domain. In fact, as a human I felt all my life that we lived in an uncaring universe, or if the universe did care, it might call upon us at any moment to justify our continued existence. Evidently Grace felt that too; maybe she got that from me. In the worst case, she was preparing to take the other universe to court for wanton unprovoked destruction. I wish I was with her now to explain that I believe that not only does Poe care, he is actually on our side and grateful for our help.

But is there indeed another universe? Proof seems elusive. What is there to prove that Poe isn't just a self-destructive teenager throwing a tantrum? "Happy Mother's

Day. I've sent your family to z8_GND_5296. Enjoy your stay!"

Or maybe Poe has a flawed coping mechanism, and responds to affronts with mayhem. I don't think so. He hasn't destroyed us. I think it is a standoff. But with whom? A parent with more experience than he has? Is that why he's involving me and Alan? Maybe it's even more serious, with mutual assured destruction in the offing. Poe knows we humans have a lot of experience with that sort of stupidity. Maybe he's having to justify *his* existence.

"Is that it, Poe?" He never tells me anything. Ralff and Benrus are arguing over a point of physics that they've gleaned from Alan's notes. But I feel useless. I swallow a lump in my throat and think again about how unfair it all is. I swirl the sand around with my forefinger, tracing out the names: Alan, Grace, Eric. The waves lap closer and gradually erase my artwork.

Annoyed, I move farther back from the shore, and write the names again; doodling helps me get my thought processes going. A gust blows up a small vortex and lays a deposit of fine silicate over the names of my loved ones.

Now I really am getting angry. Kick sand in my face, will you? I've already admitted to being a 98-pound weakling. What more do you want?

The white silicate suddenly turns black and glassy, and I'm looking at what I would swear is a television screen, its frame flush with the sand. Creepy as hell. The screen lights up, a fine high-definition image of a ferris wheel and a brightly lit arcade. A voiceover announces:

"Stressed and falling apart? Come to Platidia 9 for a once-in-a-lifetime vacation. Cool down to near-absolute zero, and tame those entropy blues. Schuss through mountains of frozen nitrogen, taste the singing electrons of Angiorum (a gustatory delight!), and contemplate the ruins of Platidia 8, which have been transported one fried wafer at a time to shock and amaze you!"

Another message on the beach. This one doesn't sound nearly so cryptic as the previous ones I've gotten. This is a planetary disaster that has been turned into an amusement park. A cosmic Spring Gardens? I don't find that so amusing somehow.

"Virginia," you have a message, Ben says.

"I do? Who would be calling me here?" I ask hopefully.

"It's an AI that calls itself QoS."

"That's an acronym for Quantum Opposable Singularity," Ralff says. "It appears to be an AI that operates at the bare minimum energy requirement, the base quantum of our universe."

"What does it want with me?" I ask.

The screen clears, and a new message appears. It simply says, "Poe sent me."

"I've gathered that, but I'm not going to go to a godforsaken planet made of frozen nitrogen. Why doesn't Poe just send you there instead? Sounds like it's right up your circuit board."

"We need two," the screen says. "And you'll do for the other one."

"Two what?"

"Shields. The universe is being attacked from all sides. I can curve through the space-time continuum to a degree, but not in all dimensions. Poe needs a respite."

Well, so do I, I think, but then I feel guilty.

"Why me?" I ask.

"Poe has inadvertently created an anomaly, and needs your assistance. Also, you are organically similar to the anomaly."

"Anomaly?" I realize that Yverra was right. "You mean Grace, don't you?"

"Yes." QoS has verified my worst fear.

I've been sitting on this beach for who knows how long now, twiddling my imaginary thumbs. I'm nothing if not foolish, and I've got to get back in the game.

"Is this going to get my family back, or am I just a pawn in the game? Oh, hell, it doesn't matter. I'm in. What do I have to do?"

"Hold the Cintamani and assume my appearance. It will be a disguise."

Hmm... I've always wanted to wear a disguise. I hoped that one day someone would walk up to me and say, "You look about the same size as Madame X. We want you to go in under cover as her." I had studied an acting book, which had been recommended to me once when I was trying to become a writer.

"Like this?" I say. Or rather, I'm a flatscreen tv lying on the beach displaying that message.

"That will do," QoS says. "Let's go."

"Before we go, could you tell me one thing? Why doesn't Poe ever talk to me directly?"

In the meantime, Ralff has walked over to the twin screens communing on the beach and caught up with the gist of the conversation.

"If I may venture a conjecture... "

Y-e-s? I spell.

"Poe isn't your human God. His job isn't to watch out for you or anyone else. But that doesn't make him less real. And if we want to continue to exist, we have to help him."

H-o-l-d t-h-e C-i-n- I start to say, but I'm already gone. And I'm really, really big.

ॐ

Golaeth probes. It feels the adhesions spread and harden like noxious tumors in the newly hatched one. It is in pain. Golaeth speeds from one edge of the new universe to the other, but it can't be everywhere at once. As physician it triages as best it can. Transient disturbances propagate across the infant's dark energy fields, creating black holes and disrupting orderly radiative activity. As far as Golaeth can tell, quantum effects such as superconductivty and superfluidity are as yet unaffected, but the amount of latent heat is concerning. Application of negative temperatures to problem spots temporarily helps. For eons, the disease is chronic but not acute. Then it begins. Disturbance of a vulnerable nexus leads to a blockage of the timeline, leading to necrosis. Instabilities develop around the obstructions, and threat of seizure is imminent. The self-repair mechanisms of recursion begin to fall behind. At this rate the universe will soon lose consciousness and collide with the brane of its brother universe, unleashing uncontrolled hot plasma. The two universes will rebound, leading to another, premature Big Bang. Golaeth will have no option but to terminate the enterprise. Wait—the boundaries between the two universes appear to be receding. There's a thickening at the edges, like scar tissue. Maybe there is still hope for the repair process. Golaeth scatters a flurry of radiation across the new borders.

☉

I'm doing it. I'm doing it. I'm stretched one molecule thin, but I'm joined to QoS like a giant football that's stitched together across the top and bottom. We wouldn't be very easy to catch, but we're aerodynamic. We seem to be in this shape because the "noses" at either end of the football are moving faster than the middle.

This reminds me of the time I spent on Tian Ming Shen and the trip to the Big Bang. There's a whole lot of dark matter and not much else in the vicinity. And cold enough to stop your heart. Poe's warmer, though. I can feel the Cintamani. Still no sign of those mythical other universes everyone keeps talking about. Suddenly I feel a stabbing probe, but I can't tell where it's coming from. I don't see anything.

"QoS, are you feeling that?"

"No, all quiet on this side. But as I mentioned, we *are* under attack."

"I don't believe you mentioned that. I think I would have remembered."

Parental Issues

"What are the symptoms?" QoS asks.

"Green laser beams—you may have heard about those?"

"Those are not the attackers. That is Golaeth."

"Well, this Golaeth is probing the hell out of me, and it hurts!"

"It is attempting to treat Poe."

"Can we tell it to stop?"

"Probably, but I'd feel safer if we let it continue. Some treatment is better than none, and besides, Golaeth will monitor the attack situation."

"Ow! If it's helping Poe, why wouldn't it help us against the attackers?"

"It may not be able to take sides. It manages many universes."

Another stinging prick invades my nether region. This is like accidentally backing into a saguaro cactus. The Cintamani is protecting me, but the stabbing is incessant and hypersonic. No wonder Poe wants a break. I feel my life's blood drain away. I grow woozy and pray for it to slow down.

It's death by a thousand cuts, and they're all coming at once.

☺

This is a fine opportunity to get to know a superintelligent AI properly, as QoS and I shake off barrage after barrage of Golaeth's "healing" lancets injecting us with dark matter.

"I'm of a mind to go give it a piece of mine," I say to QoS. "Why doesn't it simply tell Poe what he needs to do to get well?"

"As your little scientist friends have noted, it's not Golaeth's job. Its job is just to make sure Poe survives, or if that becomes impossible, to dispose of him. It has a lot of caretaker responsibility, but it doesn't care about Poe any more than you would care for a pile of laundry— simply a grudging necessity."

195

"Is Golaeth Poe's father?" A pretty uncaring parent, if you ask me. No wonder Poe is messed up.

"No—Golaeth reports to Poe's creators."

"Doesn't it care *why* Poe is getting sick?"

"Probably hasn't crossed its mind. It probably has a checklist of what's allowed and what's not."

I tell QoS about Alan and Gracie's theories about there being a saboteur on the loose.

"I know, Poe has given me all that data."

"So, you say Golaeth isn't the saboteur?"

"No."

"And it doesn't know who that is?"

"Unknown."

"Why don't I just ask it?"

"I would advise against it."

"It'll just take a sec, I'll be right back."

I unzip from QoS and hold up the proverbial white flag.

"Hello? Golaeth? Can we parlay?"

The big lunk has detected the opening in Poe's shield and begun pummeling him mercilessly again. I can't see the source of the beams. They are coming out of "nowhere."

"Stop!" I yell over and over. Then I see it. "QoS, is that Golaeth?"

"No, it is another universe. We had better clear out now. Poe's on his own."

"We've got to keep them from colliding!" I say.

"You're right. It has resumed a straight trajectory for us. Poe is saying he thinks we still may prevail if we can get your daughter to help."

"Suits me! Where is she? And where is this Golaeth anyway?"

"Golaeth is time-switching to try to be everwhere at once. You'll never catch it one place due to Heisenberg's uncertainty principle. But Poe has told me where Grace is. She is with Calaneris."

Parental Issues

Thanks, QoS, and thank you, Poe, for my little message on the Beach. I take a chance that the Cintamani will behave properly and try to picture Calaneris and Grace.

"Take me there." Please.

I am in a space station; it must be STS-99. Perhaps Calaneris is holding out here until he is forced to move by Golaeth's beams. I sprint toward the bridge, to find Calaneris, Blauw, and Eric, hunched over a table and talking excitedly.

"Where's Gracie?" I blurt out, realizing too late that I should have been more circumspect in my approach.

"Ah, the meddling mother-in-law," Blauw says. "Hello, Sunny."

"We need Grace to help defend the universe," I say.

"What do you think *we* are using her for?" Calaneris says. "We determined long ago that only your Cintamani was of any use to us, but then we found that your daughter also has power."

"How do you know that?" I ask, glancing over at Eric. He blushes.

"Your son-in-law has been very helpful. He has informed us of all your weaknesses."

"What the fuck? Eric?" He lowers his eyes. "I had to," he says. "The universe is in danger, Virginia. And the Emperor holds all the cards."

I decide that now is not the time to tell these traitors about Poe or the Beach.

"What cards are we talking about?"—as if I didn't know.

Soon Calaneris is bragging about how he snatched Alan and Grace out of the jaws of defeat and brought them here, along with Yverra of the Watchmen. I note with some satisfaction that at least he doesn't have the run of his beautiful garden planet any more. Caught in the

197

chipper/shredder. What a waste of beautiful perennials. And craft beer.

"How did you know an incursion was coming?" I ask.

"Gracie told me," Eric says. "And I informed the Emperor."

"Were you going to take me too?" I ask. Why do I ask things I don't want to know the answer to?

"You had already gone," Eric says tactfully. Same answer as Ben and Ralff gave—and patently false.

"We already had the living jewel," Calaneris said. "She is proving invaluable for helping us negotiate the maze for safe spots."

"*Temporary* safe spots, you mean."

"Yes. We know that it is hopeless in the end. We hope to hold out until the last possible moment, however, with your daughter's aid."

"Where is she?" I ask. "I know she's here."

"She's in custody. She built the facility herself. It is unescapable."

"A prisoner?" Then I'm just here to get my baby out of jail.

Blauw steps forward. "We asked Yverra to put her in a bubble of hacked time, which she very nicely consented to do. It gives us leverage, and we can interrogate Grace whenever it becomes necessary."

Apparently Alan and Yverra are incarcerated elsewhere on the station.

I'm screwed. My Cintamani is useless against time-hacked alternate dimensions. The Watchmen are the best security experts in the universe.

I try to reason with Calaneris, but it's no use. He's sure the universe is ending, and he's going to hole up in a bunker until he's the last one standing. I argue that if we fight, we might have a chance for survival. No dice. He is too cold to care for anyone else.

Parental Issues

I inspect the sparsely furnished bridge of the space station. It smells of oil and solvents, and there are stains on the industrial carpeting. Not a very impressive life raft for the last living souls.

I put some distance between me and Blauw. I know he is extremely strong and could relieve me of the Cintamani and my life in no time at all. I feel sorry for Alan and Eric. Blauw is just a charming bastard.

We all stand there staring at each other like a Tarantino standoff, none daring to attack the other. I'm not about to propose another alliance, although I was brought up that way, to always try to smooth things over, get everyone to play nice.

The Emperor's robes are looking a little the worse for wear. He hasn't had a change of clothes for a while. He really is making a sacrifice, when he could be using Grace to generate anything he desired. If he was his usual self, he'd be holding a big court with his Scientists, and showing Grace off to everyone. It dawns on me that he isn't just bunkering, he's trying to lie low.

"This is pretty pitiful, Calaneris. Here you were trying to be the hero of the ages, and now you're just trying to save yourself."

All right, time to come clean. Calaneris probably knows everything anyway.

"You know about the other universe," I opine.

"Yes."

"And you're helping it destroy ours."

"Yes. But I have to, you see. If I assist in the orderly annexation, he will provide me with a kingdom and safety. There will be at least a vestige of our universe remaining."

"He?" Calaneris knows the culprit personally. Poe's evil half-brother?

"Yes, when he coadunates with our universe, he will become immortal. There will be no more Big Bangs."

199

His parents aren't going to like that, I think. And neither is Golaeth, the nursemaid.

Calaneris turns to Blauw.

"The dimensional mine worked well."

"What's that?" I ask.

"We had enough interference from the Watchmen," Calaneris says. "We had to shut them off. And if you don't cooperate, we'll do the same for your family."

"The same what?" There's a knot in the pit of my stomach.

"They were just too trusting," Blauw says, with a slight shrug. "Once we learned their interdimensional techniques from Eric, we were able to find Yverra's home dimension and her people's physical location."

"But she would never…"

"Oh, you'd be surprised. Once she knew we held her people's fate in our hands, she was more than willing to help us," Calaneris says. She may look like an emotionless, cold-blooded statue, but when we showed her father in the crosshairs of the weapon, she caved. She helped us put Grace in an unbreakable stasis bubble. And I have the only key."

"So Yverra is here on the station?"

"Yeah," Blauw says. "Too bad she's the last of her kind." Anything for the Emperor's approval.

"It was necessary," Calaneris said. "The Black Universe only wanted to deal with me, so I had to remove the Watchmen as a threat."

"If the Black Universe made you do this—destroy the Watchmen with this mine weapon—aren't you afraid he'll kill all of us too?" I ask, shocked. I know Calaneris is not a family man, but I didn't know he was a monster.

There is no answer. I turn and run.

*****~~~~*****

Chapter 20.

Baby Blue Horizon

Thank God I've been on this godforsaken space station before. Multiple corridors lead out of the bridge like spokes in a wheel, and I take the one I know will either save me or kill me.

I remember going this way before, expecting only to see a series of anonymous-looking "hotel" rooms or crew quarters. Somewhere along the way, things got a little weird. I'm counting on that. I take a deep breath and plunge in.

"Virginia! Come back here!" Blauw sounds too close for comfort. Still moving, I look back over my shoulder and see him at the entrance to the corridor. He skids to a stop. He's been here before too.

Well, there's nothing for it. I'll try to hide out here. If Blauw's afraid to come after me, all the better. It looks like a perfectly normal hallway. Or maybe not so normal. The lights are dimmer than they were a few moments ago. One of the sconces lining the hall has turned into a bioluminescent lump, changing colors slowly. A coral, perhaps? This corridor seems alive. It makes me wonder if it has been constructed as a defense mechanism; maybe it senses the person traversing it is not authorized and pumps out psychedelic drugs. Or maybe it's full of Calaneris's failed AI experimentation, but too valuable to just eject out into the void of space. If that's the case, I decide not to touch anything.

"Show me what I need to see." Will the Cintamani do what I think it should?

A sphere about the size of a fortune teller's crystal ball rolls on the floor toward me. It's growing. What have I wished for?

The sphere expands like a balloon filling with hot air, rising until it nearly blocks the corridor. The surface shimmers, clearing a view inside. I don't want to look inside, yet I feel drawn to it. I sense that this thing knows about Grace.

"What are you?" I ask. At first there is no sound except a low hum, but it gradually is replaced by familiar music. I've heard this music before, at the Beach. Is this simply a stasis point, or a portal to the Beach? If so, I don't want to go there. I want to keep looking for Grace. When the coast is clear.

For once, the Cintamani doesn't whisk me off to the Beach. Perhaps that means I still have some latitude here.

Against my better judgment I move closer to the sphere and try to peer in. It's as though I've stepped into a high-speed elevator. I zoom up a dizzyingly high double helix with rows of tall windows along each spiral. I can't see into all of the windows, but each seems to open out onto a different world. Some reveal a starry sky. In others, it's day.

I hear a baby crying, or what sounds like a baby. I'd swear it was Grace.

*****~~~~~*****

Chapter 21.

Living Cintamani (Bang, Bang, Bang)

I can feel my mother's pain. She's looking for me. Even though I'm locked in a vise of Yverra's devising, I know she's just trying to protect me. I've shown poor judgment in trusting Calaneris again. I wish I could make up my mind. I do have a weakness for bad boys. It all started with my husband.

Eric was this cute, drunken frat boy who for some reason started following me around. I was actually flattered. I'd spent my teen years being the geek at school who everyone said hello to but no one asked for a date. Everyone assumed that since I was part Asian that I'd just naturally want to study. Nothing could be farther from the truth. I wanted to be a pioneer, to go on adventures, and live the bohemian artist life. My parents encouraged me wherever they could, but they didn't really understand me. There was so much pressure. Everyone always asking what you want to be, before you've even had a chance to live. Sometimes I think my mother must have sprung fully formed at birth, like Aphrodite. She never seemed to drop that cool facade. Always the perfect mother, the perfect homemaker. But I didn't want that. I wanted to explore new kingdoms.

When my parents dropped me off for college, Mom cried and hugged me. It was the first crack I'd ever seen in Mom's armor. College turned out to be more of the same, however. I finally decided to go to law school, since the logic component of my LSATs was off the scale. The long nights of studying were drudgery, and I spent half my time at the local Starbucks poring over some arcane bit of international treaty law, in hopes of someday landing my dream job in China or Hong Kong. As my dad would say, "a lot of being in the right place at the right time is the result of careful preparation."

But then I met Eric. He was like a breath of fresh air, always spontaneous. He had a wide circle of friends, and they all played games constantly. They welcomed me into their circle immediately, and along with many new acquaintances, I also sampled mind-expanding substances and frequented the clubs. Mark Ronson was my favorite DJ. Bang, Bang, Bang. My grades slipped accordingly.

One night Eric was driving us home from the local pub, and an SUV turned left in front of us, hitting us head-on. I remember the tremendous crash and the impression of blinding lights as I lost consciousness. I don't know how long I was out, but when I woke up, a horn was blaring and steam was hissing from the radiator through the crumpled hood of Eric's Saab. We were upside down, hanging from our seatbelts. I fumbled for the buckle and fell shoulder first onto the car roof. Dark blood dripped through Eric's sandy hair onto the dashboard, and I could smell the metallic tang of it filling the cabin. I was sobbing and crying, "God, don't let him be dead." My first aid training from high school came flooding back. I felt for his pulse, but I couldn't find one, and I fought harder to free him. Eventually, I popped his buckle, lowered his window, and began to drag him out onto the street. Some passersby helped, and I sat beside Eric until an ambulance came. The medics said he wasn't breathing, and loaded him up for the trip to the hospital.

"Can I ride with him?" I asked. On the trip, the medic talked quietly into his radio, saying they were on their way in with a probable DOA, massive head injuries, unresponsive.

I held Eric's hand and said, "Eric, you're not going to die. You're going to live, and we're going to be together." Wishful thinking.

Living Cintamani

Suddenly Eric coughed a little. The startled ET jumped from his bench, slapped an oxygen mask over Eric's face, and started an IV drip.

It turned out that Eric had only suffered a scratch.

"Amazing that all that blood came from a tiny scalp wound," Eric joked later. After that night, Eric and I made a pact that neither of us would drink any more. At the time, I was just happy that I had my fiancé back. I wanted Eric to live, and I felt lucky that he had.

At first, I didn't want to know that the odd things that began happening were my doing. Sure, I wanted to believe in a fantasy world, but that was just a world of imagination. My mother was raised a Catholic, and they believed in miracles, but after I was confirmed we rarely went to church.

But miracles continued to pop up all around me. The little girl who was found alive after falling down a well and being missing for three days. I'd been fretting over that, so I went for a walk and found her. The Carolina Panthers winning the Superbowl. Maybe that one wasn't me. My mom suddenly becoming a concert-level pianist after struggling for years on her music lessons. My friends all winning free lifetime Steam memberships at the local GameStop. My bicycle gears shifting perfectly. All my classmates getting perfect scores on their finals. That one didn't work out too well. We were accused of cheating, but all I did was wish everyone luck.

Anyway, you get the picture. A long run of excellent fortune, with me as lucky charm. I began suffering migraine headaches, like my mother. But nothing seemed so out of the ordinary that you'd think the universe was out of whack or that I had anything to do with it. Until Eric.

After the accident, Eric was a bit more somber, and I chalked that up to his being more sober. Of course, we quarreled once in awhile, but we made up and got

205

married. I had what I wanted, and I looked forward to sharing my happiness with everyone.

My first inkling of what later became known as The Unwinding (my mother's term) came the morning Eric and I went home for a visit and to join in a picnic with my parents at Nag's Head. We were sitting on a nice blue plaid tarp, and Mom was unpacking the basket that she had stuffed with soda bread, kimchee, sliced pork, cheeses, olives, cake, and raspberries. Dad joked that at least we wouldn't starve.

"Oh, damn, I forgot the champagne," she said. "I wanted to toast the happy couple."

"Not a problem," I said. It was probably best that Eric didn't drink a lot of alcohol anyway. We'd kept the accident a secret from my parents; no need to worry them unnecessarily. "Let's just have whatever's in the basket."

Mom reached in, and pulled out a tall glass bottle filled with what looked like a wicked concoction of layers of booze and orange juice interlaced with red syrup. "Wow, what's this?" she asked.

"It's a Carolina Hurricane," Eric said. "That's not very funny, Mrs. Jones."

"Please call me Virginia," my mother said. She looked puzzled. "But I didn't pack this."

That was when I was separated from my husband of two months by a storm of biblical proportions.

❂

"Welcome to the Court of Emperor Calaneris, my Lady." Having just arrived instantly from a picnic on Nag's Head, Grace said nothing. A courtier in long robes bowed in front of me.

"Where am I? Where's my husband?" she asked.

"Arrangements are being made to retrieve your husband and family," the courtier said. "I am Chen-li, here to serve you."

"Retrieve them to where?" Grace repeated.

"You are on Tian Ming Shen."

206

"A planet?"

"In the outer arm of galaxy z8_GND_5296. The Emperor will be with you shortly."

Grace found herself in what appeared to be an ancient Chinese imperial court, where she was being treated as royalty.

"Mom would have loved this," she said. "Where am I, anyway?"

A cadre of soldiers entered the room, ushering in the Emperor, a giant figure in ornate robes. The soldiers turned out to be the Emperor's Scientists, and they were studying an anomaly in the cosmos.

"Hello, Grace," Calaneris said, holding out his hand slightly. Grace took this as a cue to bow. She'd been in enough mock courtroom situations to know that you have to make a show of respect for the judge, or things will not go well for you during the trial.

"Welcome, my dear," he said. "You're very welcome."

"What can I do for you?" Grace asked. "And have you had any news of my family?"

"Don't worry, your family are on their way," Calaneris said. "I need your help to locate a tribe of advanced aliens that can help us to save the universe."

"I must admit I'm a little disappointed," Grace said. "Here I was all primed to be a lady, maybe a fairy princess, dabbling in magic—how else would I have been transported here—but don't you think saving the universe is kind of a big ask?"

"You must know by now that you have vast magical powers."

"What?"

"Surely you realize the miracles you have experienced since childhood were not just flukes."

Grace quickly settled into her life as a princess.

Months went by, and there was no sign of Grace's family, but one day, the Emperor's right-hand man, another human from Earth named Blauw, showed up with her father and Eric in tow. Grace cried with joy to see them, but Eric seemed a little down. That was understandable. He and her Dad had been cast into the past and suffered through a long, barbarous war, before being discovered by Blauw and brought here.

Calaneris's Scientists seemed to worship Grace like a goddess, and Eric became her trusted advisor and prince regent.

Grace sat in her antechamber working her way down a list of tasks that Calaneris had conjured up, when Eric walked in. She hadn't seen him in days.

"What do you want?" she said. The wind slammed the door shut behind him. He jumped.

"How's it going with finding the alien tribe? Alan calls them 'the Watchmen,'" he said.

"I haven't had much luck finding them."

"You've been under a lot of pressure. Why don't you just relax and let it run through your mind? I'm sure it will come to you."

The next day, Grace called Eric excitedly. "I've found them! They've gone back in time, like, sixty million years!"

"Congratulations, that's my Grace!" he said, and kissed her.

"It's hard to imagine something that far back in time, isn't it?" she said.

"Yes, but it's hardly a drop in the bucket compared to the age of the universe," Eric said.

"I suppose so."

That night they celebrated.

�❧

Calaneris decreed that an expedition would be sent to this nexus Grace had located many million years in the past. But first, he had another project he wanted to complete.

"I want you to build me a space station," he said.

"You want me to just drop everything about this tribe of aliens?" she asked with incredulity.

"We have some new theories, and we might not need these aliens," Calaneris replied.

"God damn him, Eric," Grace said. "I feel angry that all my work is being dismissed."

"Calm down, Grace," Eric said. "Let's just let the Emperor be the Emperor."

☺

Calaneris asked Grace to build the station just outside the event horizon of a wormhole that would lead to the calculated time vicinity of the first Big Bang of the universe.

"I have no idea where that would be," Grace said. The Emperor noted that his Scientists had for a thousand years been developing increasingly accurate telescopes that were honing in on the age and location of the first minutes.

"And what about going through a wormhole? Isn't that going to be dangerous?" Grace asked. The Scientists assured her that they had developed a method of packaging up the "souls" of travelers into a mass no larger than a photon, so they could be sent through the wormhole. Mass to reconstruct the traveler would be gleaned at the other end. The problem was that the space station was too massive to deconstruct and send that way.

"That's where you will come in, Grace," Calaneris said. "Oh, and Blauw has some changes to the specs for the floor plan of the station."

"It's going to cost you extra, your Highness," she said. Calaneris smiled indulgently.

Blauw summoned up the holo of the plans, and the changes were already marked in glowing green.

"Oh, you're adding a room? What's it for?"

"It's a brig," Blauw said. "For when we catch this bastard."

"Is this one of the aliens you're talking about?"

"No, this is for the culprit who's tinkering with the universe and trying to kill us all. That's why you have to make it escape-proof."

"Though I shudder at the thought of incarcerating a mass murderer, or a planet murderer, I'll do my very best," Grace vowed.

🌀

"I'm rather proud of STS-99, if I do say so myself," Grace said to Eric, as they prepared to send it to the time and space coordinates of the Big Bang.

"You're awesome, Gracie," he said.

Once the station was in place, Calaneris began sending Scientists through in a steady stream. They were to spend up to three minutes observing the birth of the universe for a flaw that he was sure would be easy to spot.

But Calaneris was in for an unpleasant surprise. The aliens had beaten them there. Grace knew them from her earlier forays into the era sixty million years before present. However, they looked all hazy, and they seemed to ignore Calaneris's Scientists while they went about their mysterious business. Calaneris was fit to be tied.

"Do you want me to establish contact with them?" Grace asked. "They seem like nice enough people. Why don't we try to work with them? Isn't this what you wanted?"

"It most certainly is not, young lady," Calaneris said. "And you are forbidden to try to talk with them."

🌀

*Well, that was the wrong thing to say to **this** young lady. Calaneris may have become a larger-than-lifesize father figure to me, spoiling me with lavish gifts and accommodations, but I still had a rebellious streak. I'd built his stupid space station, and he wasn't going to tell me who I could talk to. Besides, I had figured out that the*

Living Cintamani

Scientists weren't worshipping me; they were studying me. I was so naïve. I immediately popped over to the Big Bang.

The bang was just beginning, and a small egglike rock spun in the empty void. It was mind-blowing, and I actually felt like it was calling to me. I'd thought I knew everything, but this was beyond me. I must have let my guard down, because the next thing I knew, Yverra pulled me into her realm. She was not the first to point out to me that I didn't know everything; I had Mom for that, but under Yverra's tutelage, I soon realized that I needed to add dimensional travel to my bag of tricks.

I was amazed and grateful to be talking to the Watchmen, especially since I felt I was defying Calaneris's wishes. But I missed Eric immensely.

"You humans are a study in contrasts," Yverra said. "Totally promiscuous in youth yet monogamous at maturity. Quite the contradiction." I soon had Eric by my side.

Yverra indulged me in my childish desire to be treated like a princess. She taught us the Watchmen's technique for time hacking, explaining that was how they were able to visit the Big Bang. They were impressed that I could seemingly do it at will, but took the time to explain how they did it to Eric. Now if we wanted we could roam the universe together. Those were happy times, being out from under Blauw and the Emperor's thumb. So I thought.

I should have known something was up, when Eric asked me to teach him the interdimensional trick Yverra had used to bring us both there. And which he immediately used to go back and spill everything to Blauw, including time hacking.

That was the start of the competition between the Empire and the Watchmen, and the destruction of an innocent race, though I didn't know it yet.

I was shocked when Yverra told me. How had she found out? And how could my own husband keep this from

211

me? I hadn't noticed his short absences, just thinking he was granting some "me-time."

"You humans tend to form strong loyalties, but not always to causes that would be in your own self-interest," Yverra said. *Kind of a judgy bitch, but her logic was spot-on. Now I felt I couldn't really trust Eric, and I started to withhold some of the secrets that I once willingly would have told him. His probing for technical secrets became a lot more obvious now that I was looking for it. But I was totally unprepared when he walked in with the news.*

"Hey, Babe. Guess what? Your Mom's here."

*****~~~~~*****

Chapter 22.

An Opening

Well, Grace is in limbo, Alan and Yverra are in the slammer, and Eric is a spy impeding progress. I knew I should have listened to the entire tinkerbell, especially the part at the end where Blauw tortured Eric.

I decide to give it one last try. I touch the jewel at my neck and think to Eric, "Mind if we have a word?" He looks surprised. It worked. The Cintamani has made me telepathic.

"Are you on board with Calaneris and Blauw's plot to hand over our universe?"

Eric frowns. "Not really."

"Wouldn't you really rather get Gracie back?"

"That's why I did all this. For Gracie."

"Well, you know Calaneris isn't going to keep you or her alive after he gets his little kingdom, don't you?"

"Yes, but what can I do? He's already got her."

"Why don't we try a Lochinvar?"

"Virginia, would you just speak English?"

"You know—Lochinvar, the knight who courted this lady, and her father married her off to some old geezer. He walked in on the wedding and acted like he was paying his repects, then he ran off with the bride."

"Come off it. Will that work?"

"If you can wake Grace up, I'm sure she and I can get us all out of here."

Eric is starting to smile slightly.

"What's so funny?" Blauw asks. Eric jumps.

"Umm, nothing."

Blauw says, "Take her to the brig." A Scientist steps up to take me by the arm. I can tell he's no soldier.

213

We start down the hallway toward the stairs to the lower level of STS-99.

Eric talks to me. "If you let them put you in there, you'll never get out. Grace made it impregnable," he says wordlessly.

"You just wake up Grace—I'll be okay," I reply.

"Wait," Calaneris says. "The Cintamani." He holds out his hand.

I hand it over. I'm praying Poe's catching all this.

The Scientist and I reach the lower level and proceed toward the brig. I never noticed it before. It must look like all the other rooms I thought were hotel rooms.

"Which one is it?" I ask.

"They're all part of the brig," the Scientist says. Creepy. He stops in front of one of the rooms, where Chen-li is sitting watching a tennis match on a holoscreen. He jumps to his "feet" when he sees he has visitors.

"So, they've made you the jailor, Chen-li?"

"Lady Virginia!" He looks genuinely shocked. Considering he's an AI, I'm touched.

"Put her in the brig," the Scientist says curtly and floats off. The room's sparsely furnished, only a bed, bath, and flatscreen.

Speaking of AIs, I'm rather pleased to see that QoS is here. The holoscreen disintegrates into a pixelated soup and pours down to the floor, where it skitters on invisible legs and crawls up Chen-li's leg. Chen-li shrieks, but not for long. QoS's nanocytes have covered him entirely, and no sound escapes. It's horrible, but fascinating, kind of like "The Blob."

"Try not to hurt him, QoS—he's actually kind of sweet."

"I'll reserve his datastore," QoS says obligingly. "What is the status of the Living Cintamani? And... where is yours?"

"You noticed, eh? Calaneris confiscated them both. Good thing mine was a fake."

An Opening

"How did you do that, Virginia Sun-Jones?"

"Trade secret. Let's just say it takes one to know one. Blow this door, and we'll get Alan and Yverra."

"Even I cannot do that; it's been quantum locked," QoS says.

"Do I have to do everything around here? I picture a lock sliding open, and voila, there are Alan and Yverra. I flick off their electronic cuffs." Alan hugs me, while Yverra stands there looking uncomfortable.

"I'm glad to see you too, both of you. Let's move. I'll bet Eric could use some help right about now."

I cast about for Eric's thoughts. He's crawling through a utility crawlspace under the bridge. Gracie was under our feet all along! We apparate on the bridge, just in time to see Blauw looking at the floor and pointing a blaster. He must have heard Eric.

"QoS, the gun." Blauw yanks his hand back as his gun disintegrates into tiny pieces on the industrial carpet.

Calaneris and his Scientists are so engrossed in trying to track events unfolding at the Big Bang that it's not that hard to round them up into a corner.

"Hey, Sunny," Blauw says, flashing his patented grin on me again. "Don't forget I've got your jewel."

"Don't forget she's got your number," Alan says, and elbow strikes him. Blauw crumples to the ground.

"Ooh, nice one Alan," I say appreciatively. My torc shimmers into view around my neck. Calaneris looks at the one lying on the carpet beside the unconscious Blauw.

"Remember that we loved you, Virginia."

Right. He doesn't love anyone but himself. Then I hear a clunking sound below us. Eric's not much of a ninja, I'm afraid. I pull up a carpet tile, and there he is, pulling the stasis locked Gracie along behind on a bedspread from one of the rooms in the brig.

215

We all pitch in to pull up more tiles, and then hoist Grace onto the bridge. She is glowing slightly, a bit transparent, in stasis. Yverra steps up to wake Gracie.

"Oh, no you don't," Eric says. "That's my job." He bends down to kiss Grace, and probably does some other magic that I can't discuss here, and she opens her eyes.

"Hi, sleepyhead," I say.

"Mother— Dad— Eric? Is everything under control? I don't remember what happened."

"We've got you now, Babe," Eric says. She looks at him, and I can see the sparks shoot between them. About time.

"Listen, everyone, we got sidetracked, but now that we're back together, there's something I want to tell you all."

I explain what QoS and I have discovered.

"We've verified your observation that the universe is under attack, Grace," I say. "But there's more than one player involved."

"And my people have been wiped out," Yverra says. "We can be of little help now."

"I'm not talking about the Watchmen, Yverra. I'm so sorry about the last incursion—maybe the other universe felt you were too big a threat and told Calaneris to take your people out. But there's some other entity— call it an Uber Universe—that's out there.

"Whose side is it on?" Alan asked.

"Nobody's. That's the problem. QoS and I are sure it could put a stop to the damage, but we think this Uber Universe thinks our universe is at fault."

"At fault? How?"

"Poe's been expanding too fast, and we've exceeded our territory. The Uber Universe has been punishing it by destroying problematic timelines. QoS and I tried to hold Poe in and protect him, and we got a lot of lashes on our backs for our trouble."

An Opening

Despite our relative refuge here at the safety point near the Big Bang, where it's too early for Poe to get himself in trouble yet, I feel a growing sense of unease. If the Uber Universe gets completely fed up, what's to stop it from making us never happen in the first place? I think back on all the remarkable people I've met on this journey, Pauline Bernard, Violet Rain, Benrus and Ralff, and even non-people, like Chen-li and QoS, and I don't want to lose a single one of them. And every one of them is in danger of never existing.

"I think we're going to have to split up," I announce.

"You're too late. Grace is already gone." Eric stands there, tears streaming down his face. He holds up a letter. "It's for you." The envelope is addressed to "Mom" in Grace's rather childish handwriting. Shaking, I open it. Eric has probably already sneaked a peek, but I don't care.

Dear Mom—

First, I just want to tell you how great you are. I would never have had the wonderful life I've lived without my family. I'd write a letter to Dad and Eric too, but there isn't time, and I know you will let them know I love them too. Eric just asked me if I'd love him forever, if I'd love him till he's dead. I would, and I have.

When Yverra said today that she was the last of her kind, it struck me as the saddest thing I'd ever heard. I would never want to be alone like that, the Last of the Mohicans, so to speak. And it also struck me that it was all my fault. I've known for a long time that I have the power to step up, but I didn't try very hard. I was too busy being a princess and soaking up all the credit, while you were out there busting your buns to find out what has gone wrong. Sure, I found out some new laws of the universe, but when the Black Universe took Yverra's people, where was I? Getting duped by my husband and getting myself kidnapped. Now everywhere I look I see death and devastation. We're facing extinction, and I'm

217

pretty sure that I'm the only one who can do anything about it. I finally know who I am.

I know you and Dad and Yverra are strong, and I know you'll come up with a plan. But I'm afraid that will take too long. I've got to go talk to this Golaeth you talked about and convince it to spare us. I'm sure if it sees who and what's at stake, it will come around. I know you're scared, and Golaeth has already given you a beating. Now it's my turn to go to bat. Please don't feel like I'm just doing this to try to atone for anything. I'm not that noble. And please don't feel guilty. It's my choice. I owe you, and I owe Yverra, and I owe the universe. You're the best, Mom. Seeing you in action helped me break out of the bubble I've been in. I love you so very much.

Grace

I hand the letter to Alan, my hands cold and trembling. I can't believe I couldn't read her thoughts at all. Eric looks ashen.

Furious, I blurt out, "How could you let Gracie do this, Alan? This is all your fault. Treating her like a princess, making her take on all the responsibility herself, this *noblesse oblige* shit. Why didn't you discuss it with me?"

"I didn't know what she had in mind any better than you did," Alan retorts. "All I heard is that she wanted to understand the entity that's roaming around the space station. But for what it's worth, I think she's capable of doing pretty much whatever she wants."

"Yes, that's what you would say," I say, my voice cracking. "You and Gracie always leave me out of whatever's going on, and you always side with her."

"I'd say it's more the opposite," Alan replies, rising to the bait. "You think you can run everything your way, but it's just not possible any more. Everyone's got a role to play. We're not ignoring you. Get a grip."

An Opening

"Let's take this offline," I say. Maybe I realize that if I air out our dirty laundry in the open, I will lose. We retreat to the white room.

"This reminds me of the time you took Gracie hot-air ballooning without inviting me, or asking if it was all right. Then it nearly crashed. I shudder to think what nearly happened."

"Don't bring this up again. We already fought about this and settled it. Gracie wanted to go, and I knew you were afraid of heights. We agreed that I'd at least check with you next time. But this isn't the same thing. Besides, you're over your acrophobia now, after riding Hangul, aren't you?"

I ignore him. "After all of the effort I've gone through to get you and Gracie back, how could you do this to me? I've spent over a year looking for you, hoping for you, following every lead, no matter how dangerous, to be disappointed again and again, and you just flippantly throw it all away?" I start to cry.

Alan holds me. "I'm sorry, Hon. I know how hard it was. Remember, I was missing in action too. And I'm not throwing it all away. I love you and Grace more than ever, but I also know it's not just about us anymore. The stakes are higher than ever. Please, everyone looks up to you, so you've got to hold it together."

"It's so hard, Alan, I can't bear to think about it. And that cold fish Yverra and her poker face. She doesn't seem to care what happens to our family."

"Remember, she's lost her family too. Her whole civilization. Yverra's got your back. Think about her, and Ben and Ralff, and ..."

"I want my baby back," I wail.

"I know."

"But Alan, she's gone back to the future," I say, not caring that I'm echoing a movie title. "It's not safe there. It's not even safe here."

219

"She's not going there to be safe, Hon. She's a grown woman. She knows what she wants to do, and we can't stop her. Actually, I'm kind of proud."

I sniff. Damn his logical brain. You can't be rational and empathetic at the same time. I'd begun to have some irrational doubts that Alan was my husband. This banished them forever. I returned to my senses, such as they were in this odd universe. "Well, I still don't forgive you, but I know you're right. She's our daughter, and we have to let Gracie be Gracie." Though I hate to admit it, Alan has talked me down from the precipice once again. I take one last look at Grace's letter. "Let's go back."

"Wait. A kiss for good luck."

We materialize back in the common room. Nobody looks me in the eye. Yverra is assiduously checking her watch-looking thing.

"I'm sorry, everyone. I just lost it when I read Grace's letter."

"No apology is necessary, Virginia," Ben says, ever the diplomat. "Have you and Alan come up with a plan?" Alan shakes his head.

"If I could have just taken her to the Beach, she could have met Poe," I suggest. "Well, maybe not. He doesn't communicate to anyone except his pal QoS. She could have taken QoS."

As if on cue, a two-dimensional rectangle rotates in the air in front of us, and quickly morphs into an old-fashioned 2D flatscreen TV. QoS speaks. "Poe would also desire that I accompany her."

"I don't know where she is, exactly," I say, "but if you're willing to go wherever the Cintamani chooses, I'd be happy to send you. It doesn't always behave the way I expect it to."

"That would be optimal," QoS says. "The Cintamani is his agent, as are you."

An Opening

"Thanks. I'm gratified to finally receive this acknowledgment from Poe. I'll do my best to send you to Grace." Suddenly I feel all formal, like Moses receiving the Ten Commandments. I close my eyes and picture Grace alive and well. That's all. No galaxies, no planets, no supernovas, just Grace. I lay our greatest sacrifice at the altar of the universe.

*****~~~~~*****

Chapter 23.

Synergies and Dreams

Golaeth feels thinner than ever. Pent up gravity waves rippled through the Hatchery, but with no place to go. New universes waiting to be born will have to wait until the distribution and creation of matter can be stabilized, if that is even possible. Older brother and sister universes are also not stable, even after being given extra time to mature. Two in particular seem like they would **never** *mature.*

Whose fault was that? Certainly not Golaeth's. The two siblings are not merely rivals; they are locked in what can only be called a struggle to the death. Golaeth has tried everything it can: adding extra dark matter to ease the pressure of the younger to expand, as well as repairing damage wrought by the elder.

"Have you tried talking with them?"

Stunned, Golaeth has never heard the voice of one of its charges, other than the occasional cries of being born.

"Which of my universes are you?" Golaeth demands.

"I'm not a universe. I'm Grace."

"You look like a creature."

"Guilty as charged. I've come to see if I can help."

"Who sent you?"

"No one sent me. I came on my own."

"This is impossible. And unacceptable. If I find which universe has spawned you, I will report it to the Makers, and your universe will be deleted."

223

"Then I won't tell you which universe I'm from. I only want to help. Who are you, incidentally? Mom calls you the Uber Universe."

Golaeth considers yet again. It might be difficult to locate the creature's origin, then. "You may call me Golaeth. What makes you think you can help?"

"I just know that I am unusual, even for my own universe. There is no one like me, as far as I can tell. I can do some pretty amazing things, if I do say so myself."

"I'll be the judge of that." The upstart creature thinks it is a Maker. Delusional. For now, Golaeth will humor the poor insane creature.

"I know what you're thinking," Grace says. "You think I'm insane. I'm not, I assure you. Plus, I've had training in settling territorial disputes such as what I think is going on here. That's my mom's theory, by the way, she just hasn't figured it out yet."

"You're only a child," Golaeth says. A charming child, admittedly, but nonetheless a mortal child of a race of creatures that lived and died on vastly different time scales than the Makers.

"I understand your concern," Grace says. "Why don't you check with the Makers? If they know everything, like you say, they can vouch for me."

"Such hubris!" The idea is tempting, however. Golaeth is tired, tired of fighting so long with nothing to show for it and with no help from the Makers. No, this is illogical, more immature behavior from an inferior creation. Golaeth resolves to delete the silly creature.

"You don't want to do that," Grace says. "You want to stop the fighting, don't you?"

With dawning realization, Golaeth feels its resolve bending, bending to the will of the creature called Grace.

"Wow, you're almost as hard to convince as my mother," Grace says. "I feel like I've been on trial here."

You have, Golaeth thinks.

"I can hear you," Grace says with a smile. "Let's go kick some butt, as Mom would say."

☺

A waking dream. It's the same scenario, with Grace floating in the void, radiating white light and holding her palms up in supplication. The religious symbolism is unmistakable, and Grace's smile is the essence of humility. There is calm. Suddenly, an array of tentacles of brilliant green fire lashes out, but QoS throws himself in front of her as a shield. The tentacles envelop both of them, spinning a cocoon that threatens to strangle them both. QoS struggles to break through the green chrysalis. Suddenly it all vanishes from my view. I gasp. It isn't a dream. It's real.

"Something wrong, Hon?" Alan asks.

"I don't know, but I think Grace has just made contact," I say. "All we can do right now is wait."

"Is she fighting with it or something?"

"She's just— gone. The green monster's taken her and QoS somewhere else. They may not even be in our universe any more.

"Are we in danger?"

"I think that's a given, but just as a precaution, let's go to the beach."

"I'd love to see this beach of yours," Alan says with a smile.

"We're taking Eric and Yverra too," I say. "There's someone I want her to meet."

In a moment, we are on the Beach. I'm wearing shorts and sandals, and so is Alan. In spite of her reptilian appearance, Yverra is most decidedly not dressed for the beach. Her tight leather catsuit is impenetrable against the light ocean breeze, and a drop of perspiration beads on her frowning forehead. An unruly wisp of hair teases its way out of her neat French twist.

Benrus and Ralff come hurrying over. They've switched to light summer-weight robes, artfully decorated with numbers and symbols. I think Yverra will enjoy meeting some like-minded individuals.

"Ben, Ralff, I've brought my husband, Alan, and my son-in-law, Eric."

"Congratulations on retrieving your husband," Ralff says. "And who is this?" he says, looking at Yverra.

"She's the top physicist of her people. Yverra, may I introduce Benrus and Ralff."

"I can see that these beings are accustomed to quantum travel and must therefore be a more advanced race than you humans," Yverra says, nodding slightly.

"Right," I say, biting my tongue. Best not to engage with someone who's still grieving over her lost people. I wonder how she can tell about Ben and Ralff just by looking at them. Maybe they've got some sort of invisible quantum passport that gets stamped when you displace.

"We've got Calaneris and Blauw in custody, at least temporarily, and Grace is off negotiating a meet with Poe's creator."

"And QoS?" Ben inquires.

"He is a hostage, along with the Living Cintamani," Yverra says. I wish she wouldn't always be so blunt.

"You know Poe can hear us, don't you?"

"I am not convinced of the wisdom of trusting this Poe. He is not a living entity."

"He's quite alive enough for me," I retort. "And Gracie has vouched for him." I remember her statement, "The universe holds many wonders, Mommy." Or was that her statement? The child on the beach—was that really Gracie speaking? Why, of course, it was. I should know my own daughter.

"At the very least, we should put this nexus in stasis," Yverra says. "I can do this for you, with the aid of your Physicist assistants."

"Um, that won't be necessary—yet, but I'd be grateful for all your help if we need to pull out the big guns." I have no idea what kind of big guns can fight off the universe and his jealous brother and disapproving minder.

While we wait to hear from Grace, I ask to see Hangul. He rises from the sea, and I touch my torc, a sort of greeting.

"If you all don't mind, I left some unfinished business in Hangul's world."

"Where is that?" Alan asks.

"I'm really talking about Los Angeles, 400 years in our future. When I arrived there looking for you, Hangul plucked me off the side of a cliff. Los Angeles, and I gather, the rest of Earth, was nothing but a giant holodeck. The population was living in the world of their imaginations. One thing they hadn't imagined was that the world was about to end."

"So this was where you first got the Cintamani—from Hangul?"

"No, I think I've had it all along, even in Freetown in North Carolina in 1827, although I didn't do anything useful with it except kill bugs, unless you count holding back the ocean like Moses. I think I wasn't ready to meet Hangul until Los Angeles. Anyway, I met this lovely young lady named Violet Rain there, and I think she'd be good on our team. She's a master of virtual reality."

"I'll go with you," Alan says.

"Two can ride as cheaply as one," I agree. "Besides, she's your great-great-great granddaughter too."

Alan is the computer scientist of the family. In lieu of QoS, he is best equipped to understand VR. I have a hopefully wrong foreboding that if worst comes to worst, Poe will not be allowed to live, hence neither will we. But maybe we can live on in someone's imagination somewhere. Violet reminded me of Grace, but Grace had no inclination toward computers. I think there will be a synergy there. Maybe that's another reason Poe picked me. I do have a talent for mixing and matchmaking.

We climb aboard Hangul, and I picture Violet Rain alone in her empty control room. She is just beginning to receive reports of interruptions in service from all over the Southwestern quadrant of the U.S. VR net, and is frantically trying to grasp what's going on. Hangul apparates and squeezes into the back of the big room. We barely fit, and he drips water all over the floor of the concrete bunker.

"Told you I'd be back," I say, climbing off Hangul. "Oh, and be careful. Hangul's real."

I explain that we have only a few seconds. She nods, and approaches Hangul, who backs away from her. He let Alan aboard, but not Violet? Maybe he's a one-woman dragon.

"Hangul, we haven't got time for this. Let Violet ride with us. Now!"

We are about to depart, when a pulsing green tendril crashes through the roof and grabs Violet. She screams. Reality's a bitch.

Crap. This Uber thing is one step ahead of me. Now it's got three of us, and it's shutting down all of our secret meeting places.

Alan and I scramble back aboard Hangul and retreat. What did it want Violet for? Or Earth, for that matter? I hope she'll be all right.

☺

"Where is the female Earthling you were supposed to retrieve?" Yverra asks as we wink back onto the shore.

"We lost her," Alan says. "I got to see her, but that's all, before the Uber Universe swooped in and swept her away."

"That is regrettable," Yverra says. An unusual bit of empathy, for her. Maybe I should have let Yverra do the grab, but it's too late now.

I turn to Eric. "Eric, I remember your advice when gaming, about how it pays to be pragmatic rather than getting pissed off when something goes wrong. Any strategies for facing a foe that's way out of your league?"

Eric's been moping around on the beach ever since we got here. I'm hoping that bringing him in on the conversation will break him out of his funk. Of course, the best medication for that would be to get Grace back. So, okay, what would Lochinvar have done?

"I think Yverra's got a point about the green monster not being alive. It doesn't have anything to lose, so it can't be compelled to do anything it doesn't want to," Eric says.

I hear a crunching sound and look down at my feet.

"My, this beach certainly has a lot of litter," I say. "Just a little joke. It's another message from Poe." I pick up the piece of crumpled, brightly colored waxy paper. It's a food wrapper of some kind: "Old Santa Fe Burrito, Extra Hot."

"Anybody order the burrito?"

"Maybe it's something to do with heat," Alan says. "There's a narrow range of temperatures where life can exist. Any planet that's close to the Earth in size and near enough to a warming sun is what's called a 'Goldilocks' planet. Our galaxy has plenty of places that qualify."

Maybe compared to the other possible universes, ours has too many hot spots. Maybe the universe was supposed to do its Big Bang and then gradually cool back down, but it isn't doing that.

Ralff chimes in. "As I recall, we all were surprised when we found the universe is actually getting hotter. But where's it getting all of its energy?"

I'm beginning to think we're the victims of a vast cover-up.

⟳

The runaway expansion continues, despite Golaeth's best efforts. Another anomaly from the infant universe has manifested itself, requiring Golaeth to split its attention yet again. The anomaly is highly abnormal, imbued with capabilities on a par with its own, yet devoid of purpose other than to simply exist. The new universe seems to resist all efforts to examine the anomaly.

Golaeth reconsiders the situation. The recursion process is functioning properly, but with each descent, it is introducing new snippets of code, generating unbalanced dark matter. Efforts to excise the excess matter are proving fruitless, and each repair of a nexus just results in the anomaly springing up elsewhere. Slathering in copious amounts of dark energy to wall off the damage just seems to speed up the expansion. And the temperature continues to rise—it is already a degree warmer.

And now, surprisingly, the universe has allowed Golaeth access to the anomaly, dangling it like bait on a hook. The temptation is overwhelming, and Golaeth approaches cautiously. There appears to be two instances of it, each radiating at different energy levels. Could it be a binary pulsar? If so, Golaeth must be very careful not to receive a direct burst of gravitational radiation. It reacts in astonishment as the anomaly generates a third appendage. Golaeth rises to take the bait, wrapping the anomaly in a dense web of negentropy. Perhaps the deviant methods can be nullified before the other universes intervene. At last the true nature of the anomaly will be revealed.

☉

The torc around my neck is getting warmer. I've always found it comforting, sort of a balm against the cold universe, but it now is actually hot to the touch. I pull it off and fan it. I hope the Cintamani isn't overheating or something. I lean closer and blow on it, like I do with a cup of tea brewed at North Carolina sea level. I turn it

230

around. The jewel sparkles like a highly faceted diamond. It doesn't look like the setting's damaged, so I slip the torc back on. I look around at the Beach, trying to take it all in.

The cool grey light is unchanging, and the waves roll in gently. A place of sanctuary and contemplation. I feel somehow the team is closing in on the mystery of the misfortune that has befallen our universe. We are living in Poe's castle, and we are the last defenders, standing on the parapets waiting for the final invasion.

I look down and laugh. I'm wearing full battle armor from the Middle Ages. My connection with the Cintamani is now so close I don't even have to wish to make my thoughts known. I laugh, because I know that any kind of armor is useless. If it weren't for this beach, we'd all be squashed like those cotton weevils, or vaporized by the Uber Universe's snaking green whips.

"How about at least a laser gun, instead of this heavy sword?" I say to Poe. "You know, I liked it better when QoS was here. At least he talked to me. I'm going to go see if I can help Grace."

Down the beach, Alan is setting up a fireworks show to entertain us all. He's built a raft and is using that as his launch platform so that the burning rocket remains will fall harmlessly into the ocean, and he can be as wild and creative as he likes. Hangul watches from a safe distance. I track the bombshell volleys as they explode across the sky, while Eric cheers and encourages Yverra, Ralff, and Benrus to do the same. They try gamely, but showy displays of enthusiasm don't seem to be their thing. I can't feel much enthusiasm either, and I resolve to go looking for Grace as soon as the show's over.

Alan lights up a particularly fine pair of Catherine wheels, and they spin madly like mini-galaxies before eventually sputtering out.

In spite of Alan's pyrotechnical efforts to try to distract us, I find the tense feeling of helplessness while we wait to hear from Grace seems to have given me a

231

splitting migraine. I've been subject to them since I was a young girl, so I tell myself to try to relax. I sit down and try to pull off my helmet, but my hair gets caught in the visor, and I spend a painful few moments trying to untangle it. A wad of black and gray hair still sticks to the pin of the visor, punishment for my impatience. The bright lights and noises from the fireworks aren't helping.

My mouth is dry, and I'm feeling a slight tickle at the back of my throat. Even with the lovely oceanside humidity, I feel my nasal passages close up as the lining of my nostrils swell. I feel foolish, coming down with a cold after traipsing all over the universe. I rub my temples and fold my palms over my eyes. Images of the fireworks sear themselves onto my retinas, leaving me with flashbulb eyes.

The feeling of the armor is becoming oppressive, so I clumsily undo the side buckles that reach from the waist up to the underarm. There must be a dozen or more of them. Exhausted, I shed the breastplate and strip down to my shirt of chain mail. I ache all over from the effort. I look at my reflection in the pile of metal. I'm a mess. My eyes are bloodshot, and what's left of my hair is matted to my forehead.

I should be able to just wish myself free of the rest of the armor, but I don't have the strength. The torc is getting hot again. I want to tear it off, but I can't. My eyes are burning, and it's become too painful to swallow. It feels like a hot coal is lodged in my throat. I'd swear I have tonsillitis, if I had tonsils. At first, I think I should have been taking better care of myself. But now I know it's Poe. He's trying to stop me from leaving. Why was it okay to go to L.A. but not to where Grace is? It's more confusing than ever.

I give a little cough to dislodge the phlegm that's collecting in my lungs. I'm surprised to feel mucus in my mouth and quickly spit it out. It's a putrid green color. My chest begins to hurt, and my teeth begin to chatter. My heart is beating faster, and I begin to panic, knowing I have to escape before it's too late.

I cast my thoughts out to Grace. I'll go to her, and we can fight this thing together.

"You know, you can't keep doing this," I say to Poe. "You can't keep us here forever. You have to let us help. You have to let me go to Grace."

Ah, there she is. I see her. I reach out with the Cintamani.

But suddenly the cool, damp sand looks quite inviting. My head feels twice its size, and the jewel is strangling me. I decide to lie down. I can't be much help if I don't arrive rested, with my batteries fully charged. I'll probably feel much better after a little nap…

Dreaming of numbers. I can't get them to add up. I'm standing at the board, chalk in hand. The teacher is staring at me. I feel the beginning aura of my first migraine coming on. A writhing zigzag of light dances across my field of vision, and I can't see the board properly. The harder I try to focus on what I've written, the harder it is to see.

"Your answer, Miss Sun? Your answer?" My mouth goes dry, synapses begin to burn, and I feel myself unwind. I drop the chalk and run from the room.

Darkness. Stinging rain. The sea heaves, gorge threatens to rise from overtaxed stomachs. A funeral breath exhales over the souls on the stricken ship, casting a pall on the hopes of all who desire only one thing: to continue living. A light. Miraculous, a light beckons toward the safety of a safe harbor. It moves up and down, back and forth, tiny yet glorious. Sheets of rain obscure it temporily. There it is again! A cheer escapes from every throat. But perhaps it is a trap.

An alarm clock is ringing, ragged bits of music tearing at my eardrums. No, let me sleep. It's too hard. I need to save my strength. I reach out and hug my pillow closer.

The hot ectoplasm seethes, surging closer to envelope the easy prey, to dissolve it in its acid digestive juices. A gustatory victim, ready for the frying pan. How disgusting. It's nothing but an embryo. Where's its mother? It's Poe!

Someone is shaking me. I hear Alan yell, "Ginny, Ginny... Something's happening. Eric, come help me! She's burning up!"

"Not so loud, please, Alan. My head is killing me, and I can't breathe. I've got to get out of here."

"You're in no shape to go anywhere," he says. "Help me get her up."

I slowly sink again into a comfortable oblivion.

*****~~~~~*****

Chapter 24.

Unholy War

I don't know how much time has gone by. I must have passed out. When I open my eyes, I see Alan and Eric leaning over me, dabbing at my forehead. I brush Alan's hand away.

"What happened?"

"We're under attack!" Eric blurts.

"Be quiet, Eric," Alan says through clenched teeth. "How are you feeling, honey?"

"Attack?" I say, confused. "This isn't some sort of an April Fool's joke, like the time you woke me up in the middle of the night and said the cat had puppies, is it? This is just a drill, right?" Poe's beach has always been a secure place.

"It's not a drill. We were having fun shooting off fireworks, and at first we didn't realize what was going on. Then these laser beams started raking across the sky, and we've been hunkering here around you ever since."

I try to sit up. Whoa. Dizzy. The sky is crazed with fine green cracks, and the horizon is flashing. Hangul bellows at the threatening noises and thrashes about through the surf, defending his turf. It looks like Poe's secret hiding place isn't a secret any more.

I'm contrite. Sorry, Poe. I blamed you for not letting me out, when you were just trying to defend me against a breach after all.

"I'm feeling all right," I say, getting to my feet. "If someone would just get me a glass of water..." One appears in my hand. I gulp it down.

"You make the best water, Poe."

The ground shakes, and we all struggle to keep our feet. The green fire spreading across the arc of the sky seems to be getting brighter. It's not going to be long before whatever it is reaches in and grabs us like it did Violet, or kills us. Burnt cinders are raining down all around us.

Yverra comes careening up. Her long hair is loose, and she's wearing a light caftan like Ben and Ralff. Nice to see her loosen up for a change.

"Lady Virginia. You must act now. Let us devise the stasis field."

"What will that do?"

"It will protect us all until the end of the universe, and possibly beyond."

"What good would that do, if the universe ends? We'd have nothing to come back to."

"You are being illogical. It is to ensure our survival."

"*I'm* being illogical? So we'll just sit here through eternity, while Poe gets hammered out of existence?"

"Odds are good," Yverra says. Another booming crack sounds, and she glances nervously over her shoulder. "Time is short."

"That's not going to work for me," I say. Stubborn to the last. Not one of my finer points, Alan would say.

Alan. I think about who would be best to start a brave new world if Grace or I were out of the picture. He's the patriarch of the family, and he knows how to work with our Physicist friends. And if Grace or I aren't successful...

Yverra is drawing a circle on the beach, just big enough to hold seven. She is chanting quietly, a pentatonic scale, if I'm not mistaken. Greek symbols begin to appear on her caftan—pi, alpha, omega, the mathematical language of her people.

"You go on, Alan, and take Eric. I've got something to discuss with Poe, and I'll be along shortly." He turns and reluctantly steps into the circle.

"Poe, if I don't make it out of here, make sure the Cintamani goes to Alan," I say. Hangul bellows again.

"Lady Virginia! We are setting up the field. Come with us now."

I touch the torc on my neck, now warm and pulsing. I wave goodbye.

"Remember me, Alan," I say, and jump aboard Hangul.

"Virginia," he yells, but just then the stasis field pops into existence, and only a black reflective sphere remains. Steam curls off its surface as water condenses from the surrounding air. Then, slowly, it shrinks until it is no longer visible.

☉

I don't know where to go next. I already miss my family. I sit on the beach astride Hangul, dithering. We could jump back to Earth in the 25th century, or the STS-99 space station outside the Big Bang, but I know the Uber Universe is attacking there too. I can still feel the lashing from my and QoS's stint as shields. Probably just a prelude to certain death.

The sky continues to reverberate with the blows of an angry Uber Universe. Or maybe it's just determined. I sit there like a recalcitrant teenager who's stormed out and locked the door to the bedroom. I'll just sit here and sulk and consider the unfairness of it all.

A little piece of wood is sticking up out of the sand. I dismount and go over to pick it up. What is it? A riding whip? A magic wand that can whisk us all out of here and back to our normal lives? I turn it over and run my fingers along the grain. My fingers encounter an engraved surface along the shank. It says, "Virginia Jones." It's a personalized gift, a bit of wood from the great rowan. A lump forms in my throat.

"Thanks, Poe," I say, and tuck it into the waistband of my shorts.

Suddenly, the attack ceases. It grows quieter as the sky begins to cool and repair itself. Soon the only sound is the soft whoosh of the lapping waves.

"Think it's given up, Poe?" I say. Then I realize that it's only been distracted by something more interesting. I hope it's not our little stasis escape capsule.

A picture begins to draw itself in the sand. The grains rise and form a bas-relief, a portrait of a woman's face. It's Grace.

⟳

This is good news. Isn't it? I still don't know where Grace is, but apparently Poe does. Has she found the Uber Universe and talked it out of destroying us? I'm about to congratulate the universe on our good luck, when the sky begins to darken again. A tower of black clouds billows upward, and lightning flashes. Uh-oh.

The torc is getting hot again. A pelting rain begins. The grains of sand rinse away, taking the picture of Grace with them. I may have spoken too soon. I have a sickening feeling that the Uber Universe might be angry at us again. What did we do this time?

The temperature is beginning to plummet. The dark clouds in the sky look like they are bringing snow. Sure enough, flakes begin to fall. I stick out my tongue, both to sneer at the elements and to sample the snowflakes like a kid. Growing up in North Carolina, we didn't get that much snow. I shiver. Shorts and a tank top are not going to cut it. I think about one of those snow bunny outfits you see in magzines for ski resorts. That helps a little, but it's still getting colder.

And darker. I think it's gotten too cold to snow. The thin layer of snow on the beach is no longer slippery, it's crunchy. The hairs in my nose are beginning to freeze. Wow, from 70 down to zero degrees in five minutes. At this rate, I'm not going to last very long. I don't know about Hangul, but he doesn't seem to be suffering. I wonder what frostbite on a dragon claw looks like. I wish to be taken to Grace. Nothing doing. I dismount. Looks like I'm not going anywhere.

"Why don't you hide out for a bit, buddy?" He slips down under the waves, and I lose sight of him.

The sea is choppy, and the sluggish waves are beginning to freeze. I read somewhere that the salt in the ocean allows it to hold a lot of heat, so it takes a long time for it to freeze, but eventually it can freeze over, like at the North Pole. But this seems even colder. Maybe like on Mars, or an even colder place, like the moons of Jupiter. My torc seems to be the only thing keeping me alive. I'm becoming resigned that my warm little haven is going to eventually reach the ambient temperature outside. And by outside, I mean the big, empty outside. Space. A few degrees above absolute zero. Any lower than that, and everything stops. Maybe that's the idea. To stop us.

Something is eating us alive, turning us into nothingness. This isn't like the behavior of the Uber Universe, with its green lasers inflicting pain to get our attention. No, this is going to cool us down so far we go to sleep. Permanently.

I wish I was with Eric and Grace, and I could use my torc like a video game remote, and I could push buttons randomly (my usual way of learning to play a game) until I got the world to react the way I wanted it to. QoS would be my console. I'd have a streak of beginner's luck that defied all explanation. QoS would be scoring all my masterful strokes to fend off the creepy invisible demon of darkness— "And now, Vir-Gin-I-A has levelled up and defeated the Black Universe!" The sound of crowds going wild. The Black Universe dissolving before our very eyes on the display. But it's not a game, and Poe isn't changing my luck.

My little beach has turned into an ice world, mountains of ice and rock grinding along slow moving glaciers of more ice. I walk slowly, trying not to slip into one of the dark blue crevasses that stretch out in all directions. I'm not that far from the ocean's edge, and I finally manage to creep over to it and look down. Just more of the same. Wait. There's a light. Something fluorescent green is flashing by beneath the ice. The light disappears. There it is again, dimmer this time. Maybe it's Hangul, searching for a thin spot, so he can break through and join me once again. I climb down a frozen bank and step cautiously out onto the ice. I follow the lantern, like a shipwrecked sailor lured by the Breakers.

☾

I've long ago stopped hoping for rescue; I spend most of my time regretting that I didn't take a berth on Yverra's stasis lifeboat. But if I had, I'd probably outlive our universe and have very little in common with whoever I met at the other end of time. That's kind of important, as it turns out. Having a common goal. Seeking mutually beneficial outcomes. The never-finished quest.

I still can't find Hangul, although I suspect he's under the frozen nitrogen ice covering the ocean. The flicker of light has become fainter each time I see it. I stumble toward a sighting, until I reach what looks like the spot it came from, but by then, there's nothing but darkness. I'm totally lost. I wonder if I've been going in circles. Even if I had a compass, who knows if it would work anyway. I've never been sure where the beach is located, or when. It could even be before the Big Bang, and there would be no atoms yet, much less magnetic fields.

I use what little energy I have left (supplied by the last powers of Poe's jewel, I suspect) to create a little marker. If I'm out over the ocean, it might better be called a buoy. If I come around this way again, the marker will at least tell me that I've been on a fool's errand. The marker is about three feet tall, conical, and made of concrete. A large iron ring pierces the rock near the top. Reminds me of a place to loop the reins if you're parking your horse, or your dragon. It's chiming a tune, like an ice cream truck. It's playing, "Sailing, Sailing."

It would be creepy if it weren't so lovely. It's another hint from Poe. Hangul must be near, and this means I'm going to find him! If I don't get lost again. Maybe we'll be sailing out of here in no time.

After another quarter hour, I'm discouraged again. The ice cream truck music is loops over and over, beginning to annoy me no end, and there's still no sign of Hangul or the light under the frozen waves. It's still getting colder. I'm terrified that this energy drain is going to end Poe and me when we reach absolute zero.

I'd swear there was a breeze, making me feel even colder. Of course, that's just silly. There's not even any air here. Too cold for that. But when it nearly knocks me off my feet, I know the wind's real. I've heard of solar wind, but this can't be that. There's no sun.

"I'm tired. Can't we just rest?" No, nevermind. Might not ever wake up again.

A green-tinged light winks only 20 feet away. I come upon a river of green ice flowing below. A dark silhouette flashes by in the wet under the ice, golden scales and iridescent flesh writhing.

"Hangul?"

A small vortex forms, growing in height and in angular momentum, until it appears to be 100 feet high. It twists and writhes on the ice in an irregular column, finally hovering over the spot where something lurks. The ice cream truck song turns into a high whine, like a drill. Chips of ice begin to fly in all directions, and I step backwards.

With a crash, Hangul breaks through. And strapped to his back is a refrigerator-size black box.

"A package for me?"

241

Hangul settles to the ground and shakes, dislodging the big box, which tumbles and skids across the ice and stops at my feet.

The sides and top of the box begin to unfold, and the contents begin to inflate. It looks like a recliner with a built-in TV screen.

Letters begin to spell out across the screen.

"SPECIAL DELIVERY—"

"QoS! But— How did you get here? If I'm not mistaken, we are heading straight for absolute zero. The Big Chill, right?"

QoS corrects my impression.

"That is highly unlikely, Virginia, at least in our universe. Practically, the work needed to remove heat from a gas increases the colder you get, and an infinite amount of work would be needed to cool something to absolute zero. In quantum terms, by Heisenberg's uncertainty principle, the more precisely we know a particle's speed, the less we know about its position, and vice versa. If you know your atoms are inside your experiment, there must be some uncertainty in their momentum keeping them above absolute zero—unless your experiment is the size of the whole universe.

"Our theory is that in an attempt to kill you, your nexus has been moved to the Boomerang Nebula, 5,000 light years from Earth in the constellation Centaurus," QoS continues.

"Gases blowing out from a central dying star have expanded and rapidly cooled to 1 kelvin, only one degree warmer than absolute zero. But the attacker failed to realize that this nexus is protected by quantum effects, and furthermore, at such low temperatures chemistry actually works better rather than slowing to a stop."

Befuddled yet slightly reassured, I ask, "Where did you come from? And were you with Grace? I'm pretty sure I saw you two disappear into the arms of the Uber Universe."

"We were indeed beginning to commune with Golaeth, when we began to detect increasing chemical reactions from this nebula. It has sent me here to check on our universe's status."

"Was it hoping we were dead?" I ask waspishly.

"Not necessarily. It is still assessing what to do about Poe. Meanwhile I came here to generate gravity waves to repel the Black Universe. Force is the only thing it understands right now. Don't worry, we have a good counsel in Grace."

"Well, I'm sure you want to get back together with your best bud, Poe," I say. "Now that we know he's safe, and Grace is safe, can I leave you here and join her?"

"Yes, Virginia. But you are mistaken that we are all safe. I will stay here to try to defend Poe. Have a good voyage."

I hobble over to Hangul and climb into the saddle. I want to get out of this place as fast as possible. It's colder than a witch's tit.

*****〜〜〜〜*****

Chapter 25.

Capitulation

I have to admit I'm spoiled. Apparently QoS has downloaded all the necessary coordinates into Hangul, so all I have to do is hang on while we travel through what I am guessing is some sort of wormhole that stretches us thin and snaps us like a rubber band at the end. I can't describe the scenery, because there isn't much of any. Unlike my last wormhole experience going to STS-99, this one seems to take a very long time. Relatively speaking.

We arrive in a grand hall of mirrors, with Grace and a vaguely humanoid ball of light at the far end. The light is dazzling at first, but someone (I'm guessing Grace) must have hit the dimmer switch, because suddenly I can see everything. I glance in the nearest mirror and see that I'm still wearing a snow bunny outfit.

"Catch up with me, will you?" I admonish my own mind.

I'm now dressed in my most demure outfit, perfect for Sunday Mass.

"Hi, Mom. Welcome to the Fun House. You already know Violet, right?

"Hello, again, great-grandmother."

"Thanks, sweetie. And this is the minder, the Uber Universe, I presume?" I wonder if I should bow. Where do I get that? I'm American, and we don't have royalty.

"I am Golaeth. Grace has told me all about you, Virginia," Golaeth says. "She tells me that you are her creator."

"Well, it took two of us," I stammer. Alan deserves half the credit. Or more.

"Very understandable. She is the anomaly we've all been searching for. She is an impressive creation."

I can tell I'm going to like this one. I ask them to bring me up to date. "QoS told me you weren't attacking our universe but rather trying to repair it. So who's invading us, and can you help us?"

"You seem inclined to ask compound complex questions, Virginia. Let us consider them one at a time."

"Sorry," I mutter. "Go on, please."

"The aggrieved party is another universe. Your universe has been threatening to encroach upon its territory."

"We suspected that, or at least Grace did. Is there anything we can do to fix it?"

"At present, we do not have a solution. We are sorting through an infinite set of possibilities."

"Ooh. QoS is a superintelligent AI. Should I have brought him back to help?"

"It is far beyond QoS's capabilities. He is more of a plaything of your universe, as are you and your human relatives. Grace, on the other hand, has been quite helpful."

"Oh, how so?" She's more capable than the mind of the universe? My little girl?

"To put it in your terms, I was overwhelmed, and now there are two of us."

"That's good. So, I'm fairly useless too, even with the Cintamani?"

"I didn't say that," Golaeth says.

"You implied I was just Poe's plaything."

"You are still quite powerful, if your powers are applied properly."

"Well, apply me." I don't know what gets into me sometimes. No need to dispense with manners. "I mean, I'm willing to assist in any way I can."

"If you would join with us, Mom, we'd like to attempt to contact the other universe," Grace says.

Capitulation

"Golaeth will protect Violet until it's safe to return her to the universe."

My Cintamani zaps me with a little spark. It hurts so good.

☺

Golaeth reaches to the edges of its range. Its sphere of influence has increased appreciatively, good. It inspects the edges of both Virginia's and the other universe. Grace calls it the Black Universe, although truly it is made up of all wavelengths in their universe, plus a few additional ones unknown to Poe.

The Black Universe continues to assault Poe, attempting assassination by heat death, but it is beginning to realize that avenue is fruitless. It is growing wearier— and angrier. Golaeth frets that the Black Universe might remove the matter from its hands by lodging a complaint against Poe. That would be the ultimate humiliation. Golaeth has been the trusted steward of infant universes since before the beginning of time.

Grace's suggestion of a conference among the affected parties seems like a good idea. Golaeth reaches out a single tendril to the edge of the Black Universe's territory. It is expecting to find a universe that is in the peak of health, which will be a huge contrast, after all of the work that Poe has required just to keep alive. The Black Universe has obeyed all of the rules, and its growth has been orderly, unlike its unruly younger brother. But Golaeth has been remiss in ignoring the Black Universe. This universe has been infected, and it too is dying. Now it is taking matter into its own hands to steal what it can from Poe, and Golaeth's proscriptions against further attacks have been ignored.

Golaeth calls for a hiatus, sending calming pulses down the green beam to spread across the shell of the Black Universe. Virginia's Cintamani and Grace's power will surely bring it into line.

The recalcitrant imp! It is resisting the order to cease hostilities. It has opened a back door, through which it captures and refocuses all of the triad's energies into a deadly weapon of collimated gamma radiation, aimed straight at Poe's tiny nexus.

Golaeth withdraws the beam, but too late. The fatal blow has been dealt. But wait. The beam crackles over a barrier, a shield around the nexus.

An unknown entity has erected a barrier to shield the infant. The shield holds for a millisecond but crumbles, like a lump of coal turning to ash. Golaeth probes the entity's final thoughts:

Regrettably my shield has failed, but Poe will be spared. I foolishly assumed it was the monster trying to hurt us. It wasn't until a yoctosecond later that I learned that the monster was called Golaeth, that it was Poe's Minder, and that it was performing temporary repairs. I also neglected to notice the planet that was being gradually deprived of all of its heat. In some ways it was indistinguishable from all the other planets out on the edge of the universe that are cooling down to near absolute zero. But I should have noticed that this planet was colder than the coldest spot in the universe—that there was another term in the equation...

ↄ

"No!" Virginia screams. "QoS!"

The AI's quantum data stores and all of its nanocytes have been destroyed by the burst of ionizing radiation. Golaeth can feel QoS's consciousness disintegrate. There's fear, then nothing.

"Why have you done this?" Golaeth asks.

"What reason do you need to die?" the Black Universe responds.

"I've got to get back to Poe," Virginia yells. "Without QoS, he's defenseless."

ↄ

Capitulation

Without asking leave of Golaeth, I jump back onto the Beach. It is a wreck. The formerly frozen landscape has thawed, leaving heaps of debris and detritus washing up on the re-liquified shore. Thousands of dead and dying creatures lie stinking in the muddy sand. Now I'm truly afraid for our universe. Somber strings play a dirge for QoS; I recognize the strains of Warlock's Pavanne. If I ever had any doubts that I could be killed, I don't have them any longer.

"Poe! I'm here. What can I do? Golaeth was just trying to help. We're so sorry! At least, QoS didn't suffer long." I bite my tongue. That's never a consolation.

A ghost ship appears on the horizon, flying the Jolly Roger. A huge storm blows up around it, tearing its flag off the mast and ripping its sails to shreds. It crashes on a sandbar and falls to pieces, with tremendous rending and tearing sounds.

"I know, I know." What I know is that it takes time to grieve. And time is what we don't have.

"He had no right. QoS was so brave, defending you like that. Listen, I know I'm not in his league, but please, let me help you defend. He showed me how to defend against Golaeth's beams, didn't he? There's too much at stake to give up now."

The waves continue to crash, spraying high into the air and falling back into the dark sea. I back up and quiver in terror. I'm crying, no longer able to project my usually matter-of-fact practicality.

Abruptly, the storm subsides. A rain of tiny wood chips falls onto the beach. A piece of paper blows across the sand. Thank goodness, he's talking. Without QoS as his mouthpiece, I was afraid he'd never communicate again. Shaking, I unfold the scrap and read what it says.

HE HAS GRACE

*****~~~~~*****

Chapter 26.

I've Come Undone

Poe has let me know that the Black Universe has somehow gotten to Grace. This will not stand. I jump back to Golaeth's hall of mirrors. Golaeth stonewalls.

"Grace has gone on her own, to try to reason with the Black Universe."

"I don't believe you. Poe tells me, and I quote, 'He has Grace.'"

"I assure you it was of her own volition. You saw as well as I when we contacted the brother universe that it too is in danger."

It's hard to stomach, but I know Grace has a head of her own.

"Yes, but I also saw that it will kill whoever it needs to, to survive." I'll be damned if I'll let my kid die before I do. It's unnatural. But I'm afraid of dying alone, and my heart is breaking.

"And there's the little matter of my family. Can you give them back to us? They're in the lifeboat that Yverra created." Yes, I know that in a fit of nobility I said I'd put them in safe-keeping, but that was when I didn't have Grace by my side and wanted to go looking for her alone.

"Are you sure? I'm fairly certain that Grace can handle it," Golaeth says, persisting with the coverup story, when everyone can see the truth.

"Yes, if you can retrieve them, I'd be grateful, and I'm sure Poe would also."

"I will initiate the search," Golaeth says.

"Thank you. I'll be at the Beach."

☺

251

The Beach is beautiful, like it used to be. A soft, warm light shines on the horizon, and the dead fish and seaweed smell have all disappeared. The wreckage has been cleared, to heaven only knows what big landfill in the cosmos.

"I've talked to Golaeth, and it's bringing the rest of my family. Soon we'll have the whole team." I don't mention QoS, not wanting to touch on a very sore subject.

I feel a little guilty bringing my family and Yverra, Benrus, and Ralff into the line of fire again, but with QoS gone, there would be no one to tell them what happened if Poe were to end. I'd entrusted that little duty to QoS, as well as the passing down of the torc with the Cintamani.

Now, I put on my Carolina Devil outfit, a big-shouldered black leather motorcycle jacket, Doc Marten boots, wraparound shades, and gold rings carved with grinning skulls on my fingers. I slip a pair of brass knuckles into the chest pocket and zip it shut. I remember this getup from the last time I played "Chitin Carapace Warrior" with Gracie and Eric.

Carolina Devil was my avatar. Gracie was a giant carnivorous insect, and Alan was an albino alligator. It is reassuring that Poe continues to go along with my little role-playing adventures, along with the concomitant costume changes.

A chill settles on the sand, as if the warmth was again being sucked out of the nexus. "Oh, God," I start to say.

But it isn't the Black Universe. Poe is expropriating a lot of energy for another task. He is unpacking the lifeboat that Golaeth has found.

Invisible at first, a tiny opaque sphere appears and begins to grow, bright as the sun and pulsing shimmering rings of light too intense even for my sunglasses. I stand back, shielding my eyes with my hand. I put on my baseball cap with the star emblem and shut my eyes tightly.

I've Come Undone

"Hey, Ginny, are you coming with us?" It is Alan. He doesn't even realize he's already been put in stasis and been retrieved. Or that I haven't gotten in the lifeboat.

"Change of plans, Alan. Grace is in trouble, and we've been elected to do the dirty work."

Yverra steps out of the globe, as the light rapidly diminishes.

"I don't recommend this course of action," she says. "Odds are high that it will result in our deletion, and possibly the universe's." Ben and Ralff stand by, nodding and looking puzzled.

Alan says, "So, did the Uber Universe kidnap Grace and refuse to help us?"

"Long story," I say. A little revenge for the time he neglected to tell me about Grace's powers. "It calls itself Golaeth."

I turn to Yverra. "I'm sorry to break your little bubble, Yverra, and you're welcome to return to the lifeboat. But if you would be willing, we could sure use your help. The one against the many, and all."

"It's probably for the best," Yverra says. "Golaeth has identified a weakness in the stasis field that allowed it to unpack us precipitately. I can construct a much better one than that now."

"Hold that thought," I say. We may end up needing the lifeboat after all.

We can hear music, strident chords too low for the human ear, but strangely stirring nonetheless. I just hope we can improvise over this progression without hitting a wrong note.

"Coming, Alan?" Hangul rises from the water.

"I wouldn't miss it," he says.

ᕗ

The short moments I spent with Golaeth are now a part of my and Hangul's timeline. Hangul takes Alan and me to the moment when the Black Universe rejected Golaeth's advances and took Grace hostage.

"We can fix you," I say. "I know you can hear me. I know you're suffering from the same disease as Poe. Actually, it's not exactly the same disease, but rather the antimatter version of it. And Grace is key to providing enough energy to keep it stable. She's the anomaly, like a mutation." Mutations can either be good or bad, depending on the circumstances.

"Listen, if you keep up these skirmishes with our universe, we're both going to die. It'll be a really big bang, bigger than has ever occurred."

"Pay heed to the primitive life form," a voice says. It's Golaeth. I'm grateful for the vote of confidence, faint praise though it is.

"Hi, Mom," Grace chimes in. Well, I'll be. Here we all are, back together.

ⓢ

"Where are you, Grace?" Alan asks. "We've come to get you. And Eric's waiting for you too."

"Thanks, Dad, but I can't leave. You heard Mom. I'm the only thing holding the two universes apart, and they don't mix well."

I understand Alan's frustration. All this way, just to be turned back again?

"Golaeth, you've been keeping them apart up until now, haven't you?"

"Regrettably, I was preoccupied with attending to your universe, and was unaware of the degeneration of the Black Universe."

"Well, what if we take Grace back and you do whatever you were doing for *both* universes?"

"Unfortunately, that won't work. I was treating Poe with large doses of black energy, and that would be a fatal prescription for his brother. And the black energy has caused Poe to expand into a territory dangerous to them both. Luckily, Grace has the power to apply repairs, so there's a temporary truce."

I still don't understand why everything has to be in such black and white terms. Matter/antimatter, energy/dark energy, never the twain must meet. Black and white. Hmm, that reminds me of something.

"Alan, let's go talk to Yverra. I might have an idea."

☉

"The metaphor is interesting," Yverra is saying. "Let us run the numbers." She holds out her hands to Ben, Ralff, and Violet, and they form a circle, boy-girl, boy-girl. They've become the new Watchmen. Good to see.

As Yverra begins deftly drawing invisibly in the air, Greek symbols begin to burn on the sleeves of her robe, but now the symbols aren't only Greek. Some are Chinese and Korean. I smile as I recognize them. I pray this bit of magic is going to work.

☉

I don't know if this is going to turn out to be a happy reunion or a sad funeral, but I take a deep breath.

"Ride with me one last time, Hon?"

"It would be my honor, my lady," Alan replies.

We burst out of the Beach like the Four Horsemen of the Apocalypse, except it's just two horsemen on a Korean dragon.

We carry a precious cargo, the cure for two sick universes, both of which are in no mood to take their medicine.

Yverra has uploaded the antiviral pattern into the Cintamani, and I can feel it like the kind of fever you get when you get a polio shot. I tell myself it's for the good of us all, like an immunity booster shot. But I still feel wretched. Traveling at quantum speeds does nothing to settle my psyche.

Hangul stops at what can only be described as the most out-of-the-way spot in the cosmos. This must be the boundary between the two.

Careful to stay on our side, I call out:

"Grace! Can you hear me?"

"Mother! Don't come any closer!"

This is the place, all right.

"Grace, can you package up a nexus from the Black Universe and put it out here on the boundary?"

"That could be disastrous," she replies.

"Well, just keep it slightly close to the edge, then. We're going to do the same with Poe's nexus."

"No, I won't do that." Grace doesn't see where we're headed. I don't blame her. It's a lot of responsibility saving the universe.

"Please, just put it there. We need it for the coadunation."

"Two universes can't be joined like that, Mother. They will both be destroyed."

"Grace, can you just trust me this once?"

There is a long silence, while Grace communicates with the Black Universe.

"All right, we are creating a stable nexus."

"It needs to be the same size as Poe's, you understand."

"Yes, yes. I understand that the two want equal footing in this standoff."

"Is it done?"

"Yes. I'll make it visible for you." A pretty globe, kind of like the snowglobes you see in the department stores, shimmers into view, seemingly only a few feet away, but probably thousand of miles.

"Now, Grace, I'm going to put Poe's nexus right here. Don't worry—it's still on our side." I touch my torc, and the Cintamani renders Poe's stasis nexus, beach and rolling waves and all.

I explain to Grace that here's the tricky part. Golaeth begins setting both universes rotating clockwise, using the strong gravity between the two nexuses as an axis.

I've Come Undone

The two universes each grow a tail and begin warping into teardrop shapes.

"Uh, oh." Alan says. Something is happening. The beach is being destroyed. And so is the Black Universe's stasis field. This isn't right. We ride up to Poe's beach to survey the situation. The field is blinking in and out of existence. It may disappear at any moment, causing both universes to explode.

Golaeth speaks.

"Grace, push your nexus to Virginia."

"It's afraid!" she says, echoing her own universe's feelings accurately, I suspect.

"It's the only way. The Black Universe's nexus will become the property of Poe, and the Beach will reside within the Black Universe."

"So it'll be a hostage situation?"

"Yes, but more like guarantees that each will respect the treaty and continue to coexist without further altercations."

I nudge the beach out into the No Man's Land between universes.

"I'm pushing ours out too, Grace. When you see the Beach, grab it. We'll grab yours."

This is it. For what seems like an eon, nothing happens, then suddenly Grace's nexus shoots across into our universe. I give the Beach a tremendous shove, willing everything I've got into the Cintamani. I can feel Golaeth giving an assist.

I watch the Beach roll end over end like a blue marble into the Black Universe. It's hard to watch the only safe place in the universe shrink into the distance.

Like an uncle who has accepted his nephew as his new ward, Poe reaches out for the Black Universe's nexus and wraps it in a cocoon of dark energy. He took his shot like a big boy.

"Grace, you can come home, now," Alan says.

"Mom. Dad. I'm here. But where's Eric?"

257

"He's with the others at their new headquarters on STS-99. That's where Yverra likes to hang out, so Poe created a new nexus, just for the Watchmen. Oh, and even Calaneris is there."

☺

"After rummaging through every metaphor in the book, I finally hit upon the yin and yang symbol," I say, as we all share a drink aboard STS-99. "I'd forgotten that I'd displayed the divided circle for many years on a patch on my Tae Kwon Do uniform. Sometimes the thing you search for the hardest is right under your nose."

"Yin and Yang?" Alan says. "Isn't that the symbol for male versus female? Are we looking for the gender of the two universes?"

"Yes, it can mean that, but it's often used to symbolize a lot more."

"Such as what?"

I explain that it's used to describe how seemingly opposite or contrary forces are interconnected and interdependent in the natural world; and, how they give rise to each other as they interrelate to one another. Many natural dualities (such as light and dark, high and low, hot and cold, fire and water, life and death, and so on) are thought of as physical manifestations of the yin-yang concept. The concept lies at the origins of many branches of classical Chinese science and philosophy, as well as being a primary guideline of traditional Chinese medicine, and a central principle of different forms of Chinese martial arts and exercise, such as Tae Kwon Do, which is the Korean martial art.

"I can't help but think QoS would have approved of it," I add. "He was big on the idea of the two sides co-existing, and even cooperating, different as they are," I say.

"The aspect of its use in medicine by your people is especially intriguing," Yverra says. "If you look at the symbol, you can see that there is a dot of white in the black half of the circle, and a dot of black in the white. This could be a metaphor for the practice of mithridatism, in which someone takes small doses of a poison in non-lethal amounts with the idea of developing an immunity."

"I remember that from an old story, what was it called?"

"Rappaccini's Daughter," Alan says. "About a man who raises his daughter to be immune to poisons, but she becomes poisonous herself."

"That poison maiden story is ancient," Ralff pipes up. "It occurs even on our planet."

"That's it," I say. "Poe's Beach is Golaeth's poison maiden."

*****~~~~*****

Chapter 27.

Empty Nest

Though thou wert scattered to the wind,
Yet is there plenty of the kind
—Alfred, Lord Tennyson

In a person's lifetime, a lot of good things happen, a lot of surprising things happen, and, if we're lucky, only a little tragedy happens. I am beginning to see that some things I once thought were tragedies were actually blessings in disguise. Alan and my struggles to have Grace finally resulted in a beautiful, perfect daughter. Our struggles to raise her in the midst of a cruel and violent universe resulted in a place of honor that neither of us could have expected in our wildest dreams. Without Grace, we would never have had the time to find a way to save ourselves. Her strength was what healed the rift between the Black Universe and Poe.

I always believed our universe was stark, mind-bogglingly immense, and unwelcoming to lowly creatures such as myself. Yet, strangely, our universe turned to us when it needed help. Fragile as we are, we gave Poe the strength to survive his encounter with his brother. We're thankful for the chance to climb a little higher, make a few more mistakes, and to even have a future.

We've returned to STS-99 to celebrate the near-miss with disaster with the new friends we've made over the past year and to grieve over the loss of the selfless being that was QoS. The mutual assured destruction/hostage angle is working out well to calm the breach between the Black Universe and Poe. Except now we're calling them the Yin and Yang Universes. The space

261

station is at a handy location just a hop, skip, and a jump via wormhole to the Big Bang.

Yverra and her new Watchmen are busily setting about recreating an Earthlike world within the new nexus, which, like the Beach, appears to be much bigger on the inside than on the outside. She has a long list of repairs to be accomplished, and sits down with Violet to outline how the Earth of the 25th century might be rejoined to its old timeline. It may or may not be possible, and if it is possible, it will take a lot of work.

Yverra offers her critique of recent events.

"The universe has required entirely too much hands-on maintenance," she says. "While the recursive process does major repairs, Golaeth has spent too much time trying to keep little emergent events from snowballing into giant crises. I will propose that this and other universes be made Self-Winding."

The talk turns too technical for me, and I wander out of the Watchmen's lab. Spokes are being added to the space station to accommodate living and research quarters. Calaneris has agreed to administer the station, and he and Blauw reside at the center of the wheel. Blauw has already set up a courtyard area filled with exotic plant species. Everyone has forgiven them, and they are working on forgiving themselves. At the moment, at least, they seem completely at peace.

"I've had some time to learn about guilt and forgiveness," Blauw says. "At first I felt like I was barely staying afloat on top of a pile of garbage and was about to sink again. Then I recognized it was just the guilt," Blauw said. "That's the first step. The second step is to try to make amends as best you can. That's why you see me here. I can tell you in detail what we did to your family— if you want to know, that is—so you can hopefully get past the trauma and begin healing."

Calaneris cleared his throat. "Blauw is taking too much of the guilt on himself, of course. As Emperor, I ordered him to do it. Although I must say, he took to it like a fish to water. But that's in the past. We've moved on. We want to do the same with you."

I say, "I think I understand why Blauw did it for you, but I don't think I can ever forgive either of you."

"Well, guilt isn't just to make us feel bad. It's there to help us learn something and make it less likely that we'll repeat our bad behavior in the future. We were unfortunately caught up in a complex feud between competing universes. Blauw and I have removed ourselves from the Empire that I used to control, so those temptations are less seductive. We fill an important role, manning the space station here along the Yin-Yang Boundary between universes, and helping to ensure the peace."

"Yeah," Blauw said. "I was Calaneris's bad boy, and I enjoyed it. But I'm also a human, and there are damn few of us left in this timeline. I even feel guilty for putting the moves on you, Virginia. But now I'll do whatever I can for Alan—and for you. I mean that."

"I loved QoS," I reply, with a lump in my throat.

"Of course," Blauw says, putting his hand on my arm.

I can't help flinching.

"Too soon?"

"Maybe a little," I say. "Let me think a while."

I sit on a bench under a rowan tree, sampling the red berries and listening to the nightingales warble a pastoral melody. Off in the distance a boxwood hedge neatly encloses the garden. I compliment Calaneris on his work.

"It's my maze," Calaneris says proudly. "You cannot even tell, but you are seated at the center of an unsolvable maze. All of us within it will be safe throughout the life of the universe. Yverra has made me the guardian of the stasis that protects this nexus."

I am happy for the way things have turned out, but I am beginning to miss home. The universe holds many wondrous things, of course, and I can do so much more now than I ever could before. Still, there's an invisible pull, calling me to at least check in on my original life. Call it Christmas, if you like.

"Blauw, I wonder if you'd pack me a picnic and include a six-pack of your finest holiday ale."

Blauw winks, and within the hour hands me a wicker basket with a calico napkin covering the contents.

"Thanks." I rise and head off to find Alan, Gracie, and Eric.

"Hey guys, I don't want to interrupt all the good work you're doing, but what are the chances of having Christmas at home?" I hoist the picnic basket in front of me. "With global warming, it's been getting warmer every Christmas, and we can spend it on the beach, like we started to do last year," I say, hopefully.

Grace looks questioningly at Eric, and he nods. As I recall, our last picnic together was not a picnic for him either.

"Mom, we couldn't turn you down even if we wanted to."

"Where there's a will, there's a way," I reply.

☺

The North Carolina beach is brighter than I remember it. Or maybe it always was brighter than Poe's Beach. The lighthouse is visible in the distance, its black stripes like a giant licorice candy cane; I've heard they are going to put a cell antenna on top of it. I can detect the faint aroma of automobile exhaust from the cars crowding the beach parking lot. It smells like heaven. We spread a blanket and dig into the basket.

"Yum, here's a slice of fruitcake for each of us," I say, pulling out plastic plates and forks.

"Virginia, why do you persist in thinking anyone likes fruitcake?" Alan says.

"You'll like mine," I say.

With a sigh of resignation, he takes the colorful dessert, and cuts off a tiny piece. He tastes it reluctantly, and a look of surprise registers on his face.

"This is actually good," he says.

"It's the company," I reply.

A gaggle of kids come running down the beach, in hot pursuit of a clear beach ball modeled after a map of the world. Grace and Eric are digging into the fruitcake, whether out of politeness I can't tell. There's a lot of love being lost between them.

"Um, kids, what do you say about moving back here? Grace, you could start a practice, and Eric, I'm sure we could get you on at the university as a history TA."

"Mom, I would love to do that, and maybe someday it could happen," Grace says. "But right now, Poe needs us, to keep an eye on the Black Universe's nexus, and Golaeth has got us booked for a lot of diplomatic work among the other universes. It's what I always wanted to do, you know.

"And—I'm hesitant to say this, but—something like this could happen all over again. We need to work out a new set of UU Policies and Procedures." UU is our shorthand for Uber Universe, a name that Golaeth seems to rather enjoy.

"What do you mean about new policies and procedures?" I ask. "That's fine for a university or a corporation, but this is *universes* we're talking about. They have their own laws, don't they? I assume you can't change the laws of physics."

"It will be difficult, but not impossible, Mom. And it's not so much changing the laws as enforcing them. The solution you came up with, for example. Under normal circumstances, both universes would have been destroyed, but we found a way out of that."

"It was pretty miraculous, actually," Eric adds. "I've gotten a whole new appreciation for the fact that when things seem hopeless there are actually an infinite number of possibilities."

"Well, there was plenty of destruction along the way," I point out. "Like Yverra's people, the Ministry of Contemplation, and all of Golaeth and the Black Universe attacks on Earth, and—"

"Yes, there's no doubt that there was a lot of suffering. That's why it's so important to do a better job of tying up the loose pieces. Golaeth is impressed with what can be done in the way of automation. I'll be free to do a lot more coadunation between universes, and Eric will be an ambassador."

"Don't you still have the problem of different laws in different universes?"

"Yes, and that's part of the challenge, of course. We'll have to discover what those laws are and systematize them. You know, things like what's a misdemeanor in our universe might be a capital crime over there, the whole justice thing. But with the Watchmen as both architects and enforcers, I'm hoping we can open up the multiverse to a wide range of cooperation and prosperity."

"I can see that," I say. "I've heard Yverra say she has ideas for improvements. Plus, she can slip her people between dimensions, and Ben and Ralff are already old hands at interdimensional travel. What about Violet?"

"Violet is a genius at envisioning how things can be. She's a lot like you, Mom."

"A real badass, eh?" I joke.

"More like a field marshall," Alan says.

"I still worry, especially about you and Eric," I say. "I'm a mother, after all. I can't help it. And aren't you some sort of weird anomaly that really shouldn't exist?"

"We know, Mom, and we love you for it. But we'll have guidance from Golaeth and protection from the Watchmen. We don't think Poe will make the same mistake twice."

Empty Nest

So… No having the kids living close by at home, then.

"Of course, dear. It was silly of me to ask."

೨

A brightly lit solant with a golden head and black wing tips hovers overhead in the sky, selecting a strike target, then assumes an arrowlike shape to make a spectacular high-speed dive. It's just stopping off for a snack on its way to the Gulf of Mexico, then heading back to the realm we humans can't reach. The early winter sun is beginning to set already. We pack up the picnic basket and police the area for trash, scouting for any stray wrappers left on the beach. It's clean as a whistle. Our car is still where we parked it.

I know it'll be lonely without Gracie and Eric, but Alan and I've decided to stay at home for good. As soon as we make the decision, the torc and the Cintamani disappear from around my neck. I've never really understood the true nature of the Cintamani, only that Poe has imbued it with features even beyond Yverra and Ben's brilliance. It's probably now back at the Beach with Hangul. I'll miss him too. Maybe I'll write about some of the things I've seen. With what I know now, I could even write a first-hand history of wrecking and the black rebellion in North Carolina.

We give the children a hug and wish them godspeed. They're both so tall. In a twinkling, they're gone. I stare at the empty space, trying to burn every minute of today into my memory. Alan puts his arm around me.

"Cheer up, Hon," Alan says. "They'll be back. There's always next Christmas."

"Wait a minute, Alan. I think I've left my cell phone back on the beach." I run back to the picnic spot and see the tip of the black case, nearly buried in the sand. Picking it up, I swipe the sand off. The screen lights up.

I see universes repeating, infinitely.

###

About Juliana Rew

Juliana Rew is a software engineer and former science and technical writer for the National Center for Atmospheric Research (NCAR) in Boulder, Colorado. She has won more than a dozen technical writing competitions and mentored minority and female college science interns in writing scientific papers. She advocates digital preservation of literary works and has produced several public domain works for Project Gutenberg. Her blog is called The Well-Rounded Geek (https://thewell-roundedgeek.blogspot.com), and you can peruse her other fiction forays at her author website, julianarew.com.

Art Credits

Cover image and design – Keely Rew

*****〜〜〜*****

Discover other titles by Juliana Rew:

(1) Erenarch Academy: Under the Dragon Banner
(2) Daris Moon
(3) Miranda of Daris
(4) Mountain Ma'am
(5) The Adventures of Mountain Ma'am

Coming Soon:
Extremophile: Violet Rain
Book 2 in the Unwinding Series

www.julianarew.com

Sophont

www.ingramcontent.com/pod-product-compliance
Lightning Source LLC
Chambersburg PA
CBHW071505110726
47908CB00003B/731